Operation Vampyr

1941. THE RUSSIAN front. The mighty armies of Nazi Germany rampage across Europe. The beleaguered allies enter what looks to be their darkest hour. Unbeknownst to them, the night is about to get a lot darker.

Young Hans is an idealistic soldier, joining the German army along with his two brothers for what he believes is the good of his country. What he sees on the front lines will change his life forever. When the troops are joined by Rumanian allies, led by the mysterious and sinister Lord Constanta, Hans is unsure of their true loyalties but cannot fault their fighting prowess. But why are the Rumanians never seen before nightfall? Why do the corpses of Russian soldiers that are found bear looks of absolute terror? What unholy bargains has the Fuhrer made in order to win this war?

D1603095

More action from Black Flame

ABC Warriors

THE MEDUSA WAR
Pat Mills & Alan Mitchell

RAGE AGAINST THE
MACHINES
Mike Wild

Dark Future

GOLGOTHA RUN
Dave Stone

DEMON DOWNLOAD
Jack Yeovil

AMERICAN MEAT
Stuart Moore

Durham Red

THE UNQUIET GRAVE
Peter J Evans

THE OMEGA SOLUTION
Peter J Evans

THE ENCODED HEART
Peter J Evans

Judge Dredd

DREDD VS DEATH
Gordon Rennie

BAD MOON RISING
David Bishop

BLACK ATLANTIC
Simon Jowett & Peter J Evans

ECLIPSE
James Swallow

KINGDOM OF THE BLIND
David Bishop

THE FINAL CUT
Matthew Smith

SWINE FEVER
Andrew Cartmel

WHITEOUT
James Swallow

Nikolai Dante

THE STRANGELOVE GAMBIT
David Bishop

IMPERIAL BLACK
David Bishop

Rogue Trooper

CRUCIBLE
Gordon Rennie

BLOOD RELATIVE
James Swallow

Strontium Dog

BAD TIMING
Rebecca Levene

PROPHET MARGIN
Simon Spurrier

RUTHLESS
Jonathan Clements

DAY OF THE DOGS
Andrew Cartmel

A FISTFUL OF STRONTIUM
Jaspre Bark & Steve Lyons

FIENDS OF THE EASTERN FRONT
Created by Gerry Finley-Day and Carlos Ezquerra

Fiends of the Eastern Front

Operation Vampyr

DAVID BISHOP

BLACK FLAME

To Jay, for his boundless enthusiasm

Historical note:

This novel is a work of fiction set during the Second World War's conflict between Germany and Russia. As far as possible the historical details are accurate, but the story takes liberties with reality for narrative effect.

A Black Flame Publication
www.blackflame.com

First published in 2005 by BL Publishing, Games Workshop Ltd., Willow Road, Nottingham NG7 2WS, UK.

Distributed in the US by Simon & Schuster, 1230 Avenue of the Americas, New York, NY 10020, USA.

10 9 8 7 6 5 4 3 2 1

Copyright © 2005 Rebellion A/S. All rights reserved.

All 2000 AD characters and logos © and TM Rebellion A/S. "Fiends of the Eastern Front" is a trademark in the United States and other jurisdictions. "2000 AD" is a registered trademark in certain jurisdictions. All rights reserved. Used under licence.

Black Flame and the Black Flame logo are trademarks of Games Workshop Ltd., variably registered in the UK and other countries around the world. All rights reserved.

ISBN 13: 978 1 84416 274 1
ISBN 10: 1 84416 274 5

A CIP record for this book is available from the British Library.

Printed in the UK by Bookmarque, Surrey, UK.

No part of this publication may be reproduced, stored in a retrieval system, or transmitted in any form or by any means, electronic, mechanical, photocopying, recording or otherwise, without the prior permission of the publishers.

This is a work of fiction. Excepting notable historical names, all the characters and events portrayed in this book are fictional, and any resemblance to real people or incidents is purely coincidental.

Directive no. 21 [Extract]

The German Armed Forces must be prepared,
even before the conclusion of the war against
England, to crush Russia in a rapid campaign,
The army will have to employ all available formations to this end, with the reservation that
occupied territories must be insured against
surprise attacks. The air force will have to make
available for this Eastern campaign, supporting
forces of such strength the army will be able to
bring land operations to a speedy conclusion
and that Eastern Germany will be as little damaged as possible by enemy air attack. This
build-up of a focal point in the east will be limited only by the need to protect from air attack
the whole combat and arsenal area we control.

I. General Intention
The bulk of the Russian Army stationed in

Western Russia will be destroyed by daring operations led by deeply penetrating armoured spearheads. Russian forces still capable of giving battle will be prevented from withdrawing into the depths of Russia. The effective operation of the Russian Air Force is to be prevented from the beginning of the attack by powerful blows.

II. Probable Allies and their Tasks

1. On the flanks of our operations we can count on the active support of Rumania and Finland in the war against Soviet Russia. The High Command of the Armed Forces will decide and lay down in due time the manner in which the forces of these two countries will be brought under German command.

2. It will be the task of Rumania to support the attack of the German southern flank, at least at the outset, with its best troops; to hold down the enemy where German forces are not engaged; and to provide auxiliary services in the rear areas.

Signed: ADOLF HITLER
The Führer and Supreme Commander
of the Armed Forces
Führer Headquarters, 18th December 1940

Chapter One

JUNE 21ST, 1941

IT WAS THE stench of horse piss and rose oil that Private Hans Vollmer could not stomach. He had arrived in the Rumanian village of Galati three days earlier, marching into the shattered settlement with an infantry unit of young soldiers, most of them fresh from basic training. All were eager for their first taste of combat, eager to make the long weeks of drill back home in Germany count. Each man had been in the Hitlerjungen, the Hitler Youth, before joining the army – some had even been in the Jungvolk before that. None had seen more than nineteen summers, yet they had been training for war since puberty.

Like many of his brothers in arms, Hans had feared the war would be over before he could take part; such was the speed with which the Führer's glorious Blitzkrieg had rolled across Europe. He need not have worried, Hans told himself as he searched Galati for his quarry – the day of glory was mere hours away. He longed to get the stink of this place out of his nostrils, to replace it with cordite and conquest, the odours of a just war. But that would have to wait. For now he must find Sergeant Witte and deliver the message.

Hans quickened his pace as he strode along the western bank of the Prut River, proud to be seen in his uniform by the locals. His black leather jackboots gleamed in the sun, the heavily studded soles thudding into the dirt roadway. His grey tunic and trousers were just as immaculate, the five metal buttons neatly fastened down his chest. The leather waist belt was worn over the tunic, lined with six pouches for ammunition and fastened by a square alloy buckle embossed with an eagle, symbol of the Wehrmacht. So far, Hans's uniform bore only the basic insignia of an untried soldier, but he was certain these would soon be enhanced with medals reflecting his bravery and valour in the heat of battle.

If there was one thing holding him back, he decided, it was his grey steel helmet. The army issued the so-called "coal scuttle" to its men in five basic sizes, but Hans had an unusually large head, even as a child. God knows, his mother had complained often enough about the pain she suffered giving birth to him. The size of his skull was coming back to haunt him. He had been forced to remove most of the thin leather lining to fit his head inside the helmet. The other men in his unit had rejoiced in rapping their knuckles against it, to see the pained reaction on Hans's face. He had been promised a larger helmet any day, but there was no sign of it. In the meantime, he was carrying his ill-fitting helmet under his arm, letting the gentle breeze ruffle through his short, blond hair.

The locals took little notice of Hans as he walked amongst them. He was one soldier among thousands thronging that side of the river. Galati rested not far from where the Prut met the Danube, but the river's surface was unbroken by tugs or fishing smacks these days. Anyone foolish enough to venture out into the waters was soon driven back by Russian sentries, firing from the opposite bank. There stood the Soviet town of Reni, blue smoke rising from its houses and black fumes belching from factories and foundries. A cloud of crows darkened the sky, cawing to each other in the afternoon sunshine. To Hans, they sounded melancholy, almost mournful. They shall not be crying for me tomorrow, he was certain of that.

In the distance he could see a bridge across the Prut, leading from Galati to Reni, a bridge none dared to cross. On the far side was an archway bearing the symbol of Bolshevism, the hammer and sickle. Beyond that is twenty-five years of tyranny and godlessness, Hans thought. Tomorrow, we rewrite their history. Tomorrow, the might of the Wehermacht will cross the Prut.

He would not regret leaving Galati. Larger than a village, it had been rent asunder by earthquakes the previous winter, collapsing many buildings. Some still lacked a roof or a wall, some entire facades. Gaping cracks offered those passing the chance to peer within, to catch glimpses of Turkish carpets and paper screens, people with jet-black hair and huge moustaches. How could anyone live like this, the soldier wondered? How could they tolerate the stench that pervaded everything? Dogs and boys chased each other along the streets, while men sat in cafes drinking coffee and shouting at women passing on the dirt pavements. Everyone knew what was coming, but this was a Saturday – a day to see and be seen, to share news of the week and talk of all the tomorrows to come. Sunday was a lifetime away, another world yet to be born.

Hans spotted his quarry arguing with a Greek barber, their negotiation a flurry of angry hand signals and different languages. "Sergeant! Sergeant Witte!" Hans called out. "The leutnant wants you back at camp," But his cry went unacknowledged by the sergeant, who was still trading words and gestures. The barrel-chested Greek should have been an intimidating figure with his powerful arms, bristling demeanour and enormous eye-brows. By comparison, Sergeant Josef Witte was an inch shorter, with a slight physique, that was more sinew than muscle. His shock of dirty blonde hair would have made a younger man look boyish, but the sergeant's face was gaunt, every one of his thirty-eight years visible in its lined contours. His blue eyes were colder than ice, embedded with flecks of grey.

Witte and the barber did not share a common language, but the soldier's steely determination was easy to understand in any tongue. The barber gave way as Hans approached and pressed something into the sergeant's hands before hurrying inside and slamming the door behind him. Witte pocketed the item, sunlight glinting briefly on its metal surface, before acknowledging Hans's presence.

"Yes, private?"

"Vollmer. Hans Vollmer."

Witte regarded him coolly. "I was asking what you want, not your name. I'll learn that if you survive long enough to make the effort worth my while."

Hans felt himself blushing and fought back his embarrassment. "The leutnant sent me to fetch you. Our orders have come through for tomorrow."

"That's better." The sergeant was already on the move, striding briskly back in the direction from which Hans had come. The private hurried after Witte, falling quickly into step beside him. They marched out of Galati, Hans fighting the urge to ask what had transpired with the barber. I do not need to know everything to be a good soldier, he told himself. I need only the courage of my heart and the strength of my beliefs. The rest is in God's hands.

OBERGEFREITER RALF VOLLMER was busy getting drunk. For three days he and his crew had been waiting, hungry for the order to climb inside their Panzer III

tank and head east. The 13th Division was stationed
south of Zamose, in an area that two years earlier had
been part of Poland. Now the fields and forests were
awash with German men and machines: mechanised
transports, Panzer tanks and their support vehicles flat-
tening every blade of grass, crushing the life from the
land. "What a way to spend a Saturday," Ralf said,
emptying the flask of Polish vodka in his hand and
reached for another.

Since arriving, his crew had busied themselves with
routine maintenance work, checking and rechecking
every part and piece of their mighty vehicle. Cleaning
out the gun barrel, removing any grit or trace of powder
residue which might erode the quality of the bore.
Lubricating the running gear to ensure their progress
would be swift and sure along whatever passed for
roads in Soviet territory. Testing and adjusting the tension of their tank's tracks to allow for whatever terrain
the Russian steppe had in store. Most irritating for Ralf
had been the everlasting arguments between his driver
Gunther and the Panzerwarte, the tank mechanics. Gunther was the best driver in the division, but his
attachment to their vehicle verged on the obsessive. He
watched over the mechanics as they tweaked the engine
like a doting father watches a midwife with his newborn
son.

After seventy-two hours of waiting, watching and
more waiting, Ralf's patience finally snapped. He pur-
chased three flasks of vodka from the local merchants
who were hanging round the division's fringes. The
clear, odourless liquid inside each bottle tasted of fire
and potatoes, scorching an acrid path to his stomach.
Gunther had been too busy elsewhere to partake, while
the other three crewmen promptly spat the vodka back
out again. Little Martin unleashed a tirade of obscenities,
using all the curse words he had learned since joining
the crew a few weeks earlier. Their previous loader,

Jürgen, had died in Greece, shot while taking a piss outside the tank in enemy territory.

Ralf sat on top of the Panzer, his legs hanging down
inside the turret through one of its hatches. He could feel
his head throbbing, no doubt from having drunk two
flasks of vodka. He was vaguely aware of the sun
scorching his bald pate, the relentless heat searing his
features, but he did not care. "You know what I like best
about this war?" he slurred to Big Willy below.

The mountainous gun-layer had been christened
William Buchheim twenty-eight years earlier, but to the
men of Ralf's tank he would always be Big Willy, thanks
to the prodigious size of his "equipment". The burly redhead shrugged, peeling a long flake of dry skin from his
sunburnt, heavily freckled forearms.

"Absolutely nothing," Ralf concluded.

"You can say that again," Helmut Richter agreed. The
radio operator scratched one of his large, prominent ears
before spitting on the grass.

"Alright, I will," Ralf chuckled, throwing the empty
second flask over his shoulder. "Absolutely nothing. This
war is best for absolutely nothing." A cry of pain from
where the flask had landed got his attention. "Sorry," he
shouted. "My mistake."

"Don't encourage him," Willy growled at Helmut.
They were both sitting against the tank's road wheels,
enjoying the shadow cast by the vehicle.

"Why not? He's right."

"Maybe, but we don't want him starting on the last
flask, do we?"

"Too late," Ralf announced, cheerfully waving the
final bottle in the air.

Willy cursed under his breath and stood up. "Why
don't we save some for later, yes?"

"No," Ralf laughed. "Why would I want to do that?"

"Because riding in a tank with a hangover isn't much
fun."

"How would you know?"

"Remember the morning we left Athens? You spent the previous night staying goodbye to those two sisters and their bathtub of homemade ouzo?"

"That was a good night," Ralf agreed.

"Yes, but how did you feel the next day?"

"I can't remember."

"Because you were too busy throwing up to know what day it was," Helmut replied as he darned a tear in the black wool jacket of his uniform. Making repairs to the double-breasted garment was never easy, as dark thread vanished against the black material. He glanced up to see Willy looking away to one side, the prodigious man's broad shoulders and close-cropped hair cast in silhouette by the sun. "What's wrong?"

"I think we have a problem," Willy muttered. "Get up."

"Why?" Helmut asked.

"Because if you don't, I'll shove our radio so far up your arse you'll need a field surgeon's help to send a signal." Richter got hastily to his feet. Willy was a genial giant most of the time, but his anger was terrifying when roused. The twists in his nose were ample evidence of occasions when that had happened. The redhead turned his attention back to the commander.

"Ralf, now would be a good time to start sobering up." Willy said.

"It's never a good time to start sobering up," Ralf replied, awkwardly getting to his feet on the tank's turret. "How about a song instead? Something stirring and patriotic, like we used to sing over a stein back home. A real song, mind you, none of that Nazi rubbish my little brother always sings."

"I don't think that would be appropriate, commander," Willy warned.

"Commander? Willy, the only time you call me commander is when we're up to our necks in–"

"Vollmer," a gruff voice shouted. "What in God's name are you doing?"

"Scheisse," Ralf said. He twisted round to see another tank commander approaching. Feldwebel Erfurth was a humourless native of Hamburg, notorious for his by-the-book approach to all aspects of life within the Panzer division. He had a sallow, pock-marked complexion and small, beady eyes like those of a child's doll. What Erfurth lacked in physical stature was more than compensated for by his officious manner. He was almost Ralf's equal in battle, but the two men could not have been more different otherwise. Their mutual antipathy was heightened by the fact Erfurth outranked Ralf, encouraging the unsmiling Feldwebel to torment Vollmer and his crew at every opportunity.

"I asked you a question, Vollmer. I expect an answer."

Ralf swayed slightly. "I'm sorry, I thought it was rhetorical. Remind me again, what did you want to know?"

Erfurth grimaced. "Have you been throwing empty flasks at my men?"

"Not intentionally. Why, did I hit one?"

"My gunner. He's bleeding from a head wound."

Ralf shrugged. "Sorry."

"Is that all you have to say?"

"Well, I could tell you to–"

Willy stepped towards the red-faced Erfurth. "To have good luck on the battlefield tomorrow! That's what the commander wishes, isn't it, Helmut?"

"Y-yes, that's right."

"No, it isn't," Ralf insisted, jumping down from the turret to stand beside his crewmembers. "I was telling the Feldwebel to stay out on my way. I've saved his sorry skin too many times already. I can't guarantee what'll happen if he drives across my path again tomorrow."

Erfurth bristled angrily. "Are you threatening a superior officer, Vollmer?"

"You might outrank me, but you certainly aren't my superior," Ralf sneered.

Willy stepped between the two men, smiling ingratiatingly at Erfurth. "So, what opposition do you think we'll face tomorrow?"

"Get out of my way, or else I'll have you running alongside my machine as a Panzer-grenadier," Erfurth said.

"You want to attack one of my crew, you have to come through me," Ralf warned, as he reached round Willy for a handful of the Feldwebel.

"It would be my pleasure," Erfurth replied.

"Ralf," a different voice shouted. "Our orders have come through." Gunther ran into view, clutching a handful of papers. He slowed to a halt, taking in the confrontation between his commander and Erfurth. "Oh, forgive me, Feldwebel, I didn't realise you were here too." Gunther gave a decent imitation of a salute in Erfurth's direction. "I believe your driver has your orders too, sir."

The Feldwebel was still glowering at Ralf. "Very well," he said finally. "But don't think I have forgotten this incident, Vollmer. Your insubordination has been noted. It reflects badly upon the entire division, and I will not allow one rotten individual to hold me back." He swivelled on his heels and marched away.

Ralf and the others watched Erfurth until he was out of earshot, and then burst out laughing. "I swear that man's got a ramrod up his arse," Gunther said.

"Did you see the look on his face when I told him to come through me?" Ralf asked. "I thought he was going to spontaneously combust!"

"You shouldn't goad him like that," Helmut warned. "He could be in command of this division one day. What would you do then?"

"Join the Luftwaffe," Ralf said, smiling broadly. "Be worth it to see the look on my brother Klaus's face when I turned up."

SOME THREE HUNDRED kilometres north, Major Wolfgang Satzinger was studying maps on a table in his tent. A polite cough from outside got his attention. "Enter."

Oberleutnant Klaus Vollmer stepped inside and saluted crisply to his superior officer. "You sent for me, sir?"

Satzinger acknowledged the salute before studying the new arrival. Vollmer was at least a decade his junior, but the young pilot was already building a respectable tally as a flying ace. Vollmer had dark hair and chiselled features and an angular jaw line. His uniform was well turned out and his demeanour never less than respectful in the presence of a superior officer. But there was something about the Oberleutnant that Satzinger always found unnerving. It was Vollmer's brown eyes – he never seemed to blink. The major gestured for the pilot to stand easy. "I'd like you to lead the first echelon of Stukas across the border tomorrow. I'd like you to be Staffelführer."

Klaus's face broke into a smile of delight before quickly becoming serious. "It would be an honour, sir."

"Don't be so certain," Satzinger warned. "I know rumours are already circulating about what we can expect to face. Many of your fellow pilots believe the Red Air Force will make easy targets for us. What do you think?"

Klaus shrugged. "I judge our enemies by their actions, not by the gossip of those with nothing else better to fill their time with. The English flyers proved rumours are no match for reality." Vollmer's Stuka Gruppe had lost eighteen planes to the RAF in a single day during the Battle of Britain, the Ju 87 dive-bomber proving no match for the more manoeuvrable Hurricane and Spitfire fighters. Eventually the Luftwaffe had been forced to withdraw its Stukas from the skies above the English Channel. The Gruppe had subsequently been reinforced with new fliers. More than one hundred and twenty planes stood ready outside, waiting to lay claim to the clouds over Russia.

Satzinger nodded his agreement with Vollmer's comments. "We know the Red Air Force has little to match us in terms of technology or experience, but they may overcome this with weight of numbers. Our strike against their airfields tomorrow must be achieved using surgical precision. That is why I have selected you to lead the echelon. Even if hitting our enemy is like shooting fish in a barrel, we dare not allow any to escape. The Führer himself has asked to be kept notified, with hourly tallies of our successes."

"Then we shall not fail him," Klaus replied. But even with only one eye, Satzinger could see doubt still clouded the Oberleutnant's features.

"You seem troubled," the major ventured.

"Attacking planes while they are still on the ground. It hardly seems fair."

Satzinger snorted. "Remind me, how old are you, Vollmer?"

"Twenty-two, sir."

"Then you're too young to have lived through the last war. I was a boy when my father died in the trenches, machine-gunned by an enemy aircraft. I don't know what foolish ideas you have about the noble kinship of all pilots, but we are fighting a war. The days of the Red Baron are over, understand?"

"Yes, sir."

"Mark this, Vollmer. I would make a pact with the Devil himself if I thought it could end this war without another person dying. Since the Devil does not grace us with his presence, we must do our best to fulfil this mission with the fewest losses and the greatest of dispatch."

Vollner nodded, frown lines evident on his forehead.

"Very well. He 111s will drop the first bombs from high altitude at precisely 3.15 tomorrow morning. You will take the first wave of Stuka across the frontier shortly afterwards. I imagine the scream of your planes at first light will be a most unpleasant surprise for our enemy." The major handed Klaus a sheaf of papers. "Your targets are marked on these. Good luck."

The pilot stepped back and saluted. "Hals und Beinbruch!" he said before walking out of the tent and into the fading sunshine.

Satzinger shook his head. He would never get used to the traditional farewell shared by pilots about to take off: "Break your neck and legs!" How had such a saying become considered good luck? It defied reason. The major crossed to his tent's opening and watched the young Oberleutnant hurry away. Twilight would soon be upon them, but few of the Staffel would get much sleep that night. Ground crews would be busy checking and rechecking each plane, loading them with fragmentation bombs and ammunition for the machine guns. "I wish I was going with them," Satzinger whispered to himself. He rubbed a hand across the patch where his left eye had been. Behind the leather was an empty socket, a sightless black void. No, the days of honour among pilots were long gone.

KLAUS STRODE BACK to his tent and found Heinrich Bennent waiting inside. "Well?" the gunner asked, his cherubic face flushed with excitement. "Is it happening tomorrow? I hear Satzinger called you in personally." Klaus confirmed the details, showing Heinrich the orders and maps he had been given.

The gunner gave a low whistle as he surveyed the tasks allotted to StG 77, struggling to keep his sandy fringe out of his eyes. "How many sorties are they expecting us to make tomorrow? Twenty?"

"At least half a dozen, all going well." Klaus shook his head. "You should have seen Satzinger's face. He was almost green with envy."

"Can you blame him? The old man was out of action for months after his plane went down. He wants revenge. An eye for an eye – literally, in his case."

"But shooting planes on the ground, Heinrich, it doesn't seem–"

"Sporting?" The gunner slapped Klaus's back. "You want to be the most successful Stuka ace on the Russian Front, don't you?"

"Yes, but–"

"But nothing. Take your kills where you can get them, that's my advice. The glory boys in the Messer- schmitts will get most of the kills, but there's no shame in stopping an enemy plane from ever taking off. Hell, its one less red devil in the air we have to worry about, right?"

"I suppose so," Vollmer shrugged. He watched Hein- rich leave, then went back to studying the maps for the next day's mission. The well-prepared pilot is the one who comes back alive – that's what his tutors had taught him, and the lesson had proven true so far. Let tomorrow be the same.

HANS HAD VOLUNTEERED for guard duty, knowing he would be too excited to sleep before the attack, but that was three hours ago and he was beginning to regret his enthusiasm. As midnight approached, he was patrolling the perimeter of his unit's encampment, listening for sounds in the evening air. The scorching summer sun had long since fallen beneath the horizon, but the night remained warm and humid, almost sultry. Hans tugged at the collar of his uniform, a trickle of sweat sliding down his neck to his spine. He rested the butt of his bolt- action Gewehr 98 rifle on the ground and wiped the perspiration from his brow.

A cold circle of metal pressed against the back of his skull. "If I were an enemy soldier, you would be dead by now," a gruff voice whispered in Hans's left ear. He twisted round to see Sergeant Witte behind him, a Luger 9mm pistol drawn and ready to fire. "Fortunately for you, I am not an enemy soldier. In future, never take both hands off your rifle while on guard duty."

"Yes, sergeant," Hans hastily agreed.

Witte smiled, sliding his pistol back into its holster. "At least you were still awake. Most of your comrades on guard duty were asleep when I visited them. You'd think they would be too excited to sleep, tonight of all nights."

"I couldn't," Hans said. He shook his head when Witte offered a cigarette.

"You don't smoke? Well, you will. Gives you something to do while you wait for the officers to decide what to do with us next. Keeps your hands warm in winter and busy in summer."

"My grandfather smoked for fifty years. Now he coughs for an hour every morning when he gets up. I don't want to be like that when I'm his age."

"So you're going to survive this war?" the sergeant asked, a wry smile playing about his lips.

"Of course."

"Think you're immortal, is that it?"

Hans frowned. "No, but we'll be home by Christmas."

Witte shook his head dismissively. "If you believe this war will end before Christmas, you're a bigger fool than the rest of the Hitlerjungen drones. Nothing between your ears, the lot of you. We'll be lucky to make it out of Rumania alive, let alone conquer Russia."

"How can you say that?" Hans protested. "Our generals will have planned every strategy to win this war."

The sergeant laughed. "Believe that, if you want." He went back to smoking his cigarette, two fingers and a thumb clasped round it. Hans noticed a glint of metal in a gap between the buttons on Witte's tunic.

"If you don't mind my asking, what were you arguing about with that man in Galati? I saw him give you something, a piece of metal."

Witte finished his cigarette and stubbed out its butt beneath the heel of his jackboot. After exhaling the last of the fumes, he undid the top button of his tunic to reveal a silver cross on a thin chain. Hans looked at the Christian symbol, still not comprehending. Witte sighed and fastened his tunic again.

"It's to ward off evil, private. The Greek wanted to buy it from me."

"Why? I don't understand."

"Clearly." Witte frowned. "I like to get my hair cut before going into battle, it's a habit my first sergeant instilled in me. I had to take my tunic off and that's when the barber saw my cross. Have you ever read the novels of Bram Stoker?" Hans shook his head. "What about a film called *Nosferatu*? Have you seen it?"

"About the creature that drinks blood?"

"That's it. To the west of here are two ranges of mountains: the Carpathians that stretch to the north, and another in the region known as Transylvania. Many Rumanian people believe monsters live in Transylvania. Monsters who drink human blood, who can only venture outside at night."

Hans laughed out loud. "You're talking about the vampyr. But they're myths, legends. Shadows to frighten small children!"

The sergeant shrugged. "To you, yes. But to the Rumanians, these legends are real."

"Even if they were, why should the people of Galati fear such creatures? We passed nearby Transylvania on our way here. It's more than a hundred kilometres away."

"True, but a squad of Rumanian Mountain troops is joining our infantry unit once we've crossed the Prut. The squad is coming here directly from–"

"Transylvania?"

Witte nodded.

"But how do the locals know this? Surely troop movements are–"

"Hardly a secret when loose-lipped soldiers have been visiting the town for the past three days," the sergeant sighed. He was studying the night sky, but did not miss Hans trying to suppress a yawn. "Go and get some sleep, private. I'll cover this position until your relief gets here."

"Thanks." Hans shouldered his rifle, ready to depart, but one last question still lingered in his tired mind. "Sergeant, do you believe in these vampyr?"

Witte did not reply quickly. "In any other place, I would not hesitate before saying no. But here... There is a darkness about this country. The sooner we move away from the shadow of those mountains, the happier I'll be."

"But creatures that suck blood. It sounds like some medieval fairy story."

"Myths and legends sometimes hide a fragment of truth within them," the sergeant said. "You would do well to remember that. Now, get to your bed."

Hans saluted. "Yes, sire."

Witte abruptly clamped a hand over the private's mouth. "Don't say that word here, private. Not even in jest. If what the Greek told me is true, that word has a meaning you did not suspect." He withdrew his hand. "Now, go."

Hans marched away, bewildered by the sergeant's words. Moving through the trees, he paused to look back. Witte was kneeling on the ground, looking up into the sky. Both his hands were clasped around the silver cross at his neck and Hans could see the sergeant's lips moving. It was years since Hans had been inside a church, but he still recognised the sight of someone praying.

Chapter Two

JUNE 22ND, 1941

FIRST LIGHT WAS beginning to colour the horizon when Klaus led three Stukas over the frontier and into enemy territory. A handful of He 111s had already completed one sortie against Russian fighter bases, scattering hundreds of small fragmentation bombs. Now, as the sky was shifting from black to blue, Klaus and his Schwarm were next to enter the unknown. The first wave of bombers had surely alerted the Russians that we are coming, he thought. It was simply a matter of time before enemy fighters appeared in the sky, machine gun and cannon fire scything death through the air.

Heinrich sat behind Klaus in the Ju 87's cockpit, the two men back to back inside the glass-panelled canopy. The gunner twisted round, searching the azure sky for a Russian response. "Where are they?"

"I don't know," Klaus replied, bemusement in his voice. "Before we took off, Satzinger said to expect a hornet's nest. But there's nothing in the sky except us." The pilot called one of the Bf 109 fighters escorting the

Schwarm. "Vollmer to Lang, can you see anything on our approach?"

Horst Lang's voice was accompanied by a crackle of static, but his words were clear enough. "Nothing. You think the Bolsheviks have slept in? It is Sunday. They could be having a day of rest."

A Stuka pilot, Theodor Bruck, joined the transmission. "The Reds don't believe in God. Perhaps the first sortie did more damage than we realised."

"Perhaps," Klaus agreed, uncertainty still clouding his voice.

"We're coming up on our first target," Heinrich prompted.

"Tighten up for attack formation," Klaus commanded. "I'll take the lead, Bruck comes next and the rest of you follow us down. Horst, stay back as cover if the Russians appear." The gull-winged Ju 87 was a highly accurate dive-bomber, but it was also most vulnerable while pulling out after an attack. Stuka pilots had paid dearly to learn that fact during earlier phases of the war.

Klaus glanced round to confirm the Schwarm was taking attack formation, then turned back to study his instrument panel. "I'm going in," he announced, focusing his concentration on the target below. Beneath the Luftwaffe planes lay a Russian airfield, its runways clearly visible in the thin light of dawn. Klaus began the procedures he had practised countless times in training, a precise sequence of actions that had served him well in previous sorties. His hands went through the drill automatically, all outside distractions cut from his thoughts. There was the target below and nothing else – it was all that mattered.

Close radiator flap – check. Turn off supercharger – check. Tip over to port – done. Set angle of dive to seventy degrees. His eyes flicked to the instrument panel of his plane, confirming that everything was as expected. In truth, he didn't need to look, the attainment of this angle was achieved purely by instinct, but the urge to check was involuntarily. Now, to accelerate: two hundred and twenty miles per hour, then two hundred and fifty. The altimeter was dancing before his eyes, such was the vibration of the plane as it raced ever faster toward the swelling target below. More power and the Stuka was plummeting to earth at three hundred miles per hour. Klaus applied the air brakes, a slatted length of metal beneath each wing folding forward. The siren on the undercarriage emitted its characteristic scream that so unnerved enemy troops and civilians on the ground.

Down and down the plane dived, the airfield growing so large it seemed to fill the cockpit's rectangular front window. Klaus could hardly believe his eyes. Row after row of Russian reconnaissance planes, bombers and fighters were lined up on the ground, as if on parade. Their numbers were astonishing, but even more astounding was the fact that none had been scrambled to repel the German attack. For a moment, Klaus wondered if the planes were dummies, an elaborate hoax to catch the Luftwaffe off guard. He brushed the idea aside and closed a finger over the release button on his central column.

At three thousand and fifty feet he pressed the button, feeling a shudder run through the plane as its payload released. A moment later Klaus broke away in a climbing turn, taking evasive action against any enemy flak as all his training taught him to do. But no anti-aircraft fire was firing from below and no fighters were hungrily pursuing the Stuka as it pulled sharply away. Satisfied with his manoeuvre, Klaus looked back at the target as a rain of four-pound fragmentation bombs – nicknamed Devil's Eggs – blew rows of Soviet aircraft apart. Each direct hit on a parked plane was devastatingly effective, a plume of black smoke rising from the point of impact.

Klaus watched proudly as the rest of his Schwarm completed its first bombing run, each Stuka laying claim to several Russian aircraft. "Satzinger was right," the pilot murmured to himself. "Like shooting fish in a barrel."

"Sorry Klaus, were you talking to me?" Heinrich asked.

"Just thinking out loud. Let's get back to base." Klaus called the other Stukas into formation and they headed back to refill their bomb magazines. It was going to be a long, long day in the sky.

ON THE GROUND the 13th Panzer Division was encountering some resistance, but nothing to trouble the armoured spearhead. A barrage of artillery before dawn had softened the Soviet defences along the front line, creating confusion and fear among the enemy. The infantry were then thrown into battle, overrunning Russian border positions to seize bridges and river crossings. The Panzers came next, punching a hole in the places where reconnaissance suggested the Russian defences were strongest. Once these were penetrated, the tanks were charged with striking deep behind the old frontier. As the Panzers advanced more armoured vehicles could follow, with the cavalry and infantry following behind. This was the Blitzkrieg that had swept across Western Europe. This was the fabled lightning war in action – swift, brutal and merciless.

Inside Ralf's Panzer III, it was Willy who took the crew's first shot of the new campaign, opening fire with the tank's fifty millimetre main gun. A Russian machine gun nest targeted the Panzer as it rolled towards the Soviet defensive position. The rounds pinged uselessly against the tank's armour like stones from a slingshot, but the noise was loud enough to irritate Ralf. All of his crew were wearing headphones with radio microphones so they could communicate above the din from the tank's engines and weaponry. "God in heaven," Ralf snapped, adding a few saltier curses. "Don't those Bolshevik bastards know I've got a hangover?"

"Perhaps we should stop and tell them," Gunther suggested cheerfully from the driver's seat. His hands deftly controlled the tank's forward momentum with twin steering levers and a gear lever, while his feet danced between the three pedals for accelerator, brake and clutch. Gunther's eyes remained fixed on the visor in the tank's front left armour plating, peering through thick, shellproof glass.

"I've got a better idea," Ralf scowled. "Willy, let's give them a hangover of their own."

"My pleasure," the gunner replied. He pressed his eye against the gun sight, while his hands spun a wheel to traverse the turret towards the machine gun nest. Another wheel was twisted to lower the gun's elevation, bringing it to bear on the target. "Martin, get ready."

The young loader was crouched beside Willy, the next shell already out of its storage bin and cradled in his arms, waiting to be slotted into the breech. "Ready."

"Good. Commander?"

Ralf peered through one of the vision ports in his cupola, its green glass casting an emerald hue over what he was seeing. He reached forward and slapped the gunner on the back. "Fire!" Willy pushed down a foot pedal, triggering the main gun's electronic firing mechanism. The Panzer's momentum was fleetingly slowed by recoil before it leapt forwards. The spent shell jumped from the breech into a waiting bag, while fumes from the gun were sucked away by an overhead fan in the turret roof. Martin was already reloading the mighty weapon, while Willy watched the effects of his shot. The machine gun emplacement exploded, an orange ball of flame mushrooming up into the sky, accompanied by black smoke, shrapnel and numerous Russian body parts. There may have been screaming, but nobody heard it.

Ralf smiled grimly. "Good shot. Helmut, any word of significant resistance ahead?"

The radio operator was sat on Gunther's right at the front of the tank, his attention focused on the Panzer's short wave FuG5 receiver and transmitter. "Nothing of consequence. It's as if they weren't expecting us."

"Did you forget to send out invitations?" Gunther jested.

"Just my luck," Ralf growled. "The worst hangover of my life and these godforsaken Bolsheviks haven't the good grace to hurry up and kill me." After checking they were past the Russian's front line defences, Ralf opened the hatch in the cupola, enjoying the rush of cool air.

The morning was still young, but the Panzer's interior would become unbearably hot long before the sun reached its zenith. Ralf pushed his head and shoulders out through the circular hatch, resting his arms on top of the cupola.

Ahead were the frontrunners of the armoured spearhead, Feldwebel Erfurth no doubt helping to lead the charge. Each vehicle was creating a cloud of red dust, mingling with the fumes from their exhaust. Behind Ralf's tank were more Panzers, then a succession of black smoke plumes darkening the sky, ample evidence of their path to this point. The commander sighed heavily. "Let's hope we hit some real roads soon," he said. "Otherwise this dust is going to play havoc with our engines."

HANS CROUCHED BESIDE Sergeant Witte as they waited for the signal to advance. Ahead stretched the bridge across the River Prut, leading from Galati to Reni where the enemy troops were stationed. Beyond was the land known as Bessarabia, an area of Rumania claimed by the Russians. The infantry's first task was to liberate Bessarabia, before surging onwards to the Dnestr River. That was where the Soviet defences were strongest, the eastern bank guarded by a formidable set of defences known as the Stalin Line.

Galati's streets were deserted, a stark contrast to the hustle and bustle of the previous afternoon. This early on a Sunday morning, they would have been empty, Hans reasoned, but the silence around the bridge was unnerving. "Anyone who could leave got out last night," Witte whispered.

The private started, not realising his thinking was so transparent. "How did you know?"

"You haven't learned to keep your feelings off your face. You want to survive today, you better start, boy." The sergeant consulted his watch. "Our artillery should be opening fire about." Mechanical thunder filled the air behind the soldiers, a terrifying cacophony that rebounded along the narrow streets of Galati. "Now." The barrage continued for nine minutes, the German gunners finding their range swiftly.

Reni's triumphal arch with its hammer and sickle emblem was the first to fall, taking several direct hits before crumbling in a cloud of dust and debris. More shells rained down upon the Russian positions, pulverising most structures within a hundred metres of the bridge. The crossing itself remained untouched. Through it all, Hans had kept both hands clamped over his ears, his helmet resting on the ground in front of him. Even after the guns stopped, their mighty roar lingered in Hans's mind, as if the explosive concussions were still echoing within his thoughts.

Witte pointed at the bridge. "See those wires?"

Hans peered to where the sergeant was pointing. A cluster of thin black cables led away from the bridge, back towards the nearest building in Galati. "We're going to blow it up?" Hans asked, confused.

"A safety measure, in case the Russians attacked first. I saw the Rumanian engineers laying them last night. The Reds will have done the same thing on their side. Hopefully our artillery has taken out the man with the detonator."

Hans swallowed hard. "And if it hasn't?"

"Then you'll get to experience 'death or glory' any minute now." Witte rapped his knuckles on the private's discarded helmet. "Put this back on. Take it off again today and I'll have you on report."

"Yes, sergeant." Hans wedged his helmet on his head, fastening the black leather strap beneath his chin.

A low whistle was blown nearby. Witte smiled grimly. "Time to go." He rose to his feet and ran, crouching low to the ground. Hans found himself running in the sergeant's shadow. He clutched his rifle in both hands, one finger resting on the trigger, ready to fire. From numerous positions, dozens more German soldiers were running towards bridge. All had the same intense look of fear and determination in their eyes. Witte reached the river crossing and pressed into its metalwork, waiting for the others to join him. He signalled silently for the first ten men to follow him on to the bridge, motioning at the rest to hold position.

Hans found himself among the ten men. A strange thumping noise crowded his brain, battering at his hearing. He glanced round quickly for the source and realised it was his own heart beating, the blood in his ears throbbing, his every sense heightened. All the activity around him was fading away, becoming distant as if he alone was standing on the bridge. The others were like wraiths, blurred shadows at the edges of his vision. All he could see was the far end of the river crossing, inviting and calling him forwards.

"Breathe," the sergeant said gruffly at Hans, resting a hand on his shoulder. "Your heart will be racing, you need the extra oxygen."

Hans nodded and took two deep breaths. The pressure gripping his chest relaxed, pressure he hadn't even been aware of before Witte spoke.

"Let's go," the sergeant whispered, creeping forwards, hugging the left side of the bridge.

A dark-haired conscript fell into step behind Witte. What was his name, Hans wondered? Hammel? Hagemeister? Yes, it was Hagemeister. Fritz Hagemeister. Buck-toothed, with pimples and bad breath – he would never feature on a recruiting poster. Hans was next to step forwards, followed by a surly individual called Groth. Nobody knew Groth's surname, only that he had a foul temperament and a short fuse. The other seven followed along behind, all holding their weapons like loved ones, wide eyes studying every battered building and broken window on the Russian side of the Prut, waiting for the first shot, hoping against hope not to be its target.

They were halfway across the bridge when Witte dropped to a crouch, signalling for the others to do the same. Hans pressed his legs together, wishing he had been able to take a piss before the artillery began its barrage. He had stood in an alleyway for five minutes, feeling like a fool, waiting for something to happen. Having Hagemeister beside him hadn't helped, merrily whistling the "Horst Wessel Song" while spraying the walls with his urine – so much so, that Hans had done up his flies and gone back to waiting with the others. Now his bladder was crying out for the chance to empty itself, threatening to darken the front of his trousers.

Hans grimaced and gave Hagemeister on his left a nudge. "How do you do that?" he whispered. "How can you take a piss while somebody else is watching?"

Hagemeister didn't reply, so Hans gave him another nudge. The long-limbed private pitched forwards face-first on to the bridge, a neat puncture hole visible in the back of his helmet. Blood pooled beneath the dead body. "Scheisse," Hans gasped.

Witte glanced back, took in the corpse and grabbed Hans by the collar. "Snipers! Move it!" The sergeant had sprinted along the bridge towards Reni, dragging Hans behind him. The others were hard on their heels, all

searching the buildings ahead to see where the shot that
killed Hagemeister had originated from. As they neared
the end of the bridge, Hans saw a fistful of wires skirting
the edge of the structure. He ran faster, his jackboots
stomping along the dusty surface, mindful of what Witte
had said. As they neared the Russian side of the river,
bullets began spitting into the ground ahead, defying
them to come any closer. Witte skidded to a halt and
dived out of the way as more bullets thudded in a
straight line towards him.

Hans was overcome by the strangest of sensations.
Moments before, everything had been a juddering, jerky
blur of movement. Time was slowing down around him,
seconds extending languidly. His senses perceived everything around him, as if seconds were minutes. The
sergeant was diving to one side, shouting at his men to
take cover. The enemy rounds stabbed into the ground,
one after another, each impact throwing up a puff of dirt,
each impact getting closer to Hans as he ran forwards. In
the distance he could see clouds of smoke from the
Russian position in a first floor window.

Something flashed past Hans left ear and a scream
confirmed that another of his brothers in arms had been
hit. Hans could not help looking back to see who it was,
and as he did so, he tripped over, let go of his rifle and
fell to the ground like a rag doll.

Hans landed on top of his rifle, its length smacking
into his solar plexus, driving the air from his body. He
slid forward another metre, then rolled to one side, the
line of bullets passing beside him. As Hans rolled over,
he saw Groth take seven bullets in three seconds, the private's body twisting. Several more men went down
screaming, fingers clawing at wounds, some with lifeless
eyes as they fell to the ground, their bodies peppered
with bullets.

Only two were unhurt, twins from Dresden, Ulrich and
Siegfried Held. They had been at the rear, giving them

enough time to avoid the Russian gunfire. The pair flung themselves in the same direction as Witte, clinging together for comfort. The sergeant was surveying the way forward, searching the battered buildings. "Vollmer. Did you see where that came from?"

Hans pointed at the upper floor of a two-storey building close to the ruined archway, forty metres away. "I saw smoke in that window," he gasped, fighting to regain his breath.

"Good," Witte said. While the privates had all been armed with rifles, the sergeant was carrying a MP 38 machine pistol. He fired a burst at the window Hans had indicated, emptying a thirty-two round magazine in a little over ten seconds. While the sergeant was reloading, he ordered Hans to throw a Stielhandgranate – a stick grenade – short of the enemy position.

"Why?"

"The chances of you getting it through that window from here aren't great. But throw it halfway and the explosion should throw up enough dust to distract our Russian friends and give us time to get off this bridge before they detonate."

"Can't we defuse the charges?"

"They'll have booby-trapped them. I would have." Witte slapped the a magazine into the base of his machine pistol. "Ready?"

Hans pulled a stick grenade from his waist belt. He gripped its wooden shaft in his left hand, while unscrewing the alloy cap at its base. A looped cord and blue bead fell into Han's right hand. Using his elbows to push himself up into a seated position, Hans pulled on the cord, activating the fuse. He counted to two and then threw the grenade halfway towards the Russian position. A cloud of dust and debris billowed up from the explosion, creating a smoke-screen between the Germans and their enemy.

Witte was already up and sprinting towards the shat-tered arch with Hans scrambling after him. The private

could hear Ulrich and Siegfried close behind, their
breath coming in short gasps like his own. As the noise
from the explosion died away, the Russians resumed
their machine gun fire, bullets zipping through the
cloudy air. Hans felt something ping off the side of his
helmet but he kept running, trying not to think, letting
training guide his actions. He reached the shattered
stone columns of the archway, surprised to still be alive.
The twins dove to the ground beside him, smiling at
each other. So far, so good.

"Now you can try for the window," Witte ordered.

Hans nodded, extracting another stick grenade from
his waist belt. Siegfried and Ulrich did the same, nodding when they were ready. The trio tugged on the
cords, then tossed their grenades at the nearby window.
One bounced off the shattered frame, but the other two
flew inside. Someone had time to utter a Russian curse
before the grenades exploded, screams accompanying
the detonations.

The sergeant peered round the rubble of the ruined
arch, studying the blackened building. "We should make
sure there are no more surprises," he decided, pointing
at Hans. "Vollmer, you're with me. You two stay here
and keep under cover, understand?" The twins nodded.
Witte signalled for the men back on the Rumanian edge
of the bridge to hold position for now. Satisfied his order
had been received, the sergeant stood, motioning for
Hans to do the same. "On the count of three... One...
Two... Three!"

The two men ran out from behind the broken archway
and sprinted towards the building where the Russians had
been. They paused on either side of its shattered doorway,
Witte signalling he would go in first. Hans nodded, still
fighting to control his breathing, as the sergeant ducked
into the dark interior. Hans waited a second and then followed him in. He stopped in the doorway to let his eyes
adjust, but a hand yanked him further inside.

"Stay in the light and you make yourself an easier target," Witte said. "Didn't they teach you anything in basic training?"

Hans studied the building's interior. It had been a tavern in the past, but was now a blackened, burnt out ruin.

The sergeant pointed at a staircase on the far wall, leading upwards. "There."

Hans nodded and followed Witte across the room, careful to follow his sergeant's footsteps. Basic training had at least taught him to avoid hidden booby traps by following the footsteps of the man in front. They advanced slowly up the stairs, sweeping their weapons from side to side, ready to open fire at the slightest sound or movement. On the first floor a doorway stood between them and the room facing the bridge.

Witte was the first to examine the room. "They're all dead," he said, no hint of pride in his voice.

Hans was joining the sergeant when he noticed a shadow fall across Witte's back. "Behind you!"

The sergeant spun round, firing his machine pistol as he did so. Bullets shredded the body of the Russian who was creeping up on Witte, his bayonet falling to the floor. Witte stood his ground, glaring at the would-be assassin, the stench of blood and cordite thick in the air. Hans looked down at his rifle. He hadn't fired a shot, he realised, but he'd saved a life.

The sergeant patted Hans on the shoulder. "Good work, Vollmer. Remember, in future, check every corner of a room as you enter, even if you believe all those inside are already dead. I should know better myself."

Hans nodded. "You know my name."

"What?"

"Yesterday, you said you'd only bother learning my name if I survived long enough to make it worth your while."

Witte smiled grimly. "I have to know all your names, whether I like it or not. How else would I know what name to write on the letters of condolence to your families?"

Hans pointed at the Russian's corpse. "He fought to the death. He could have surrendered, but he didn't."

"Remember that," the sergeant said. "You may be passionate about fighting for the Fatherland and our glorious Führer, but the Russians are just as committed to winning this war. If they all fight like him, then the communists are not the weak-willed, inferior foe our propagandists would have us believe." Witte went to the window and signalled an "all-clear" to the Held twins.

"What about the charges on the bridge?" Hans asked as more German soldiers began crossing the Prut.

The sergeant pointed at a nearby crater. A cluster of wires stopped at its edge, frayed ends visible amid the dirt and debris. "We got lucky," Witte said. "Our artillery must have severed the cables in the first wave of shelling. Otherwise we'd be dead by now." He moved away, ignoring the smoking corpses of the dead Russians smeared across the charred floor.

Hans fought back the urge to vomit.

KLAUS'S SCHWARM HAD returned to base, been reloaded with bombs and sent straight back into the air. This time the mission was to bomb Russian fortifications along the River Bug. Once the Stukas had dropped their payload, they returned to base without seeing a single enemy plane in the air. Klaus reported this fact to Major Satzinger while waiting for his Ju 87 to be refuelled and rearmed for another sortie. "At this rate, we'll own the skies before nightfall," he said, bemused at how easy the day's activities had been.

"Don't complain," Satzinger replied. "Would you rather be dead?"

"No, but–" Klaus's reply was cut short by a cluster of explosions on the opposite side of the airfield. Five black mushrooms of smoke were rising from the ground.

Above them half a dozen twin-engine bombers were turning in a wide circle.

"Looks like you might get your wish yet!" Satzinger shouted, already running towards the radio tent. Before he could reach it, three German fighters sped over the base, only six metres above the ground as they passed. Luftwaffe ground crew paused from reloading the Ju 87s to cheer them on.

Klaus shielded his eyes from the midday sun to watch the ongoing dogfight. As the nimble German planes approached the Russian bombers, thin threads of smoke shot forwards at the enemy aircraft. One of the bombers flashed silver, and then fell to the ground with its engines screaming. A second Soviet plane was engulfed by a red glare as it exploded, shedding its parts like autumn leaves. A third flipped over backwards, flames smearing the sky around it. The remaining Russian planes tumbled from the air in less than a minute, six columns of smoke on the horizon – the sole evidence of their doomed attack. Klaus cheered each triumph with his comrades, applauding the devastating accuracy of the fighters.

Satzinger joined him, having been inside the radio tent to report to nearby Luftwaffe air bases. "I hear the same thing's happened all along the frontier. The Reds fly in, never shifting off course, making no attempt to evade our fighters or flak. Their losses must be frightful. It's like they've got a death wish." The major handed Klaus a new sheaf of maps and instructions. "Here's your next target."

Klaus felt the smile slip from his features. This is not war, he thought bleakly. This is something else, something without honour or glory.

BY DUSK, THE Russian town of Reni had officially been liberated, with the few final pockets of resistance remaining stifled by roving infantry units. After his involvement in the early action, Hans had spent the rest of the day stationed close to the bridge crossing the Prut. Witte had put him and the Held twins in charge of guarding the Russian end. "You never know when our enemy might launch a counter-attack," the sergeant had insisted. "As we surge forwards, our flanks are exposed to any Russian units hidden among the rubble. Keep your eyes open and your wits about you."

Hans and the twins had saluted, their fervour matched by relief at being spared frontline duty for the rest of the day. Watching seven of your comrades cut down before your eyes was a sobering experience. Yes, they had seized the bridge, but the cost was not insignificant. Hans had done his basic training with the dead men, suffered and sweated, drilled and practised with them. He might not have liked them all, but that sort of intense activity created a bond, an allegiance. Enemy bullets paid such bonds no heed. Death was death, nothing more and nothing less on the battlefield, Hans told himself. I must get used to the fact. One day it may come to claim me too.

He saluted as another company of cavalry reached the Reni end of the bridge, its commanding officer stiff and upright on his horse. In a war where Panzers and planes had inflicted the most damage, Hans found the idea of cavalry units old fashioned, almost quaint. Of course, he had not yet faced enemy cavalry on the battlefield. No doubt that would change his opinion, he thought, especially if the Cossacks were the equal of their infamous reputation.

His attention was brought back to the present by noise from a German truck on the bridge, stuck behind the cavalry horses. Hans edged along the bridge to the truck, careful to stay clear of the increasingly agitated animals.

When he reached the vehicle, Hans noticed an unusual insignia on the driver's door – a bat with wings unfurled, its talons clutching a swastika. Beneath this was a black pyramid, like the peak of a mountain. The same insignia was also emblazoned on the khaki tarpaulin covering the truck's cargo tray. A surly soldier sat in the driver's seat, hammering a fist against the horn. "Move yourselves!" he shouted, leaning out of the window to berate the cavalry. "I must get through by nightfall, on orders from Hauptmann Constanta."

"You'll have to be patient," Hans suggested. "The cavalry is going as fast as it can. The commotion you're creating is unsettling the horses, making matters worse, not better."

The driver glared down at him. "Did I ask for your opinion?"

Hans had run out of patience with this goon. "Papers," he demanded.

The driver gave his truck's horn another battering.

Hans aimed his rifle at the driver. "I said papers. Now."

Grudgingly, the driver thrust a handful of documentation at Hans. "I am Obergefreiter Cringu – personal orderly to Hauptmann Constanta of the 1st Rumanian Mountain Troop. You would do well not to threaten me."

"Where in Rumania was your unit formed?"

"Sighisoara, in Transylvania."

Witte's comments from the previous night flooded back into Hans's mind, about a troop of mountain soldiers joining the infantry. Hans returned the driver's papers, his thoughts dwelling on what the sergeant had hinted about the Rumanians. The cavalry was beginning to move off the bridge into Reni. Cringu eased his vehicle forward slowly and once it had passed, Hans took the opportunity to open the tarpaulin covering and peer within. Inside were ten long boxes, stacked on top of each other in a pyramid formation. Handles were bolted to the end of each box. Each box was more like a

casket, with slanted sides forming a hexagonal shape.
No, not like a casket, Hans thought, a chill of fear travelling along his spine.

The boxes resembled coffins.

The truck halted abruptly, startling Hans. Hurriedly,
he closed the tarpaulin as Cringu appeared beside him.
"What are you doing back here?" the Rumanian
demanded, his thick accent hard for Hans to understand.

"What kind of equipment do you transport in such
caskets?"

"That is none of your concern," the Obergefreiter
snarled while tying the tarpaulin down, concealing
the caskets from prying eyes. Satisfied, he stepped
closer to Hans, his foul breath invading the young soldier's nostrils. "The Hauptmann allows no one but me
to touch his supplies. I am his most loyal servant.
Unless you wish to join his service, you would do well
to keep away." Cringu strode back to the driver's
cabin and climbed inside. The cavalry had cleared the
bridge and the truck sped away over the river
crossing. As the vehicle passed the cavalry on the far
side, Hans noticed several of the horses almost
unseating their riders, such was the apprehension
caused by the truck's presence. Maybe it's not the
truck, Hans thought. Maybe it's what is inside the
truck. No, that's ridiculous. There are no such things
as vampyrs.

Hans rejoined the Held twins on sentry duty at the
Reni end of the bridge. "What was all that about?"
Siegfried inquired.

"Nothing," Hans replied, shaking his head. "Some
Rumanian Obergefreiter throwing his weight around.
You know how it is, give some nobody a rank and next
thing you know they think they're the Führer."
Siegfried laughed knowingly and even Hans smiled at
his own humour. But he still felt an inward shudder as
the setting sun dipped towards the horizon. Monsters

that can only venture outside during night, Witte had said.

Soon night would be upon them.

Chapter Three

JUNE 23RD, 1941

IT WAS A few minutes past midnight when Hans stumbled into a Soviet counter-attack. He had been sleeping soundly, when a fellow conscript woke him while returning from patrol. Hans cursed the bumbling fool, squinting to identify the culprit in the darkness. "God in heaven. Some of us are trying to sleep here," he said angrily.

"Sorry, Hans. I missed my footing," Franz Kral said apologetically. He was the shortest man in the unit, a cheerful lad from Hamburg who had wanted to join the Kriegsmarine, the German Navy. Why? Because Hamburg has more canals than Venice, as Kral told anybody who asked about his thwarted ambition. Alas, wartime bureaucracy and an inability to swim led to him being stuck on dry land with the Landser, the infantry.

"Go back to sleep," Franz urged.

Hans did his best, but the discomfort of a full bladder soon proved too much for him. After ten minutes of failing to fall back to sleep, Hans pulled on his jackboots, shrugged on his tunic and went to find a latrine.

Overhead, clouds crept across the night sky, black on
dark blue. The scent of burning rubber and tobacco
hung in the air, a reminder of the previous day's battles
and the ubiquitous cigarettes smoked by most soldiers.
Hans tried to find a sentry who could say where the
latrines had been dug, but all the guards were conspicuous by their absence. They had better not let the
sergeant catch them slacking off, otherwise their lives
wouldn't be worth living, Hans thought with a smile.

When he discovered the first bloody corpse, Hans
realised Witte was the least of the sentry's problems. A
dark red stain ran down the dead soldier's tunic from a
deep wound to the throat. Hans crouched by the body,
studying the victim's pallid face. Terror and pain had
twisted the features, but Hans still recognised Private
Fedder, another member of their unit. Fedder's rifle was
not to be found, nor were the spare ammunition clips,
but his bayonet was still unsheathed on his left hip.
Hans found the dead man's identity disc – a perforated
oval of zinc worn around the neck by a thin chain. He
snapped off the bottom half. He would give it to Witte
so that the Army Records Department could pass on the
sad news to Fedder's next of kin. Hans pressed his fingers against the dead man's face to close the lifeless
eyes. The corpse was still warm, suggesting Fedder had
died soon after relieving Kral.

That meant the enemy must be close, probably within
a few hundred metres.

The sergeant had been right yet again, Hans thought.
Russians have hidden themselves in the remains of Reni,
letting us move past them. Now they are using the cover
of darkness to attack our flanks. Do I raise the alarm
from here and risk being killed by the Russian insurgents, or try making it back to the others before calling
out?

The decision was taken away from him by the sound
of a rifle bolt being slotted into position, ready to fire.

Someone close by spoke to him in an unfamiliar language.

"I don't understand what you're saying," Hans replied quietly. A Russian soldier stepped from the shadows, motioning with Fedder's rifle for the German to raise his hands. Hans did as directed, all too aware that the only weapon he could hope to use against the Russian was Fedder's sheathed bayonet. I'd be shot and killed long before I could reach for it, Hans concluded. The Russian looked down at the corpse and grinned, muttering something under his breath. His uniform was splashed with blood, no doubt from cutting Fedder's throat.

Hans jerked his head towards the corpse. "You did that?"

The Russian's grin broadened further.

"And you're proud of it too, aren't you?" Hans grimaced, his hatred for the enemy growing stronger by the moment. He judged the distance from himself to the enemy soldier: three metres, maybe four.

Can I make it to him before he shoots me, he thought? Perhaps. Not much to pin a life on, but it's all the hope I've got right now.

He edged one leg backwards and crouched slightly, preparing to launch himself at the smirking Russian, but the other soldier was no fool. He saw Hans's movements and raised his rifle, aiming it squarely at the German's chest. The Russian said something towards the shadows and three of his comrades appeared from the darkness, all armed and ready to fire.

Hans breathed slowly, forcing himself to relax. His opportunity to save himself has passed and his life was in the hands of the enemy – hands that were covered in German blood.

I'm going to die in the dark and I still haven't fired my rifle in anger, Hans thought.

He remembered the day he left his mother back home and how tearful she had been when he marched off to war, following in the footsteps of his older brothers. Hans knew she was proud at having all three of her sons fighting for the glorious Fatherland. He offered a silent prayer that the Russians killed him quickly and that he did not disgrace himself in death.

But there was no killing blow. No mercy killing. To Hans's surprise, the first Russian lowered his rifle and began talking to the others. The four soldiers produced hand-rolled cigarettes from inside their uniforms and lit them, apparently unafraid of being discovered by other German sentries. They must have killed the other guards, Hans decided, chilled by this realisation. Studying the new arrivals, he noticed they also had fresh blood spattered on their tunics.

"What are you waiting for?" he yelled. "Why don't you kill me, like you murdered the others? Go on, put me out of my misery!"

The Russians looked at him uncomprehendingly, before shrugging and muttering to each other. They must be waiting for something or someone, Hans realised. He felt like a fool to be caught with his guard down. One of the first things he had been taught was to always carry a weapon, no matter the place, time or circumstances. Now he knew why, for all the good it would do him.

The scent of the Russians' cigarettes hung in the air. He thought that their tobacco smelled harsher than German cigarettes. He smiled at the absurdity of this observation, when death was only a few seconds away, waiting to claim him.

I've nothing better to do with my time, he admitted. All I can do is wait to see what happens next, then something strange caught his eye.

Tendrils of mist were creeping across the ground, snaking out of the darkness like growths on a vine, insinuating themselves around the four enemy soldiers' legs. It was not cigarette smoke creating a fug. If Hans had not known better, he would have thought that mist

had a will of its own. But such things were impossible –
mist was mist, nothing more. This must have come from
the nearby rivers. He knew they were not far from the
lagoons of both the Danube and the Prut.

Suddenly, one of the Russians disappeared, vanishing
from where he stood in a blur of movement. He gave a
brief cry of surprise before he faded away. Hans was as
shocked as his captors, uncertain of what had happened,
bewildered by the speed of this startling occurrence. The
three remaining Russians spun round, searching the
shadows for their missing comrade, but there was no
trace of him, merely a gap in the swirling mist where he
had been standing.

The soldier who had taken Hans by surprise reacted
angrily to the German's smiling expression. He hurled
abuse at Hans, gesticulating with his rifle. The words
were incomprehensible, but their meaning was clear:
what have you done with our comrade? Hans shrugged,
doing his best to convey the fact he also had no idea
what was going on. He noticed the creeping mist
growing thicker round the ankles of another Russian, a
swarthy soldier with a black, oily moustache worthy of
Stalin himself. Hans was about to point this out, but
events overtook all of them before he could.

In a flash the soldier was gone, disappearing from
sight as quickly as the first. The two remaining Russians
jumped. It would have been comical to Hans, had his life
not hung in the balance. The Russians jabbered at each
other, tension etched into their faces. Having come to a
decision, the pair stood back to back, rifles ready to fire
at anything that came close to them. They had forgotten
about Hans for the moment as he watched, fascinated,
as the mist began to coalesce once more around the Russians' legs.

Before the third soldier disappeared, Hans thought
he saw a figure form in the swirling mist. Then
another Russian was gone, leaving a single man

behind – the same soldier who had caught Hans. He spun round and round on the spot, searching for some clue to explain the disappearances. When he found none, the Russian tossed his rifle to one side and produced a knife, its blade glistening with blood. He launched himself at Hans, knocking him to the ground. The Russian pressed the edge of his blade against Hans's throat, snarling threats and questions, his eyes bulging, his breath rancid. Hans protested his innocence, tried to plead for his life, but the Russian was close to hysteria. He pulled back the knife, ready to plunge it into Hans's throat.

A blood-curdling cry sundered the air. Hans knew this was his chance. He grabbed hold of the Russian's right arm, twisting the hand that clutched the bloody blade. The Russian flailed at him uselessly, but Hans had the advantage and he wasn't giving way. Another savage twist and he felt something snap inside his captor's wrist – a popping sound clearly audible in the night. The Russian cried out and dropped the knife, his face showing his agony.

Hans smashed the base of his hand up into the Russian's face. Blood poured from his nose, spattering warm droplets across Hans's features, the coppery tang of gore filling his nostrils. Hans wrenched the Russian sideways, the two men rolling across the dusty ground, grappling desperately. Somehow the Russian got the upper hand, pinning Hans down once more. He punched a fist into the German's cheekbone, pain exploding in Hans's head.

The Russian grabbed hold of the discarded knife, a smile of triumph on his bloody features, but he stopped abruptly, his eyes peering down at his chest. Two wisps of mist were clamped across his torso, visibly tightening, as if they were clotting in thin air. Within moments, the mist was thick as a man's arm. Strangest of all, each section was forming shapes like human hands, fingers extending out from them. "Bojemoi!" the Russian gasped. His eyes locked with those of Hans, utter terror and bewilderment forming a bond between them.

Hans could feel time slowing around him, as it had done on the bridge. Behind the Russian he could see the sinister mist coalescing into a humanoid shape, with shoulders and a head. Most disturbing of all, he could make out the outlines of a face, complete with a wolfishly grinning mouthful of teeth.

Not teeth... They were fangs.

Then the Russian was gone, vanishing from view just like his comrades. Hans was left alone on the ground, panting for breath, every muscle and sinew in his body tensed and ready to fight for his life. A bitter, metallic taste filled his mouth, but he didn't know if it was down to his blood or the adrenalin pumping through his system. Falling to the ground, Hans groped in the darkness and found the knife the Russian had dropped. Crouching on one knee, the terrified German waited for the mist to claim him as well.

A howl of torment and pain ripped through the air, the cry of a slaughtered animal, but with an unmistakeably human voice. Then another sound replaced it: wet, slurping, like a hungry piglet suckling at the teat of its mother. Hans shuddered, profoundly disturbed for reasons he couldn't adequately explain. Whatever happened to the four Russians, they had been powerless to stop it. What hope could he have against this invisible enemy, this unseen terror?

Movement nearby caught Hans's attention. Tendrils of mist returned from the shadows, gathering in front of him, forming into individual shapes. Hans balanced the knife in his right hand, all too aware how feeble one blade would be against whatever had consumed the Russians. In the distance. he heard approaching footsteps.

"Over here," Hans called, praying whoever was approaching was one of his own. "I'm over here." He realised the footsteps were approaching from behind and turned to face them.

A lone man emerged from the darkness, walking out of the shadows as if taking a casual stroll in the night air. Tall and upright, with an aristocratic bearing, he wore the peaked cap of an officer. A voluminous black cloak with a high collar hung on his shoulders, a clasp fastening it across his chest. The dark, silk-lined fabric opened to reveal a tunic and jodhpurs similar to those worn by cavalry officers. A pistol was holstered on a black leather waist belt, but the new arrival did not appear to carry any other visible weaponry. He wore black leather gloves.

Hans looked at the officer's face and shuddered inwardly. The features were precise, almost haughty, with hooded eyes and a neatly trimmed black moustache. The lips had a cruel, sardonic smile about them and there were no wrinkles on the officer's face to betray his age. Hans thought the officer was austere, almost forbidding, until he smiled. The German's blood ran cold, his spirit chilled by the shameless hunger in the officer's expression. He looks at me the same way that I would a rare steak he thought.

"What have we here?" the newcomer sighed. His speech carried an accent unfamiliar to Hans, but the words were precisely spoken. It had a warm, sensuous quality, completely persuasive. Hans found himself wanting to stare deep into the officer's eyes, but tore his gaze away, focusing instead on the peaked cap. Its insignia badge was the same as the one Hans had seen the day before, on the truck driven by Cringu: a bat with wings outstretched, carrying a swastika in its talons, above a black triangle. Other markings on the officer's uniform clearly identified his rank.

"Hauptmann Constanta?" Hans asked.

The officer stopped, surprised and perplexed. "You know me?"

"We've never met, but I recognised the Rumanian Mountain Troop emblem on your cap. I met your orderly, Cringu, yesterday."

"Hmm," Constanta pondered to himself, lost in thought. His eyes moved to something behind Hans. When the German glanced over his shoulder, he saw four more men bearing the same insignia as their Rumanian leader, standing where the mist had formed into humanoid shapes. They were brushing a hand across each of their mouths. Hans couldn't be sure, but thought he glimpsed a smear of crimson being wiped away from each man's lips.

"What is your name?" Constanta asked, forcing Hans to turn back.

"Vollmer. Private Hans Vollmer."

"Your supposition is correct, Private Vollmer. I am Hauptmann Constanta, leader of the 1st Rumanian Mountain Troop. In my native Transylvania I bear the title Lord Constanta of Sighisoara, but such distinctions have little meaning on a battlefield." The officer stepped closer to Hans, motioning for the German to stand. "My men have been hunting a squad of Russian insurgents. Our intelligence report suggests they were to rendezvous at this location, before attacking the German unit nearby as its soldiers slept. What are you doing here after dark, alone and all but unarmed?"

Hans quickly retold all that had happened since venturing from his tent, concluding with the mysterious disappearance of the four Russians. "I don't know what took them," he said fearfully. "It was almost... supernatural."

To Hans's surprise, Constanta did not dismiss such a fanciful notion. "There are more things in heaven and earth than any of us can hope to understand," the officer replied. "I suggest you return to your tent, private. My men will find and deal with any remaining Russians. They shall not escape our wrath, shall they, men?" The other Rumanians growled in agreement.

Hans saluted Constanta, grateful for the opportunity to leave the Rumanians behind. There was something both mesmerising and repulsive about him, a charismatic charm masking something else, something almost sinister. Being in Constanta's presence disquieted Hans in a way he had never felt before, a feeling that defied easy description. Despite wanting to flee the five Rumanians, Hans found himself stopping to ask a question that had nagged him since first encountering Cringu. "Excuse me asking, Hauptmann, but why are you Rumanians fighting alongside us?"

Constanta smiled, showing a little of his gleaming white teeth. "We kill Rumania's enemies. In this war, that means Russians. You Germans have the same enemy, so we fight alongside you. It's a noble alliance that we are making."

Hans nodded, saluting once more before stumbling away, eager to put as much distance between himself and the Rumanians as possible. It was not Constanta's words that had disturbed Hans, it was the flash of elongated, canine teeth inside the officer's mouth. They weren't teeth – they were fangs. Lord Constanta had a mouthful of fangs, the same as the mist creature that tore away the Russian intent on killing Hans. A coincidence, Hans told himself. It's a coincidence, nothing more. You've been through a terrifying ordeal. Don't let your mind play tricks upon you.

TWELVE HOURS LATER, Hans was having a drink of water from his Feldflasche when the Held twins returned from patrolling the outskirts of Reni. The infantry unit would soon be leaving, but its men were still required to check the devastated settlement for Russian soldiers lingering among the ruins. The incident during the night had been a salutary lesson for all the Germans not to let their guard slip. As a result, all patrols had to be made up of at least two men, in an effort to prevent any reoccurrence.

Ulrich was ashen-faced when he came back from patrol, while his brother was muttering something under his breath. Hans saw their distress and approached the pair, asking aboutwhat had happened. Siegfried shook his head, refusing to discuss it, continuing his nonsensical ramblings. Hans realised the anxious soldier was reciting the Catholic Rosary, mumbling prayer after prayer, his hands trembling.

Hans let Siegfried stumble away, and then questioned the other brother. Ulrich was trying to roll a cigarette but his fingers were shaking too much. Hans took hold of the tobacco and paper and quickly produced a slender, tightly rolled cigarette.

Ulrich looked at him quizzically. "How did you...? You don't smoke."

Hans smiled. "I used to roll them for my grandfather, when his arthritis got too bad for him to do it himself. Do anything often enough, you get the knack." Hans passed across the cigarette, waiting for Ulrich to take a first, deep drag before asking again what the twins had witnessed.

"We were down by the river," Ulrich said, the quivering in his hands subsiding slowly. "Siegfried saw something floating in the water and called me over. But when I got there, I could see the shape was that of a corpse."

In the background Hans could hear Siegfried still reciting the Rosary, rocking back and forth. "Go on."

Ulrich frowned. "I waded out into the water and tipped the body over. Its skin was pale, whiter than fresh snow. The uniform was Russian, so I dragged it on to dry land. God, it was heavy. Waterlogged, I suppose."

"The Russian had drowned?"

"That's what I thought, at first. I was checking for a dog tag, see if I could find out what unit he was with. Instead I found two holes. Well, to be accurate, they weren't really holes. More like puncture marks, as if he'd been stabbed in the neck twice with the point of bayonet, then the blade was twisted round inside to make the wound bigger. I've never seen anything like it before." Ulrich sucked on the end of his cigarette, gratefully filling his lungs with smoke.

Hans frowned, trying to picture what the other soldier had described. "Why would anyone do that with their bayonet? It doesn't make sense. There are easier ways of killing."

Ulrich snorted derisively at Hans. "They didn't use a bayonet."

"They didn't? But you said–"

"I told you what the wounds looked like. I think somebody used their teeth to make those wounds."

"Their teeth? How can you be sure of that?"

Ulrich held up the thumb and forefinger of his left hand, keeping them about thirty millimetres apart. "This was the distance between the two wounds. Between them I could see four individual tooth marks on the skin, where somebody had bitten down on the Russian's neck." He finished his cigarette, crushing its still smouldering end in the dirt beneath his jackboot. "It was after noticing the tooth marks I realised how the communists had died."

"Communists? You found more than one body?"

The grimfaced private jerked a thumb at his trembling brother. "Siegfried did. Three more. All the same as the one I fished out of the Prut. Puncture wounds in the neck, teeth marks between each wound."

Hans was struggling to take in the implications of what Ulrich was saying. "Some kind of ritual, maybe? Perhaps the locals were taking revenge on the Russians for invading Bessarabia…" His voice trailed away, lacking any conviction in what he was suggesting.

Ulrich shook his head. "All four Russians were white as my mother's china plates back home. They had been drained of blood, Hans. Whatever attacked those poor bastards, it sucked the life right out of them." Ulrich stood up and shivered. "I'll tell you this for nothing. The sooner we get away from this accursed place, the better. I don't know what kind of monsters walk the night here, but I don't want to meet them." He went to his mumbling brother and gently ushered Siegfried away.

Hans hurried after them, stopping Ulrich momentarily. "Have you told anyone else what you saw, what you think happened?"

"The sergeant. Witte made us swear not to tell anyone else, but I couldn't keep it bottled up – not that." Ulrich gripped Han's arm, his fingers squeezing the skin like a vice. "You should have seen the fear in their eyes, Hans. Whatever did that to them, it wasn't human. Nothing human could have done that." The twins stumbled away, Siegfried still reciting his Rosary, Ulrich trying to soothe his brother.

HANS FOUND WITTE an hour later, standing beside a bonfire on the banks of the Prut. "I know what Ulrich and Siegfried found."

"I should have known those two couldn't keep their mouths shut for long."

"Don't blame them. Siegfried is too scared to say anything and I had to bully Ulrich into talking."

The sergeant gave him a sideways glance. "You'd make a good interrogator, Vollmer. Perhaps you should be enrolled in the SS, not the Landser."

Hans ignored the comment. "Where are the Russian bodies? I want to see them, to know if they are the same men I saw last night."

"They're gone."

"Gone? Gone where?"

Witte nodded towards the flames. Hans looked closer at the mass of burning wood, realising slowly that there were other shapes within the scorching mass. Four corpses were secreted among the flames. The sergeant was tending a funeral pyre, not a bonfire. Hans took a step towards the blazed but its heat drove him back. "In God's name, why burn their bodies? That's evidence of a war crime and you've set it on fire."

"It's in God's name I'm burning them," Witte said coolly. He opened his hands to reveal the silver cross inside them. "It's one of the few ways to ensure this infection doesn't spread."

"Infection? What infection?"

"Don't make me say the word again, Vollmer."

Hans frowned. "Vampyr?"

The sergeant concealed the silver cross inside his tunic once more. "And it would be safer if you did not say that word out loud."

"This is ridiculous. Ulrich claims the Russians had been drained of blood, so you burn the bodies. Why?"

"If you believe the legends, whoever sucks the life from a human body gains the power to resurrect the corpse. Burning is supposed to prevent that from happening. We have enough real enemies to fight. I don't need our so-called allies creating new fiends for us to face."

"You're referring to Constanta and his mountain troops."

Witte scowled. "You've seen him?"

"He and four of his men arrived just after the Russians vanished."

"What a coincidence."

Hans shook his head. "Sergeant, I believe in the Führer and in his love for the Fatherland. He would never form an alliance with the sort of creatures you're talking about!"

"Lower your voice," Witte warned as a pair of soldiers passed. He resumed talking once the patrol was out of earshot. "You want to know what I believe in, Vollmer? I believe in my country, I believe in fighting for Germany and its people. I'm proud to have taken part in wars across Europe for the Fatherland, proud to be part of the Landser. The Luftwaffe and the Panzer crews may get all the glory, but we're the ones who do the real soldiering. I know most of the men under my command will die long before the fighting is over, but I don't plan on joining them in the grave. I'll do whatever it takes to survive this war. I'll do my duty too, but when this is over I'm going home to my wife and little girl, Frieda. And nothing and nobody is going to stop me, be they from heaven, Earth or hell. Do you understand me, Vollmer?"

Hans blinked at the sergeant's outburst. He'd never seen Witte speak so passionately nor for so long on any subject. "I think so."

The sergeant sighed. "What I'm saying is that you shouldn't put so much blind faith in our glorious leader. Look with your own eyes if you want to see the truth." The heat from the funeral pyre was decreasing as the flames burnt down. "You should be preparing to move out. We march within the hour."

"Are the Rumanians coming with us?"

"No, thank God. Constanta and his men are being redeployed further north along the Ostfront. They'll be somebody else's problem after today."

Chapter Four

JULY 1ST, 1941

RALF WAS SLEEPING inside his tank when someone shook him awake, interrupting a most enjoyable dream involving Marlene Dietrich, two nuns and a bottle of peach schnapps. He jolted awake, slamming his head against a corner of the hull. He cursed loud and long, waking Willy and Gunther, who were also sleeping inside.

"What is it? What's happening?" Gunther asked blearily.

"Good question," Ralf replied testily. Martin was peering in through the cupola hatchway, looking suitably contrite at having woken the crew.

"Erfurth's sent a runner to fetch you."

"What does that pig-eyed, chinless wonder want?"

Martin shrugged. "Your presence, right now. That's all the runner said."

Ralf muttered a few more curses under his breath while gathering his uniform, then clambered out of the tank. Many Panzer crews were in the habit of sleeping inside their vehicles at night, despite the

cramped conditions. The tank was their home away
from home, with most of the crew's belongings draped
across the grey metal exterior. Steel helmets hung
from hooks on the turret, crates of rations were
stowed on the engine decking and fabricated racks
held spare cans of fuel. The temperature inside was
unbearably hot during the day, but the same interior
provided some insulation from the cold at night.

Ralf emerged to find the runner still waiting patiently
by the Panzer. The moon was setting in the west, suggesting dawn could not be far away, but the tank
commander was still not amused at being roused from
his slumber. "The Feldwebel sent you? Why does he
need me at this bloody hour?"

"I don't know. He did say there was some urgency in
the matter."

"Some urgency?"

"Yes."

"Well, in that case…" Ralf sat down on the front of his
tank and extracted a pipe from one of his tunic pockets.
"You got any tobacco?"

"No, sorry. I don't smoke."

"You will, soon enough." Ralf pressed his hands
against the pockets of his uniform, but could not find
the slim tin of tobacco he habitually carried. It must
have fallen out inside the Panzer while he was
dressing in the darkness. "So be it," he growled,
replacing the pipe in his pocket and jumping down to
the ground. "Let's go and get this over and done with,
shall we?"

"If you'll follow me."

Ralf nodded, rolling his eyes in exasperation once the
runner had looked away. The Hitlerjungen might be
good at instilling disciple in future soldiers, but it was
less successful at giving them a sense of humour. Ralf
sauntered after the runner, deliberately taking his time
over the short walk to see Erfurth.

The Feldwebel bore a distinctly sour expression when Ralf finally arrived. "Vollmer! What the hell has taken so long? I sent that runner half an hour ago."

"What did you want?" Ralf replied, ignoring the accusation.

"I've been delegated to brief the division's tank commanders on our forthcoming movements. All the others have come and gone in the time it took you to get here. Don't think your insolence or slackness has gone unnoticed."

"Heaven forbid," Ralf said, yawning. He glanced at a folding table on which maps of the local terrain had been spread, a complex series of arrows and notations indicating the positions of their forces and those of the enemy. "So, what's the schedule for today? More gentle drives through sunflower fields, or will be get to see some action for once?"

Since bursting through the Soviet frontier positions, the 13th Panzer Division had met limited resistance. The sky overhead was almost devoid of enemy planes thanks to the mighty Luftwaffe and the Russian armour had also been seen off in furious fighting outside Lutsk. The Panzers had skirted north of Rovno and crossed the River Ustiye the previous day. By Ralf's reckoning, the division had covered at least two hundred kilometres in a week and a half, despite the absence of sealed roads.

Erfurth gestured grandly at his diagrams. "We're expecting a more formidable foe today – the Red Army's 9th Mechanized Corps, made up of 20th and 35th Tank Divisions, along with the 131st Motorized Division."

Ralf studied the maps carefully, his eyes following the contours and quirks of the surrounding topography. "What are their strengths, relative to ours?"

"Unknown, but the Luftwaffe has agreed to start using their Stukas as tank busters, targeting the Soviet armour ranged against us."

Klaus should enjoy that, Ralf thought. The light Russian tanks seen on the battlefield so far were no match for a Ju 87 diving at them out of the blue.

"I want you to lead a Panzerkeil against the Bolshevik armour using the wedge formation to draw them into an attack," Erfurth continued. "The rest of the division will encircle the Russians, then we can crush them within the Kessel." He clenched his fist triumphantly, savouring a victory not yet won.

"And what about my crew and the other tanks in my wedge?" Ralf asked.

"Our Schwerpunkt is destroying the 9th Russian Mechanized Corps. Some sacrifices may have to be made in achieving that effort, but a commander of your... guile. should have no problems." Erfurth smiled broadly.

Ralf bit his tongue, refusing to give voice to his feelings. He knew the role assigned him was verging on suicidal. This was the Feldwebel's revenge and now Ralf's crew were to suffer for his insubordinate streak. He would have to make amends with them somehow. "Anything else?"

"Yes, there is, actually," Erfurth replied. "Some genius has decided our Rumanian allies need to be trained in the art of armoured warfare. As a result, a member of the Rumanian army has been assigned to our division, so he can learn from our tactics and expertise. I was asked to name the best tank commander in our ranks, so the Rumanian could be added to their crew. I put forward your name. God forbid I should be stuck with such a backward peasant in my Panzer."

"Feldwebel, you know full well there's hardly enough room inside our tanks for the five crew. Now you want me to squeeze some outsider in as well?" Ralf said.

"Exactly. You'll find him waiting when you get back to your tank."

"What's his name?"

"His name? I'm not sure," Erfurth admitted. He shuffled through his papers, eventually discovering the relevant notation. "Ah, here it is. Sergeant Valentin Gorgo, of the 1st Rumanian Mountain Troop."

"Why would a mountain troop be training its men to drive Panzers?"

"Vollmer, you have an unfortunate habit of questioning almost every order you receive," the Feldwebel said archly. "Perhaps today's tasks will make you understand the value of accepting orders from your superiors without question."

Ralf strode away, resisting the urge to beat the smirk from Erfurth's pockmarked, officious face. By the time he reached the tank, the rest of the crew were gathered alongside it. Dawn was breaking over the horizon, threatening to deliver another scorching day. "Good. You're all up," Ralf said. He quickly outlined their orders to act as bait for a trap.

"But that's selbstmörderisch," Willy protested. "Even if we survive the Russian onslaught, we'll be trapped in the Kessel with them."

"Not if I can help it," Ralf replied, making eye contact with each member of his crew in the grey light of dawn. "I give you my word, none of us are going to die this day." Satisfied by their silence, he moved on to the second part of Erfurth's surprise. "We're apparently getting lumbered with a Rumanian observer in our tank, as well. I don't know how long we're expected to put up with him, but we'll have to watch our words from now on. For all we know he's a plant from the Feldwebel, gathering evidence against us." Ralf frowned. "He was supposed to be here by the time I got back, but I guess–"

"He's already here," Gunther interrupted.

Ralf could see no evidence to confirm this. "Where?"

"Inside the tank," Helmut replied, shaking his head in disbelief. "Must be keen to make an early start. At least he's polite. He wouldn't get inside until he'd been invited."

Ralf raised an eyebrow at this. He climbed into the hull and raised the driver's hatch to look inside. A solitary figure within scuttled to one side, avoiding the pale morning light that filtered in. "Is your name Gorgo? Valentin Gorgo?"

"Yes," the Rumanian replied, his speech accented heavily. Thickset and mordant of expression, his only distinguishing feature was a bushy eyebrow that extended from one side of his face to the other, without a break above the nose.

"Did you want to come out and have breakfast before we set off?"

"I have… eaten. already," Gorgo said.

"Have it your own way." Ralf sighed and slammed the hatch shut and jumping back beside the others. "Not exactly talkative, is he?"

"Suits me," Willy announced. "I get enough chatter over my headset from Gunther and Helmut. I don't need another voice in my head."

"Are you saying I talk too much?" Gunther protested cheerfully.

"My mother-in-law talks too much," Willy replied. "You talk twice as much as her!"

"Well, he's never one to do things by halves," Helmut chipped in.

"Shut up, the lot of you," Ralf commanded. Once they were silent, he rested a hand on Martin's left shoulder. "I need you to talk with the other crews, find out which two are helping us bait the trap. If we're to get out of it alive, we'll all need to work together." The young loader nodded before scurrying away. Ralf regarded Helmut and Gunther. "You two have twenty minutes to make sure everything is working efficiently. I need the tank and everyone in it at their peak."

"Of course," Gunther replied.

Helmut was already clambering on to the Panzer. "You check the tracks, road wheels, sprockets and barrel, I'll check inside. The trigger on my MG has been sticking, probably from the dust." As radio operator he was also charged with firing a ball-mounted 7.92mm machine gun set into the tank's hull where he sat. Dust from Russia's dirt roads had become a significant problem for all German vehicles, particularly the armoured ones. Everything that moved propelled a cloud of red powder into the air. Unless you were at the front of an armoured column, that meant driving all day through a permanent dust storm. The Panzerwarte did their best to ease the problems caused by these conditions, but individual tank crews were also responsible for keeping their vehicles on the road worthy.

"What about me? What do I do?" Willy asked.

"You and I are going to have breakfast," Ralf replied, wrapping an arm round the gunner's broad shoulders. "And talk some tactics."

HUNDREDS OF KILOMETRES to the south, Hans and his unit were marching across Bessarabia as part of a long column of Landser. It felt as though they had been marching forever yet they were still some distance from the River Dnestr. Only once had they crossed its waters and breached the Stalin Line would the invasion of Russia truly have begun. All their efforts of the past ten days were merely a prelude to the real conflict still to come. Some men in the unit were already complaining about the monotony of their task as they marched mile after mile of dusty roads, with either side lined by fields of golden corn that nodded gently in the breeze. The first few hours after leaving the ruin that was Reni had been joyful. Now it was tedious as open mouths filled with dust, their irritating particles causing eyeballs to bleed.

Hans looked over his shoulder as he marched. A red cloud was rising into the sky, as if some chemical had been set alight to torture the air. Such sights had baffled him at first, until an armoured column had roared past, scattering the infantry off the path. As the vehicles vanished out of view, the column left a crimson dust wake to darken the green hills. For the most part, Soviet counter-attacks or skirmishes were over by the time the Landser reached the scene of battle. These enemy feints were delaying tactics, Hans realised, designed to give themselves time to bolster their defences at the Stalin Line. That would be the real battle, the true test of strength.

The voice of Sergeant Witte brought the men to a halt. The sun was directly overhead, roasting them in its heat. A small copse of trees one side of the road offered a little shelter, so they would rest there. Most of the men headed for the shade, content to shrug off their heavier equipment, but Hans and a few others were more interested in the evidence of a battle that had taken place on the other side of the road – the ground was pitted with shell-holes and retreating Red Army soldiers had dug a few trenches. But the big point of interest was the sight of a Soviet tank on its side amongst the corn.

A mighty gash in its hull showed entrails of twisted steel, mute evidence of the recent conflict. Hoping to get a better look, Hans took off his new helmet. It had taken more than a week of trying on helmets from dead soldiers before he'd finally found one that fitted comfortably. Witte encouraged all his men to scavenge from their fallen comrades, explaining that the better the weapons and equipment they had, the better their chances of survival. Hans peered into the ruptured tank, but could see none of its dead crew. Straightening up again, he glanced round the field but could see no graves nearby.

"Wherever possible, the Bolshevik troops take their dead with them," a voice said from nearby. Hans glanced across the tilted tank to see a man in an Italian officer's uniform using a pencil to take notes. "They always remove their papers and regimental badges too. Keeps the enemy guessing about what exactly is the size of the threat still to be faced." The newcomer walked round the tank, offering to shake Hans's hand. "Sorry, I didn't mean to surprise you. My name's Giovanni Brunetti, I'm an Italian war correspondent. One of few on the Ostfront, as you Germans like to call it."

"What are you doing here?" Hans asked.

"I'm between rides, you might say. I depend upon the kindness of motorized divisions to get from place to place. It's a fitful existence, but not without compensations." Brunetti produced a bar of chocolate from a pocket, broke it in half and gave one end to Hans. "It's melted and reset several times, but should still taste all right. Never know when you'll see a solid meal, so I always carry a fistful of these. They're useful for getting people to talk, too."

Hans could not help but smile at the Italian's disarming honesty. Brunetti was almost two metres tall, with a drooping black moustache that accentuated his dogged expression. A mass of unruly black hair swept back from his face, while his eyes were a comforting shade of hazel.

"What did you want to know?" Hans replied.

Brunetti smiled. "Tell me where you've been and what you've seen. I'm fascinated by this war. To my eyes the soldiers are more like engineers, tending a mighty machine, driving it forwards into battle. This is the new industrial age, fighting for the future of Europe." He pursed his lips. "Sorry. I've a tendency to wax lyrical whenever I get the chance, much to my editor's chagrin. I'll shut up and let you answer."

So Hans talked, relating his experiences since leaving Reni. Brunetti nodded, sometimes taking notes, but most of all he listened. As Hans's words wound down, the Italian stroked his moustache thoughtfully. "There's something else, isn't there? Something you're not telling me."

"Why do you say that?"

"It's my job to know the difference between somebody telling the truth and somebody telling the whole truth."

Hans grimaced. "It's not my place to talk about what happened in Reni. I don't know the full story, only my part in it and that wasn't much."

"Nobody ever knows the full story, especially a war correspondent like me. I get told lies by officers and bravado by the men on the ground. The truth is somewhere in between. But then I've also heard it said that truth is the first casualty of war, so who knows?" Brunetti put his notebook and pencil away. "I've heard a little about what happened in Reni, but you're the first person I've met who was there. Tell me what you saw. I won't take any notes, I won't use your name. I'm trying to put the pieces together. Maybe you could help me see what size the puzzle is."

Hans wanted to help the war correspondent but felt it would be a betrayal of sorts. "I'm sorry, I can't. To be honest, I still don't know what I witnessed."

The Italian shrugged and smiled. "I understand. Well, it looks like your unit is ready to move on and you'd better rejoin them. I hope you enjoy the chocolate."

Hans looked round and saw Witte assembling the others beside the dirt road. The German shouldered his equipment quickly and bid farewell to Brunetti. As he turned to go, the war correspondent made a final comment.

"It's a shame we didn't get the chance to talk for longer, as I suspect your experience in Reni had something to do with a Rumanian officer called Constanta. Am I right?"

Hans could not help being startled by the Italian's comment. He spun round to hiss at Brunetti. "How did you know that?"

"I didn't," the Italian said. "I was guessing. But I've had my own encounters with the 1st Rumanian Mountain Troop and its enigmatic leader, so I know what a disquieting effect he has upon those he meets."

"Vollmer. Get yourself over here," Witte bellowed from the dirt track.

Brunetti stepped closer to Hans. "I'll find you tonight. We can talk further then. I have information that could save your life, private."

Hans ran to catch up with the column of Landser as it marched away. He glanced back once to see the war correspondent walking around the ruptured Russian tank, examining its broken carcass. What did Brunetti know about the Rumanians? Did he share Witte's suspicions about them?

RALF WAS SOON despairing of the new addition to his crew. Sergeant Gorgo had refused to leave the tank under any circumstances, saying he wanted to watch and observe the movements of every man inside. He even refused an offer to take Ralf's place in the commander's seat, because the hatch was open. "We normally drive with all the hatches open, unless we know the enemy is nearby," Ralf told the Rumanian observer. "We'd die of heat exhaustion otherwise. It gets hotter than an oven inside this thing during summer."

"I understand," Gorgo replied, choosing his words carefully. "But I have an... What do you call it? An allergy. Too much sunlight is not good for me."

"Have it your own way," Ralf shrugged, exchanging a look with Martin. Gorgo had taken the loader's foldaway seat inside the Panzer, so the crew's youngest member was forced to remain standing in the cramped space. "Helmut, any more intelligence reports on the Soviet positions?"

The radio operator shook his head, attention focused on listening to incoming signals. "Nein. They are still–"

He stopped, holding one finger aloft to indicate he was receiving a transmission. Helmut started to scribble notes furiously, then sent back a report before glancing over his shoulder at Ralf. "Our reconnaissance aircraft report the bulk of the Russian armour is a mile ahead, in the next valley. Dive-bombers should be approaching them now."

As he finished speaking, a Schwarm of four Ju 87s appeared in the sky, escorted by a pair of Bf 109 fighters. Ralf watched them pass from his position in the cupola, leaning back against the rim of his escape hatch. He pushed the goggles away from his eyes, instead using his 6x30 binoculars to study the planes streaking across the azure sky. Ralf knew his brother could be one of the pilots inside the Stukas. Klaus was seven years his junior, having been born after the First World War. Ralf was born before that doomed conflict, but the Panzer commander felt closer to Klaus than to Hans. As the youngest Hans had grown up knowing little else besides Hitler's Germany and the escalation toward the war. There was eleven years between Ralf and Hans, but it felt more like a lifetime to Ralf.

He admired the Stukas as they screamed past, their characteristic gull-wing configuration and fixed under-carriages making them easy to identify from the ground. Do your job well today, Ralf urged. Our lives may depend upon you. He pulled his throat microphone closer, ensuring all the crew could hear his orders clearly. "Full speed ahead. I want to hit those Bolshevik bastards when our Stukas have finished with them, before the Soviet armour can regroup. Gunther, give me maximum accel-eration. Helmut, pass the word to the rest of our Panzerkeil – we're to go in hard and fast. Willy and Martin, get ready. If we're going to pull this off, you both need to be at your best. Everybody understand?"

The crew responded as one, reporting back in perfect unison. Ralf permitted himself a smile of satisfaction as the Panzer surged forward, two more tanks following behind to form an armoured wedge. The three tanks cut a swathe across a field of golden sunflowers, crushing the cheerful blooms beneath their relentless tracks. Ralf lowered himself fully into the commander's seat, closing the overhead hatch. He noticed Gorgo gripping the foldaway seat's edge, holding on grimly as the tank bounced and bounded across the uneven terrain.

"You are not waiting until the Stukas have finished attacking the Russians?" he asked, confusion evident on his taciturn features. "Aren't you afraid they could hit you too?"

Ralf smirked. "Gunther. Rule twenty of Panzer combat training."

The driver laughed. "Make use of supporting artillery or dive-bomber attacks immediately. Do not wait until such attacks cease. They only have a suppressive, not destructive effect. It is better to risk friendly fire than rush into an actively anti-tank defence," he shouted, hands and feet working the tank's controls.

Gorgo nodded. "But why rush into battle?"

"Martin. Rule eight, if you please," Ralf requested.

The loader tilted his head to face the Rumanian. "During an attack, move as fast as possible. You are much more likely to be hit at slow speed. There are only two speeds: slow for firing and full speed ahead."

"Very good," Ralf said. "In essence, we will drive directly at the Russians, blowing the Godless communists to kingdom come as we pass and emerge on their far side victorious and unscathed. At least, that's the plan. The resulting confusion will allow other tanks from the division to encircle the Soviet armour and decimate those trapped within the Kessel."

"Kessel?" Gorgo asked, uncomprehendingly.

"A cauldron. A crucible you might call it."

"I see," the Rumanian muttered. "A bold strategy."

Ralf nodded. "Willy. Rule thirty for our observer's benefit."

The gunner grinned, reciting the phrases like a child saying their catechism. "The Panzer division is the modern equivalent of the cavalry. Panzer officers must carry on the cavalry traditions and its aggressive spirit. Remember the motto of Marshal Blucher: 'Forwards and through – but sensibly'."

Helmut interrupted the crew's refresher course in battle tactics. "We should be able to see the Soviet positions any second now."

The Panzer crested the top of a hill and rolled quickly down the other side. Ralf peered through the glass blocks of his visor ports, taking in the carnage spread across the valley of green and gold. Strewn about the fields of corn were the gutted hulks of nearly a dozen Soviet tanks, several lying on their side. Blackened craters marked the positions where bombs dropped by the Stukas had missed their targets, creating a patchwork of holes in the battered crop. Russian soldiers stood in isolated groups, still watching the skies as the last of the Stukas departed the valley, the scream of the planes still echoing in the shocked atmosphere. Despite suffering heavy losses, half a dozen Soviet tanks remained operational, carving elliptical paths across the verdant cornfield. Another three Russian tanks were motionless on the brow of the opposite hill, as if waiting for orders.

"Forward!" Ralf shouted, marvelling at the suicidal tactics of the Bolshevik tank crews. It's as if they want to be killed, he thought, unable to grasp such a pointless sacrifice. He reached forward and clapped a hand on Willy's broad back. "Target the three tanks up on that hill."

The gunner spun the wheels around him, twisting the Panzer's turret sideways to take aim at the left tank of the three. The three vehicles had stopped in a line, one after another, like a stationary column. Disable the tank at the front and the other two would be stymied, their escape route blocked.

With the Panzer now rolling down into the valley, Willy fought to bring the main gun up to bear on his target. "Ready!" he shouted at last.

"Fire," Ralf snarled.

The gun boomed in response, spitting out its spent casing a moment later. Martin was already loading the next shell into position, while Ralf peered through his vision ports at their target.

A black tear appeared in the turret of the Russian tank and then its hatches exploded outwards, the shriek of metal audible a moment later. Amazingly, the Soviet tank began rolling forwards, as if someone was still alive inside and attempting an evasive manoeuvre.

"Again. Hit it again," Ralf commanded.

Another boom from the Panzer's main gun and the enemy vehicle flipped over sideways, smoke and flame belching from its tattered interior. The other two tanks in its formation were trying to move away from their fallen leader, but the suicidal choice of positions was to be their undoing.

"Target the rear tank," Ralf said, but Willy had anticipated the order and was already traversing the turret sideways to his new target. Another shot and the third tank was history, wedging the middle vehicle in position between the blazing hulks of its travelling companions.

"We seem to be attracting attention," Gunther called out. Ralf's gaze shifted to the cluster of Russian troops and tanks on the valley floor, getting ever closer as the Panzer barrelled down the hill towards them.

"Dissuade them," Ralf replied. "All machine guns, open fire!" Helmut abandoned the radio to aim his MG34 at the Russian soldiers. Ralf twisted his head to glare at the Rumanian observer. "That means you too, Gorgo. No passengers in my Panzer."

The sergeant nodded, grabbing hold of the turret's machine gun and fired a fusillade of bullets at the Soviet infantrymen, mowing them down as they fled through the corn. Martin maintained his cramped position, feeding the main gun with shells as Willy began targeting the Soviet armour still moving within the valley. Machine gun fire from one of the Russian tanks speckled the Panzer's exterior as it rolled toward the German vehicle.

"Remember, the Bolsheviks often stop to fire their front cannon. If one of them even slows down, blow the bastards back to Moscow!" Ralf snarled. He watched one of the Russian armoured vehicles explode, the victim of concentrated fire from the other Panzers that had invaded the valley. "Keep going," Ralf said. "Forward and through, remember – forward and through."

None of the others replied, as they were too intent on their individual tasks to say anything. The only voice audible within the tank was a cackle of laughter coming from Ralf's right. He pulled his eyes away from the vision port to look for the source; Gorgo was laughing manically to himself as he fired the turret machine gun, blazing away at the remaining Russians. God in heaven, he's enjoying this slaughter, Ralf realised. Imagine what this sadistic bastard would be like if given his own Panzer. The very thought chilled Ralf's blood.

As THE SUN dipped over the horizon, Hans and his infantry unit sought shelter for the night in a village that had been abandoned by the Russian Army earlier that day. The Russians, who razed the handful of buildings as they retreated, left a blackened and charred mess for the Germans to occupy. Hans was eating tinned tomatoes and dry black bread when he heard an Italian voice asking for him by name. In the distance Hans could see Brunetti talking with Witte, the sergeant's face cold and resolute. Whatever stories the war correspondent was pursuing, he would get little help from Witte.

Eventually, Brunetti saw Hans and strolled towards him, smiling. "We meet again, Private Vollmer. How went the day?"

Hans shrugged. "Monotonous. Marching and dust. Marching and dust. The Russians always retreating before us. It feels like this war still hasn't started."

Brunetti laughed. "Don't worry, there'll be plenty for everyone." He nodded at the meagre rations. "Not much of a meal for a day's marching."

"The goulash cannon was coming by another road, but they got stuck in mud caused by a passing shower. So, no hot meal tonight."

The Italian grimaced. "These roads – red dust that stings your eyes when it's dry, mud that sticks like glue when there's one drop of rain in the air. One of the armoured columns I've travelled with calls it Buna."

"That's a brand of synthetic rubber, back home." Hans abandoned his rations, sick of eating the same food for the third meal in succession. He moved closer to Brunetti, speaking conspiratorially with the war correspondent. "This morning, you were trying to tell me about Hauptmann Constanta and his Mountain Troop."

"These are not things to be discussed in the open air at night."

"There's an abandoned church at the other end of the village," Hans volunteered. "The Russians bombed it, but half the roof is still intact."

"That will have to do," Brunetti replied. "Show me." The two men made their way through the few remaining farmhouses in the small settlement. The church was much as Hans had described, one corner remaining in one piece while the rest was a shattered ruin. There were no crosses or religious icons in the building, its religious architecture the sole remaining evidence of its original purpose.

"I stood outside a place like this two days ago," the Italian said. "The sort of rustic chapel you see at any mountain crossroads. But there was no cross, no representation of Christ to be found. The building had been given a fresh coat of varnish, but all other trace of religion was missing, removed. An old peasant came up to the front doors and crossed himself, the same as any pilgrim in Rome." Brunetti mimicked the gesture, bringing three fingers up to his face. He touched them to his forehead, then moved them down to his chest, across to pause over his heart, then back across to touch his right breast. Finally, he raised the three fingers and kissed their tips, completing the ritual. "I asked him where God had gone. The old man told me the Bolsheviks wouldn't allow any icons or images of Christ in the church, and then he laughed." Brunetti smiled at the memory. "It was as if the peasant could not help but laugh at such impiety, as if banishing the sight of God would have any effect upon the feelings and beliefs inside these people, within their hearts and minds."

"But what does this have to do with Constanta?" Hans asked.

The war correspondent's face saddened. "I will come to that soon enough. Let a storyteller have his way." Brunetti sat on a length of fallen masonry. "The villagers told me that the communists had turned the church into a repository for sunflower seeds, waiting collection to have the oil extracted. As I watched, a group of old women appeared, carrying a silver crucifix. They told me it had been hidden from the Bolsheviks, wrapped in cloth and buried beneath one of their houses. The cross was being returned to its rightful home. As dusk fell, the villagers broke open the doors of the church and began shovelling all the seeds into sacks. That was when Hauptmann Constanta arrived, driven to the village in a truck by some surly Obergefreiter." When the Italian described the vehicle and its driver, Hans recognised them as Cringu and his covered truck.

"To be honest, I don't know why Constanta had come to that place," Brunetti continued. "Perhaps it was chance or bad luck that brought him and his men there at that time. Perhaps they had heard tell about the church being reclaimed by the villagers. But their reaction when they saw the crucifix–"

"How many men did Constanta have with him?" Hans interrupted.

"At least half a dozen. They jumped out of the back of the truck, armed to the teeth. The Hauptmann never produced a weapon, but he did not seem to need one. The command in his voice, the authority with which he held himself... It was awe-inspiring, almost messianic, you might say. I imagine few men could resist him." Brunetti paused. "Where was I? Oh yes, the crucifix. Constanta saw it and cried out, as if someone was holding a knife to his throat. The reaction by his men was even more extreme, as if they feared for their lives. Constanta muttered something to one of his men in a language I didn't understand, Rumanian I guess. The soldier shot and killed the old woman carrying the cross, murdered her in cold blood. Some of the villagers screamed at Constanta in anger, saying the old woman had never hurt a soul. Others broke down in tears. A few said nothing, the shock was too much for them, I suppose."

Hans could not stop himself from interrupting the war correspondent again. "Surely the ranking German officer in the village did not allow this to go unpunished?"

"He did try to stop it," Brunetti replied. "His name was Oberleutnant Karl Eschenbach. I had been travelling with his unit for two days, hitching a ride from one battle zone to the next. One of the privates must have fetched Eschenbach, told him what happened. The Oberleutnant confronted Constanta in the village square, demanded to know what justification there could possibly be for slaying an old, unarmed woman. Constanta said he had evidence the settlement was a stronghold for partisan fighters. Being a Hauptmann, the Rumanian outranked the Oberleutnant, but that didn't stop Eschenbach. He threatened to radio a higher authority and check the veracity of Constanta's claims. Eschenbach left to find his signals man, but never came back. They found his body an hour later, pale and drained of blood, two puncture marks in the neck. Like the four Russian soldiers you encountered in Reni."

"How did you know?"

The Italian silenced Hans with a gesture. "People tell me things they wouldn't confess to their priest – they always have. It's a useful talent to have as a reporter. Must be something about my face," he said. "While Eschenbach was gone, Constanta ordered the villagers to rebury their silver crucifix or face the same fate as the old woman. Once it had been removed, the Hauptmann had the church burnt to the ground, then set his men to work torching all the other houses in the village. Constanta said an example had to be made of them, to ensure others nearby did not contemplate offering comfort or aid to partisan fighters. When Eschenbach's body was discovered by one of the Rumanians, Constanta announced that the atrocity was proof of a partisan presence nearby. I believe the German troops had been sceptical up until then, but when Eschenbach's body was paraded before them, well... That sealed the villagers' fate."

"I'm surprised Constanta let you witness all of this," Hans commented.

"I don't think he had registered my presence, not until one of the Germans pointed it out. I was pushed into the back of the Rumanians' truck and kept there until dawn. I couldn't see what happened, but I heard what was said, what was done to those villagers – the screaming, the terror. Most of them were over fifty, some as old as seventy. The women were forced to stand in the square all night, without food or water, while the men dug a mass grave. As dawn approached Constanta ordered the Germans to execute every villager. The Rumanians drove me away in their truck as the shooting started. Just before the sun came up, the truck stopped in the middle of an open plain and I was ordered out. Constanta pressed a pistol against my forehead and warned me against ever trying to report what I had seen. 'We have friends at the highest level in Berlin. They will not look kindly upon anyone who threatens the war effort along the Ostfront,' he said. Then Constanta got in the back of the truck with his men and was driven away."

Hans thought about what Brunetti had said. It all sounded fantastical, beyond belief. But had he not witnessed things that defied rational explanation, heard stories that bore more resemblance to legend than reality? "I stopped that truck when it was being driven into Reni on the first day of fighting. When I looked in the back, it seemed to be carrying–"

"Coffins?" the Italian asked.

"Yes."

Brunetti nodded. "When they threw me into the back of the truck, it was so dark I couldn't see what I was sitting on. I took the boxes to be caskets of some sort, for storing rifles or ammunition. It was only as the first light of day began filtering inside that I saw the coffins for what they were." The war correspondent gave the sign of the cross and kissed his fingertips again, but this time it was no mere imitation. "At that moment I believed I was as good as dead. Why these creatures let me go, I still do not understand. But I have spent every second since gathering what information I can about their movements, gleaning what little I can about their activities. Knowledge is power. Even if I can never write about what I have seen and heard, I can still warn others."

"You said you had information that could save my life," Hans prompted.

"Yes. But first, tell me what you witnessed in Reni. Fill in the blanks for me."

Reluctantly, Hans recalled his late night encounter with Constanta, the mist creatures that snatched the Russian insurgents out of thin air and the enlarged canine teeth that resembled fangs in the Hauptmann's mouth. "My sergeant, he suspects the 1st Rumanian Mountain Troop could be..." Hans's voice trailed away, unable to continue.

"Don't be embarrassed," Brunetti urged. "I won't laugh if you say the word."

"He suspects they could be vampyrs."

The Italian nodded. "The undead, nightwalkers, servants of the twilight. They are a legend in my country too, a story told to send children to bed early, for fear of what might come for them in the dark. I never believed before coming to Bessarabia, but now... Now I find myself praying for the first time since I was a child." Brunetti stared at Hans. "Do you believe in God, Private Vollmer?"

"I was brought up within the church."

"Good, that will help. Do you carry a cross or religious icon?"

Hans shook his head. His mother had tried to press one into his hands the day he left for the Landser, but he had refused it, saying he was a man now and had no need of such childish things. The hurtful expression on her face had haunted him as much as her tears at his departure. Now, more than ever, he wished he could turn back time and accept her heartfelt gift.

"Find one," Brunetti urged. "Constanta and his men cannot stand to look upon such objects, things of faith, possessions imbued by belief. In daylight you are safe from him too. It seems that nobody has ever seen them walking around in the hours between dawn and dusk."

"What about Constanta's orderly, Cringu? He drives that truck full of coffins around in daylight."

"He may be in league with them, but I believe he is not a true vampyr. He must be in their thrall, doing their dirty work when they cannot," the Italian speculated. "I do not know all the facts yet, I am still discovering more every day." The sound of movement outside the church startled him. "Who was that?"

Sergeant Witte appeared in the shattered doorway. "I've been looking for you, Vollmer. You were due on sentry duty twenty minutes ago. Get to your post!"

"Yes, sergeant," Hans responded. He nodded to Brunetti and went outside, pausing long enough to hear the two men talking.

"I told you to stay away," Witte growled.

"He deserves to know the truth. They all do, otherwise how can your men hope to protect themselves from those creatures?"

"Those creatures are on our side in this war. While that remains the case, we have no need of protection. The Russians are the ones who should be scared of Constanta and his men, not us."

"Your words are brave, sergeant, but your eyes tell another story," the war correspondent replied.

Hans realised he had lingered too long and hurried away, his mind abuzz with all that Brunetti had told him. There was no doubt Witte also believed the Rumanians were evil, but he did not consider them a threat.

I pray to God he is right, Hans thought bleakly.

Chapter Five

JULY 7TH, 1941

As DUSK APPROACHED, Klaus circled his Staffel's airfield, intrigued by the sight of three unfamiliar planes parked on the grass below. He called back to his gunner. "Am I imagining things, or is that a Kette of Hurricanes down there?" Klaus dipped one wing so Heinrich could get a better look at the single-seat fighters, turning the Stuka into a banking manoeuvre.

The gunner peered down at the three aircraft. They had stubby, angular fuselages with large, rounded fins. Like Klaus, Heinrich had previously encountered Hurricanes to instantly recognise the robust fighter. "My God, you're right. I thought we'd seen enough of them over the English Channel. What the hell are they doing on the Ostfront?"

Klaus shrugged. "Do you recognise their markings?"

"They've all got RAF camouflage, but the engine cowling has been painted chrome yellow, the Axis recognition colour. There's a yellow band on rear fuselage too. Stripes of blue, yellow and red on the rear rudders – they look familiar. Must be some of our allies, come to join the fun."

"Hardly any fun left to be had," Klaus commented. The Luftwaffe had effectively claimed dominion of the sky; destroying nearly two thousand Soviet planes on the first day of Operation Barbarossa. Most of their sorties since then had been mopping-up operations or acting as flying artillery for the Landser. The airfield was abuzz with rumours that half the Staffel would soon be sent south to protect the oil fields at Ploesti in Rumania. "Let's land and get a closer look."

The second the Stuka's propeller stopped spinning, Klaus slid back the cockpit and jumped onto the plane's wing. A fuelling truck rolled towards the Ju 87. "Where's Satzinger?" Klaus called to the ground crew.

One of them jerked a thumb across the airfield. "In his tent, talking to the new arrivals: three flyers from the Royal Rumanian Air Force."

The pilot jumped down on to the grass, Heinrich following him. "Rumanian! That's where I've seen those rudder markings before," the gunner exclaimed. "They're a long way from home."

"Perhaps they're not getting enough action with Army Group South," Klaus said, striding briskly towards the three Hurricanes.

Heinrich followed, pointing at the cockpits. "That's odd," he said. "They're all black. How can they see out?"

Klaus shared his puzzlement. "Some Ju 87s are having protective sun-blinds fitted as tropical equipment, but I've never seen black glass canopies before. What purpose can they serve?" The two men walked around the Hurricanes, enjoying the opportunity to study up close an aircraft they had previously met as an enemy in the sky. Four machine guns were mounted in each wing, far enough from the propeller to avoid the need for synchronisation.

"Getting an eyeful, eh?" a stern voice asked. The two flyers turned to find Satzinger marching towards them, his face like thunder. "It's bad enough the brains in Berlin want to send half our planes south. Now the Royal Rumanian Air Force are sending us their cast-offs on some ludicrous exchange scheme!"

"Why are they flying British planes?" Heinrich asked.

"They bought them in thirty-nine, before the war began," the major replied.

Klaus was more interested in the fate of his Staffel. "Is Berlin definitely dividing us up?"

"It seems we've been too successful for our own good. So we're getting Rumania's finest to plug the gaps," the major snarled. "You want to know the best part? This lot specialise in flying night missions. In fact, our Axis friends are refusing to leave their tent until the sun goes down. Have you ever heard such nonsense in your life?" Klaus and Heinrich shook their heads. Satzinger handed across the documentation for their next sortie.

"The Soviets are bringing up reinforcements by train, so we have to stop them before they can reach the frontline. Your target is a railway line, a hundred and fifty kilometres due east of here. I'm not expecting much aerial resistance, and if you can believe Berlin, we've already destroyed the entire Red Air Force. Anyway, you can have one of the Rumanians as fighter escort. See how they do." The major stomped away, still muttering under his breath.

Heinrich smiled sardonically. "That went well."

AN HOUR LATER Klaus was taking off in his Ju 87, one of the Rumanian Hurricanes following him. The two Luftwaffe crew had been given the briefest of introductions to their escort, a thin-faced pilot called Căpitan aviator Stefan Toma. While Klaus had restricted himself to polite small talk, Heinrich could not resist asking the Rumanian a question. "Your canopy, it's painted black. How can you fly like that?"

"Is not painted," Toma said, his words heavily accented. "Is tinted glass."

"Yes, but why?"

The fighter pilot grinned wolfishly, flashing a mouthful of disconcertingly sharp teeth. "We can see out, but enemy cannot see in. It unnerves them." With that he left to prepare his aircraft for the night sortie.

As the Stuka left the ground, Heinrich was still pondering their brief encounter with the new arrival. "Tell you what unnerved me: his teeth. My father's Alsatian didn't have fangs like that."

"Let's concentrate on the mission and worry about Toma later, okay?" Klaus said, his tone making it clear this was a command, not a question.

"Jawohl," Heinrich replied cheerfully. The Stuka levelled out from its ascent and headed east, the Rumanian Hurricane staying a discrete distance behind the Ju 87's left wing. Within thirty minutes the two planes were approaching their target, the railway line clearly visible in the moonlight, its tracks cutting a swathe through the countryside. Klaus signalled for the Rumanian to stay back as cover, then tipped over to port and began to accelerate downwards, pointing the plane's nose at the twin tracks below.

As the Stuka screamed through the air Klaus heard a new noise, the sound of another plane nearby, then another, and another.

"We've got company!" Heinrich shouted. "Three Ratas, closing in fast!" He opened fire with his machine gun, quickly firing off a drum of seventy-five rounds.

Klaus knew better than to look back. He had seen enough of the Russian fighters to be aware of the threat they posed. All his attention had to be focused on the target, otherwise their payload would be wasted. "Nearly there," he said as the Stuka continued accelerating, the ground below rising up to fill the cockpit. "Nearly there..." Klaus pressed the release button on his central column, then broke away, climbing, climbing, all the while waiting for the fateful sound of enemy fire shredding the metal skin of his plane. As the Stuka climbed, it shook violently as the concussion blast from his bombs detonated below.

"Here they come," Heinrich warned, firing off another drum.

"Another few seconds and we'll–" Klaus began. But his words were cut short by the sudden appearance of the Rumanian Hurricane flying directly at him, moments away from a mid-air collision. "God in heaven!" he screamed, yanking back his control stick, straining to get his Stuka out of the way.

"What the–?" Heinrich exclaimed as the Hurricane flew mere metres below the slowly ascending Stuka, charging head-on at the Russian planes. Two of the Ratas twisted away in opposite directions, escaping the oncoming fighter, but the third was decimated by the Hurricane's machine guns as it flew past. The severely damaged Soviet plane plummeted to earth, trailing black smoke, its impact complimenting the damage already made by the Stuka's bombing run.

"He's insane," Klaus gasped, glancing over his shoulder at the Rumanian's daredevil flying. "Toma must have a death wish!"

"Then his wish will be fulfilled, unless we get back in there and help him out," Heinrich urged.

"I'm on it." Klaus thrust the Ju 87 into a steep banking manoeuvre, pushing the aircraft to its limits and beyond in the hope of engaging the enemy planes. The two Ratas had recovered from their high-speed turn and were rounding on the Hurricane. Toma was good, Klaus grudgingly admitted, but he couldn't evade the Reds indefinitely. The Axis pilot twisted and twirled the British-built fighter, extracting every ounce of maneuverability from its sturdy frame and resolute engine. The Ratas were older and their fat radial engines were slower, but they were far more nimble. It was only a matter of time before the Russian pair got the better of the Hurricane.

Klaus finished his turn and urged the Stuka forwards, eager to engage the enemy. He opened fire with both machine guns, the bullets tracing their forward trajectory through the sky, clipping one of the Rata's rear wings and fuselage. The wounded plane limped away, leaving its comrade to face the Hurricane alone. But Toma's plane was firmly in the other Russian's sight, unable to shake him loose. Klaus knew he could never turn the Ju 87 around in time to make a difference. The Rumanian's fate was in his own hands.

The two Germans watched as the Rata opened fire, plumes of smoke escaping from the crippled Hurricane. Flames burst from the engine and the cockpit snapped open and something escaped, flapping up into the air. The Rumanian's plane fell into a terminal dive, plunging relentlessly towards the black and blue ground below, but the victorious Rata pilot had limited time to celebrate his kill. Klaus watched in amazement as the Soviet plane began to twitch in the air, violently jolting from side to side. "What the hell is he doing?" Hans sent the Stuka in a full power dive after the Rata, determined to finish off the Russian flyer.

"It looks like he's fighting something," Heinrich said. "But what?"

Suddenly the Rata twisted over into a barrel roll, plunging at full throttle towards the ground below. As it did, Klaus thought he saw something small and dark escape the cockpit and flap away. The Rata exploded furiously as it hit the ground, a cloud of orange flame mushrooming upwards from its point of impact. Klaus shook his head, unable to comprehend what had happened. There was no obvious reason for the Russian's demise, yet something had clearly intervened to tip the balance.

"Let's head back to base," Heinrich suggested. "We've got two more bombing runs to finish tonight and then Satzinger will want a full report on what happened to our friend in the Hurricane."

"That's not a conversation I'm looking forward to," Klaus commented, turning the Ju 87 back the west.

IT WAS ALMOST dawn when the pair finished their night sorties. Klaus and Heinrich did not discuss what had happened over the Russian railway line with each other. Like many flyers, they did not enjoy dwelling on the loss of a fellow airman, knowing it could be their turn next. Instead, they waited until Satzinger was ready for their report before mentioning out loud the events of that first sortie.

Klaus briefly outlined what had occurred, offering praise for the unconventional but fearless flying of Toma. "It's a shame he didn't make it back. He could have been a useful man to have on the wing."

The major looked at the pair with a puzzled expression. "What do you mean, didn't make it back? Toma walked into my tent an hour ago, apologising for having lost his plane. Another of the Rumanian Hurricanes saw him on the ground, landed and brought him back."

Klaus and Heinrich glanced at each other in disbelief. "He's alive?" Klaus spluttered. "B-but that's impossible! I saw his plane burst into flames before it hit at full speed. Nobody could have got out of that crash."

"Toma said he parachuted clear. All the smoke from his burning engine probably masked his descent from you," Satzinger replied.

"We watched the Hurricane all the way down. Nothing got out," Heinrich said.

"Except for–" Klaus began, but stopped himself.

The major raised an eyebrow. "Except for what, Vollmer?"

Klaus shrugged. "Nothing. We must have been mistaken. Will there be anything else, tonight?"

"No, that will be all. Dismissed," Satzinger said, his attention already focused on the next day's targets and troubles. Klaus saluted and left the major's tent, followed by a curious Heinrich.

"Except for what, Klaus?"

The pilot frowned. "Before the Hurricane went into its dive, the canopy opened and something escaped, flapping into the air. I saw it."

"What? Documents, paperwork?"

"It was brown," Klaus said.

"Perhaps Toma keeps his documents in a leather folder."

"I thought... I thought it had wings."

That gave Heinrich pause. "Wings? Like a bird?"

"Like a bat."

"A bat." The gunner scratched his head, his face clouded by doubt. "You think a bat was flapping around the Hurricane's canopy before it crashed?"

Klaus shrugged. "That's what it looked like. I saw the same thing again with the Rata just before it crashed. It was as if a bat had got into the cockpit and was, well, attacking the pilot. Then it flew away again."

"You're saying a bat brought down the fighter?"

"I know it sounds crazy, but how else do you explain the Rata suddenly flying into the ground for no apparent reason?"

It was Heinrich's turn to shrug. "I don't know. I just consider myself lucky."

"Maybe," Klaus said reluctantly. "But I didn't see any parachutes over that railway line. Did you?"

"No, but–"

"But nothing. Our Rumanian friend is lying. There's no way he could have escaped from that Hurricane as it went down. We'd have seen him get out."

"Maybe. Or maybe the major is right," Heinrich ventured. "We were flying hell for leather up there, trying to stay alive. He might have made it out and we missed it in the heat of battle."

Klaus shook his head but doubt clouded his face. "I don't get it."

His gunner slapped Klaus on the back. "Come on, let's get something to eat. We're still alive to fly another day. That's all that matters now, right?"

Chapter Six

JULY 12ˢᵀ, 1941

IN THE THREE weeks since Operation Barbarossa began, Ralf and his Panzer crew had travelled hundreds of kilometres into enemy territory. They had punched through frontier positions, then overrun Soviet defensive lines time and time again. They had accounted for nearly two-dozen Russian tanks, dealing easily with elderly T-35s, T-26s and thin-skinned BTs. The 13th Panzer Division had skirted beneath the forbidding, calamitous swampland of the Pripyat Marshes while destroying all resistance the Bolsheviks set against them. Now, only twenty miles from the centre of Kiev and another famous victory, they were helplessly stuck.

Two days before, Ralf had seen the Ukrainian capital's kremlin spires in the distance. The 14th Panzer Division had joined them yesterday and the 25th Motorized Division was due to arrive any day. But the daring Blitzkrieg was fast becoming a victim of its own success. Such was the speed of the Panzers' advance that it was leaving infantry and artillery support behind in the accursed red dust. Supplies were running low, ammunition stocks were becoming increasingly scarce and a Soviet counter-attack could occur at any hour.

All of this was incidental to Ralf and his crew, for their Panzer had a more urgent problem. The tank was stuck, wedged in the centre of a narrow village square on the outskirts of Kiev, along with two other Panzer IIIs. They had been lured into the courtyard not long after midday by a Russian armoured vehicle, apparently fleeing from their wrath. Feldwebel Erfurth had been leading the pursuit in the baking sun. He had ordered Ralf's tank and another to form a Panzerkeil behind him to hunt down the enemy.

Ralf had tried to warn the impetuous Erfurth as they drove towards the village, all too aware of how narrow the streets of such settlements could be, but the Feldwebel would not listen. "I am in command of this strike, not you!" he snarled via the Panzers' shared radio frequency. "Follow me in, and that's a direct order." Rashly, Erfurth had charged his tank into the heart of the village and Ralf and the other Panzer were obliged to follow.

A few moments later all three tanks were stuck, Erfurth's tracks hopelessly wedged against solid stonewalls on either side of the vehicle. He had tried traversing the tank's turret, sweeping its main gun from side to side so the long metal barrel slammed into the surrounding walls. Such actions weakened the structures of the bombed-out buildings that eventually collapsed, showering the narrow square with rubble and did nothing to free his Panzer. Ralf's Panzer was immediately behind Erfurth and had nowhere to go. Behind Ralf was the third tank, commanded by freckle-faced Obergefreiter Martin Fuchs.

It was Fuchs who died first when he opened his hatch to see what was impeding their progress. Ralf was emerging from his own cupola when the sound of rifle fire cut through the air, rounds pinging against the armour of the trapped tanks. A cry of pain and Fuchs was dead, slumped backwards over the rim of his escape hatch, half of his head blown away, blood and brain matter splattered against the metalwork. One dead eye remained in its socket, staring lifelessly upwards at the sky.

"Sniper! Everyone down!" Ralf cried, dropping back into his tank, pulling the hatch shut after him. "Scheisse. It's a trap. It's a bloody trap!"

"What do we do?" Gorgo asked, clasping his Feld-flasche. In the eleven days he had been with the Panzer, none of the crew had seen him eat a meal. He sometimes slipped away from them during the night, returning a few hours later with a broad smirk on his face, but the Rumanian sergeant never appeared to be hungry. He sipped frequently from his water bottle, never letting it out of his sight. The crew had started a sweepstake to see who could guess what was inside the Feldflasche, such was their curiosity about it. First prize was well past a hundred cigarettes, with vodka or ouzo the most common guesses. All the crew needed was a chance to see who had guessed correctly. Gorgo's time in the Panzer was ending tomorrow, so they were running out of opportunities to learn of the truth.

"We keep our heads down, " Ralf said tersely. "Their rifles are no match for our armour. Helmut, call Fuchs's men. Tell them not to move his body. They'll only get themselves shot, too."

The radio operator nodded, his hands urgently working the machine at his side.

Ralf twisted round to look through the vision ports at the rear of his cupola; his warning was not being heeded. He could see Fuchs's loader and gunner strug-gling with the dead weight of their commander, trying to pull the corpse down into the safety of the tank's inte-rior. "No, you bloody fools," Ralf screamed. "He's already dead, leave him!"

Another crack of sniper fire and both men were hit. The loader's head exploded into a crimson mist, his headless body spraying an arterial fountain into the air, while the gunner was shot in the hand, losing three fingers. Screaming, he fell back into the Panzer. The sound of running feet became audible, scurrying towards the three tanks. Ralf watched in horror as a Russian soldier sprinted past and lobbed a hand grenade into the open hatch of the rear Panzer. Screams echoed within the tank, followed by a deafening roar of an explosion inside the confined interior. Black smoke belched from the tank and then roaring flames took hold. It did not take long for the sickening odour of burning human flesh to drift into Ralf's Panzer.

"Fuchs's men have had it," the commander said numbly, shaking his head. "That means we're stuck here until reinforcements arrive. Our idiot of a Feldwebel is wedged fast, so we can't go forward, and now we can't go backwards. As long as we sit tight, we should be okay."

"Unless the Russians start an artillery bombardment," Gunther pointed out.

"The glass is always half empty with you, isn't it?" Willy asked angrily.

"I was only saying what we were all thinking," the driver protested weakly.

"Stow it, all of you," Ralf shouted, silencing them. "Helmut, call our glorious leader and see if Erfurth's got any brilliant plans to get us out of this."

The radio operator nodded, transmitting the message. A few seconds later he scribbled down a reply and handed it to Ralf. The commander read it, then crumpled the paper and tossed it aside. "He suggests we stay put. What a genius. Now, why didn't we think of that?"

THREE HOURS LATER the temperature within the Panzer was unbearable, together with the thick stench of body odour and fear. All five crewmen had stripped off their tops, sweat soaking the waistbands of their trousers. Only Gorgo remained fully dressed, apparently unaffected by the sweltering heat. He sipped at his Feldflasche and waited patiently, listening as the others bickered. It was Martin who finally engaged the Rumanian in conversation, the young loader squatting in a cramped corner.

"Don't you ever sweat?"

Gorgo shook his head.

"Not at all?"

"No." The observer took another sip from his water bottle.

Martin sighed and gave up, but Gunther was not so shy. "Why don't you tell us what's inside that flask? We see you drinking out of it every day, but you never offer us a taste. Maybe we'd like to try some."

"You would not enjoy it," Gorgo replied. "It is drink favoured by many in the province where I live, but few outsiders like the taste."

"What province do you come from?"

The Rumanian smiled thinly. "Transylvania."

Gunther laughed at his mention of the myth-shrouded region. "Most of this crew have got drunk on everything from the finest schnapps to the roughest ouzo, so I'm guessing we can handle whatever you Transylvanians drink."

"I think not."

"Why? What are you drinking? Blood?" Gunther asked, the others laughing at his jest. But Gorgo did not join their good humour.

"What is it?" the driver asked wearily.

"Listen." The radio operator peeled off his headphones, eyes squinting as he concentrated on noises from outside the Panzer's hull.

Ralf leaned to one side, pressing his ear against the warm metal of the tank's cupola. "I don't hear any–" he began, but an almighty detonation drowned the rest of his words. Another explosion followed, closer than the first, then another. All three came from behind the Panzer, beyond Fuchs's disabled vehicle, but the shells were landing closer.

"Artillery," Willy whispered tensely.

"Ours or theirs?" Martin asked.

"Theirs," the others replied, speaking as one. The four men had been in enough battles to know the sound of German artillery better than the voices of their sweethearts back home.

"It's a creeping barrage," Ralf decided. "Grab what you need and get out!" The others were already scrambling to collect their Luger pistols and tunics, all except for Gorgo. He remained in his seat, as always clutching his Feldflasche. Ralf noticed the Rumanian's inactivity and pointed at a MP 38/40 machine pistol held in a bracket on the turret wall. "Gorgo, unclip that and bring it with you. The Russians might still have snipers nearby, lying in wait for us."

"I'm not leaving the tank," Gorgo replied. The others stopped, staring in amazement at the Rumanian sergeant. Another wave of nearby explosions shook the twenty-ton vehicle, stark evidence of how close the shelling was getting.

"Are you insane?" Willy demanded. "Can't you hear that artillery? The Russians are finding their range. It's only a matter of minutes before they start scoring direct hits. We're sitting ducks out here!"

"I will not leave the Panzer," Gorgo maintained.

"If this thing takes a direct hit from the best the Bolsheviks have to offer, we'll struggle to find any pieces of you to send home," Gunther said.

"I am not leaving."

"Fine," Ralf snapped. "Stay here, take your chances. We're pulling out." He drew his Luger from its holster, checking that the eight round magazine was fully loaded before clicking off the manual safety on the left side of the slide. Satisfied, he glanced round the faces of his crew. "Once the hatches are open, we're liable to attract sniper fire. Keep low and keep apart. No point making ourselves into a single, easy target."

"Rule twelve," Gunther said wryly. "Keep a good distance between vehicles. This divides the enemy's fire. Avoid narrow gaps between vehicles at all costs."

"What about our helmets?" Martin asked nervously. Like most Panzer crews they had been issued with standard army steel helmets, but these were habitually hung from hooks on the tank's exterior to save on space inside. That need was even more pressing with the unwanted addition of Gorgo to their number.

"Grab them if you get the chance. Otherwise, keep your head down and try not to get killed," Ralf said. "Everybody ready?"

The others nodded.

"Let's go!"

Hatches were flung open and the five men scrambled out of the Panzer, throwing themselves off its metal hull and on to the dirt of the courtyard. Ralf was the last out, pushing Martin through the hatchway on the cupola before clambering free. He reached for a nearby helmet but decided betterof it when a bullet pinged off its grey steel.

"Sniper! Move it!" he yelled, propelling the youth off the turret to the ground.

Ralf jumped next, his body somersaulting into a forward roll as he hit the dirt – he was then up and running, dragging Martin along beside him to the nearest piece of cover. The pair dived through a burnt out doorway and into darkness as more sniper fire kicked up earth and perforated the ground behind them. Ralf flung himself back against the wall, still gripping his Luger firmly, waiting for the sound of Russian soldiers. But none came. Instead, the artillery fire was getting closer, shells landing just outside the village.

Ralf smiled at Martin. "You all right?"

The loader nodded.

"Your first time getting shot at outside the tank?"

Another, nervous nod.

Ralf smiled. "Throw up if you want. I did the first time. Scared the the hell out of me."

Martin nodded once more and retched his lunch on to the ground, while Ralf studied their surroundings. They had found refuge in what must have been the local Univermag, a co-operative store with branches in almost every Soviet-controlled village. It had been looted, either by the villagers before they fled the fighting, or by Russian troops as they retreated through this area. The floor was strewn with cartridge paper, cardboard boxes, broken crockery and packing-straw. Nothing of value remained, the store having been hit by an incendiary bomb in the last twenty-four hours. The smell of burning and despair still hung in the air, pungent and unforgiving. Ralf shook his head sadly. Why the Bolsheviks felt obliged to destroy everything in their path was beyond him. If they ever hoped to pre-vail in this conflict, would it not be easier to leave something standing for the survivors? But generals and politicians thousands of kilometres away make such decisions from the front, not the likes of me, he thought bleakly.

"Ralf, are you in there?" a familiar voice whispered from nearby.

"Gunther?"

"Just coming." Seconds later, the driver sprinted into the store, his path traced by a line of sniper's bullets. Once he was safely inside and away from the line of fire, Gunther brushed himself down. Unlike the others he had managed to grab a helmet while fleeing the Panzer, but his pistol was conspicuous by its absence. Ralf pointed at the empty holster. "Sorry. Must have dropped it in the rush to get out."

Ralf rolled his eyes. For a soldier in the mighty Wehrmacht, Gunther had a peculiar dislike of handling guns. That didn't stop him from driving what was effectively a big gun on wheels, but rare was the occasion when Gunther laid hands on any other sort of weapon. "Where are the others?"

"Gorgo was as good as his word. He's still skulking in the Panzer. I can't decide if he's brave or obstinate. Erfurth and his crew haven't budged either. Willy and Helmut are pinned down behind some masonry in the courtyard."

Ralf peered at the narrow square outside. An earlier explosion had dislodged a hefty piece of stonework, dumping it in the centre of the village courtyard. They had been forced to drive around the masonry as they entered the square, a factor that contributed to the Feldwebel's Panzer becoming wedged between two walls. Ralf could see the rest of his crew pressing themselves into the stonework, trying to stay out of sight. They were safe for the moment, but if the Russian snipers shifted to fresh firing positions, the pair would be easy targets. At least the artillery barrage had ceased firing.

"The Soviets must be talking to their snipers, asking for better bearings. It won't be long before the shelling resumes," Ralf said. "We need to get Willy and Helmut to safety."

"How many snipers did you count?" Gunther asked, edging nearer Ralf.

"Two, at the most. Probably partisans, left behind to help close the trap." The commander glanced around the Univermag's floor. "Martin, slide that plate over to me." The loader finished wiping flecks of vomit from his lips and then shoved a miraculously unbroken plate across the floor. Ralf snatched it up and flung the circle of crockery out into the courtyard. He smiling grimly as the plate shattered over Willy's head, blown apart by sniper fire.

The gunner swore loudly at the sky. "Now what, you Bolshevik bastards? Run out of bullets, so you're throwing crockery at us, is that it?"

"Over here, you dolt," Ralf said.

"Oh. It's you," Willy said, a smile spreading across his dusty features. "How did you get over there?"

"We ran."

"And how do you suggest we join you?"

"You run."

"What about the snipers?" Helmut called from beside Willy.

"They'll be the least of your problems in a minute," Ralf replied. "Listen."

A faint whistling hung in the air, getting louder by the second. Helmut cursed and started running towards them, dragging Willy along behind him. The Russian snipers opened fire, bullets flaying the air around the fleeing duo. Then the fallen masonry where Willy and Helmut had previously been hiding exploded, ripped apart by a direct hit from the Soviet artillery. The concussion blast lifted the pair off the ground and hurled them towards the Univermag's doorway. In the resulting confusion of smoke and sound, Ralf and Gunther were able to pull the fallen pair inside. Helmut was out cold, while Willy staggered dizzily about, shaking his head as if trying to dislodge water from his ear.

"What happened?" he asked blearily.

"Worry about that later," Ralf said. "Sit down and rest for now."

Martin helped the gunner find an empty corner, while Gunther tended to Helmut. Outside, the shelling continued, each explosion tearing a fresh hole in the crumbling, devastated village. The final shell of the barrage hit Fuchs's tank. The Panzer flipped over backwards and crushed a wall behind it. Once the smoke

had cleared, Ralf could see a clear path for his tank to
escape, thanks to the Soviet artillery. The only problem
was reclaiming their Panzer without being shredded by
the snipers.

Gunther joined him by the doorway. "You'll never
make it," he said, his eyes following the direction of
Ralf's gaze. "Not if those snipers are still waiting."

"The shelling might have eliminated them."

"We're not that lucky."

"You think?" Ralf asked. "One direct hit on this
building, we'd all be dead."

"Good point," Gunther conceded. "Why has Erfurth
stayed in his tank?"

"There are two possible reasons. No, three, I've
thought of another. First, the hatches could well be
jammed shut, weighted down with rubble from the
buildings he collapsed either side of his Panzer. Alterna-
tively, he figures it is safer inside the tank than running
the gauntlet of sniper fire."

"He could be right about that," Gunther said. "And the
third reason?"

"Erfurth and his men are already dead. We simply
didn't see their demise."

"That's a cheerful thought."

The shelling resumed, more Soviet shells raining down
on the village from further east. Dust fell on the Panzer
crew from the ceiling of their refuge, but none of the
shells found their target.

Once the cacophony of destruction had eased again,
Gunther nudged his commander. "What do you think
Gorgo is doing inside our tank?"

"The same thing as us," Ralf replied. "Waiting."

THE TEMPERATURE WITHIN the Univermag began to
plummet as the sun dropped below the horizon. Ralf
and his crew had spent the intervening hours watching,
searching the buildings surrounding the village square

for any sign of the snipers. But there had been no movement in the battered structures or from the two tanks parked in the courtyard. Overhead the sky faded slowly from the faintest of blues to a deeper shade of azure, then indigo. Finally, darkness ate at the heavens, black spreading across the firmament like a stain.

Helmut had recovered from his close encounter with the Russian shelling. Of the five crewmen he had the best hearing, so he had been trained as a Funker, a radio operator. He was using those superior aural abilities to listen for movement within the village, his head cocked to one side. "There's something close by," he whispered. "Scrabbling claws or nails. Something sucking on the air, sniffing the breeze."

"Probably vermin," Willy grumbled. "No doubt this place is crawling with rats."

"Good," Gunther commented. "Where there's rats, there's food."

"You want to eat the rats?" Martin asked, his face aghast at the thought. "I mean, I'm hungry too, but eating rats…"

"No," Gunther replied. "I meant there must be food nearby, food that the rats are feeding on."

"Oh."

"Of course, a well cooked rat has its merits."

"Quiet, the lot of you," Ralf said. He was standing beside Helmut, trying to hear what the radio operator could. "Where's the sound coming from?"

"I'm not certain," Helmut whispered. "But I think it's inside our tank."

"Perfect," Willy protested. "Now we've got vermin in the Panzer."

"Besides Gorgo, you mean?"

"I said be quiet," Ralf snapped. Once the others were silent, he went to the doorway and stared across the village square at his armoured vehicle. The tank's commander was not hearing what Helmut had, but he could see something happening inside the Panzer. Thin wisps of mist were curling out from within the vehicle, escaping slowly from the vents and hatchways. A thin stream of mist was even falling from the end of the main gun, collecting on the surface of the courtyard.

To Ralf's amazement, the wisps coalesced gradually, blending together into a translucent haze above the ground. The tank commander gestured for the others to join him in the shadow of the doorway. "Watch that mist," he whispered, pointing towards the vapour. "Tell me I'm not seeing things."

The others looked where he was pointing. After a few moments the mist floated away from the tanks, as if a zephyr had blown through it. "What are we looking for?" Gunther asked quietly.

"I'm not sure," Ralf admitted. He explained what he had seen, feeling ever more foolish as he tried to describe the phenomenon.

"Perhaps Gorgo is having a sly cigarette inside the tank?" Willy suggested.

"I've never seen him smoke," Ralf countered.

"Now the sun has gone down, maybe the heat from inside the Panzer is seeping out, escaping as a haze," Gunther offered.

"Have you ever seen that before, in all our time in tanks?"

"No," the driver admitted.

"I can't explain it either," Ralf said. "But that mist moved as if it had a purpose, as if it was being controlled. I know that sounds crazy, but that's what it–"

His embarrassed words were cut short by a cry from one of the battered, broken buildings overlooking the courtyard. It was a man's voice, his scream a terrible sound in the bleak twilight. All five crewmen could hear him begging, though they did not understand his language. Two words were clearly audible, repeated over and over again: "Bojemoi!" and "Djavoli!"

Then there was silence.

"That must have been one of the snipers," Martin observed. "Someone must have got to him."

"Someone," Ralf said grimly. "Or something."

"What do you mean?" the young loader asked.

"Quiet," Helmut urged them. "Listen."

A gun was fired once, twice, three times. Another Russian screamed in the dusk, the word "Djavoli!" heard before his voice was also cut short. Moments later a body was thrown from one of the buildings down into village square, hitting the ground like a wet sack of sand.

"You can come out now, my German friends." a familiar voice called. It was Sergeant Gorgo, his tone gleeful and triumphant. "The Soviet snipers are dead."

Ralf moved to leave but Gunther grabbed his sleeve, holding him back. "It could be a trap. The Russians could have captured Gorgo, got him out of the Panzer and forced him to call for us."

"Perhaps. But those screams sounded all too real to me," Ralf replied. He drew his Luger and walked carefully out into the open, tensed to dive aside at the first hint of a sniper opening fire – but no shot came. He walked to the corpse in the courtyard, crouching to examine the broken body. It was a Russian soldier, his face a mask of terror, his neck snapped, broken and mutilated; somebody had hacked at the throat with a knife, slashed and stabbed repeatedly. Ralf turned the head aside to get a better look in what light remained. The corpse had also suffered another major injury.

There were two puncture marks in the neck, over the path of the carotid artery.

They looked deeper than the other wounds, as if the knife marks were inflicted earlier. Did Gorgo attack the Bolshevik with a knife, to hide the real killing wound? The thought sent a chill through Ralf's bones, as he pondered what could cause such puncture wounds in a neck.

He studied the body with fresh eyes, ignoring the mess of blood around the neck wounds. Aside from the crimson stains, the corpse was pale, almost blue – as if the sniper had been terribly anaemic. Or as if someone had recently drained it of all its blood, a quiet voice said at the back of Ralf's mind. He pushed the thought aside, not wanting to give it any credence for now. "It's safe," he called back to his crewmen. "This is definitely one of the Russians."

The others emerged into the courtyard, Willy and Helmut joining him beside the corpse while Gunther returned to the Panzer. Ralf sent Martin to check if Erfurth and his crew were still alive and give them the all clear. Once the youth had gone, Ralf pointed out to Willy and Helmut what he had noticed about the sniper's body. "I see it, too," the gunner confirmed. "Whatever killed him, it wasn't the knife wounds. They were an afterthought."

"Helmut?"

"Agreed. If Gorgo did this, the sooner he leaves us tomorrow, the better."

Ralf nodded. He swivelled round to see the Rumanian strolling across the courtyard towards them. The front of Gorgo's uniform was stained with blood, still wet and glistening. He had a satisfied smirk on his face, the most joyous expression since being let loose with the turret machine gun.

"The snipers put up quite a fight, but I got the better of them," he boasted.

"How did you get out of the Panzer without being seen?" Willy asked.

Gorgo shrugged. "I waited until nightfall, then slipped out in the dark."

"A neat trick," Helmut observed. "You should teach it to us."

The Rumanian tilted his head to one side. "Maybe I will one day. But tomorrow I must report back to my commander, Hauptmann Constanta. I have learned much about tactics and tank combat from you. They should prove most useful if the Rumanian Army ever decides to form a tank division of its own."

Gunther popped his head through one of the hatches in the Panzer. He was clutching Gorgo's coveted Feld-flasche, unscrewing the lid. "Let's see if I can acquire a taste for your Transylvania beverage."

"No!" The Rumanian ran towards the tank, his hands outstretched. Gunther took a deep swallow from the drinking bottle and then spat the mouthful out into the air, spraying dark liquid from his lips. Gorgo snatched the flask from the driver's hands and began screwing the lid back on.

"Gah," Gunther spluttered, still choking on what he had swallowed from the Feldflasche. "That tasted like blood."

"I said you wouldn't enjoy it," Gorgo replied. He glanced at the others as they gathered around him and then smiled. The Rumanian removed the lid and drank gratefully from it. "Ah, that's better," he said, wiping a dribble of crimson from his lower lip. "Thirsty work, this war."

Erfurth had emerged cautiously from his own Panzer and was studying the walls impeding its progress. He shouted at his crew to get the tank unstuck and then strode back to talk with Gorgo. "I understand we have you to thank for eliminating the Bolshevik snipers?"

The two men walked away, leaving Ralf with his own crew.

Gunther spat out the last traces of Gorgo's drink. "I swear there's blood inside that flask, mixed with some-thing else, possibly red wine. But it definitely contains blood."

Willy was watching the Rumanian carefully. "What manner of creature are we harbouring?" he wondered aloud.

"There is a name for such monsters," Ralf muttered. "But I shall not speak it during the hours of darkness. We talk about this with nobody else, understand? If we try to say what we've witnessed, others will think us mad." The crewmen nodded their agreement. "Gorgo leaves us tomorrow, so we must act as if nothing out of the ordinary has happened. The sooner he leaves our Panzer, the safer we'll be. Now, let's help Erfurth's men get their tank free, since the Feldwebel is too busy making a new friend to get his hands dirty."

Chapter Seven

JULY 15ᵀᴴ, 1941

A WEEK AFTER Klaus's encounter with Cāpitan aviator Stefan Toma, the Stuka pilot found himself flying alongside another member of the Rumanian trio. Toma was still grounded while waiting for a new aircraft, but his two compatriots had been active as fighter escorts for bombing raids by the Staffel's Ju 87s. Satzinger had even persuaded the reluctant Rumanians to begin making sorties during the hours of daylight.

The day's target was a cluster of defensive positions along the Soviet Union's pre-1939 western frontier. The Russian 5th, 6th, 12th and 25th armies had fallen back to these fortifications, after concentrated Stuka attacks had routed the Red Army's armoured formations. The retreat had enabled the Wehrmacht to push into the Dnestr valley. Soon, the battle of the Stalin Line would begin in earnest, but first the Bolshevik strongholds had to be softened up.

When Klaus and Heinrich emerged from an early morning briefing with Satzinger, they discovered their escort was already waiting inside his Hurricane. Locotenent aviator Cristu Droc waved to them from the cockpit, his outline visible through the heavily tinted glass, but he did not open the canopy.

"Your friend's been in there since before dawn, burning through his fuel," a member of the ground crew said as they passed. "None of those Rumanians is in danger of getting a tan."

"You'd almost think they were afraid of the sun," Heinrich joked.

"Maybe they are," Klaus muttered.

His gunner sighed. "Now, don't start all that again, I don't want to hear it. How Toma got out of that Hurricane is much a mystery to me as it is to you, but I don't think there's anything sinister about his explanation." The two men had spent plenty of time debating what they had witnessed, but Klaus still could not convince his gunner anything out of the ordinary had happened.

"Fine," the pilot snapped. "Let's get in the air, okay?"

The mission itself proved uneventful. The Luftwaffe's overwhelming air superiority had been a decisive factor driving back Russian forces, so enemy attacks against the Staffel's bombing runs were rare. The return trip was another matter, with Droc calling from his Hurricane about handling difficulties. "The engine is misfiring," he said.

Klaus remembered what the ground crew had told him. "How long was your engine running before we took off?"

"I am not knowing," the Rumanian replied, struggling to understand the German's words.

"Look at your fuel gauge," Klaus urged. "How much do you have left?"

Both men in the Stuka heard Droc gasp and then hiss in what sounded like a curse in his native tongue. "Nothing," he finally replied. "It shows nothing."

"He must be flying on fumes," Heinrich said. "How far back to the field?"

Klaus studied the terrain for familiar landmarks. "At least another five minutes," he whispered. "Droc'll never make it, not at full throttle." The German pilot called his Rumanian counterpart. "You need to cut back your engine. Do you understand?"

"Cut back my engine."

"Yes, that will stretch out your fuel a little."

"I will try," Droc said.

"It won't be enough," Heinrich said quietly.

"I know, but if he can get close, maybe he can glide in," Klaus replied. His switched his focus back to the Hurricane, lowering his own speed to keep pace with the slowing fighter, but the Rumanian was throttling back too much, his plane decelerating too quickly. "Scheisse! He's going to stall."

No sooner had Klaus spoken the words than the Hurricane fell from the sky, its fuselage tipping to an awkward angle. "Droc! You've got to get the nose back up. You can still land your plane."

"I... am... trying!" the Rumanian said in a low voice, a mighty effort evident in his clenched words.

Klaus studied the landscape ahead. A long, grassy strip of flat land stretched away to the northwest. "Aim for that field on your right, but you must get the nose up. It's your only chance!"

The Rumanian shouted in what Klaus presumed was a curse, then the Hurricane suddenly folded in the air before plummeting to the ground. Both its main wings snapped off upon impact, while the fuselage bounced and skidded along the ground, ploughing through earth and grass.

Klaus called ahead to the airbase beyond the next hill, telling them what had happened. "We're going to take a closer look, see if Droc's still alive." The pilot glanced over his shoulder at Heinrich. "You ready?"

The gunner had been peering out the canopy at the long field where the Hurricane had crashed. There was just enough room for the Stuka to set down safely. "It'll be a bumpy landing, but I've had worse. Let's do it."

Within minutes the two flyers were running towards the Hurricane's remains. Toma might have survived his plane's demise, but there was no way Droc had got out alive. As Klaus neared the fuselage, he sniffed the air. Freshly ploughed earth mingled with leaking fuel to create a heady mixture. "Amazing the Hurricane didn't explode on impact."

Heinrich pointed at a tear along the fuselage when the plane had creased in the sky. "Tank ruptured in mid-air, so the fumes escaped." He caught sight of something else. "The canopy must have shattered at the same time."

The Hurricane's cockpit was a mess of torn metal and blackened glass fragments. Klaus pulled himself up to look inside, bracing for the sight of Droc's, broken corpse. "Poor bastard probably died in seconds. Never knew–" His voice stopped abruptly, abandoning his words.

Heinrich peered up at his pilot. "What is it, Klaus?"

"There's no body."

"What?"

"There's no body, nothing. It's as if he simply… vanished."

The gunner scratched his head. "We didn't see a parachute this time."

"We didn't see a parachute last time, but Toma got out."

"That was night. This is broad daylight," Heinrich replied. "Maybe Droc got sucked out of the cockpit when the fuselage folded in the air?"

Klaus studied the edges of the canopy's fractured metal framework. "No sign of blood or scraps of fabric. You'd expect him to leave some traces behind on his way out." The pilot stretched an arm inside the cockpit and pulled out a bundle of tightly wrapped cloth. "That settles things. His parachute is still inside." As Klaus removed it, a cloud of dust exploded from beneath the parachute, which blew into his face. He coughed and choked violently on the thin particles, letting himself slide back down to the grass beside Heinrich.

The gunner helped wipe the grey powder from Klaus's face. "What is this? Dust?" He dabbed the end of one finger against his tongue to taste the powder and then spat it out. "That's not dust. That's ashes! Human ashes!"

Klaus looked aghast at Heinrich. "How do you know?"

"My uncle worked in a crematorium, before the war. I know how human ashes smell." Once again, Heinrich spat onto the floor to cleanse his mouth of the flavour.

Klaus studied the Hurricane's fuselage again. "If those are human ashes, what are they doing inside the cockpit? I didn't find any trace of a fire. No burning, no scorch marks, except those ashes."

Heinrich shook his head. "None of this makes sense."

"Not unless…" Klaus's face grew grimmer as his thoughts reached a conclusion. "Not unless it was exposure to sunlight that turned Droc to ashes."

The gunner frowned. "What, you think he was allergic to the sun?"

"Not just him – his kind."

"His kind?"

Klaus nodded. "All three Rumanians had black tinted glass in the canopy of their planes when they arrived at the Staffel. They said it was to intimidate the Russians. Maybe it was more about protecting themselves. Have you ever seen any of them outside in the hours of daylight?"

"I must have done," Heinrich said, uncertainly clouding his words.

"I haven't," Klaus insisted. "Satzinger had to bully them into taking any missions in daylight, but even then they have made certain to be inside their planes before dawn, with the cockpit closed. Don't you understand, Heinrich? The Rumanians, they aren't like you or me. They aren't normal. They're something else, something sinister."

The gunner was still shaking his head, but less vigorously now. "Okay, so they're not fond of sunlight. That doesn't stop them being–"

"Human? How many humans do you know turn into ash when exposed to sunlight?" Klaus demanded. Heinrich stumbled away, back towards the Ju 87, so the pilot followed him. "When Toma's plane was hit, you know what I thought came out of the cockpit? A winged creature, like a bat. I saw the same thing attack the Rata pilot." Heinrich kept walking, so Klaus grabbed the gunner's arm and spun him round. "Listen to me. Toma and Droc, I think both of them were–"

"Don't say it," Heinrich pleaded, closing his eyes.

"Vampyrs," Klaus insisted. "The undead. Creatures of the night. You've heard the legends, you know the stories, same as I do. Beings that only come out in the darkness, beings that can turn themselves into other creatures, like bats. Beings that feed on human blood for sustenance. Beings that can be destroyed if exposed to direct sunlight." He pointed at the downed Hurricane. "Beings like the pilot who flew that plane. Droc was a vampyr and I'm betting Toma and the other Rumanian pilot are as well."

"Klaus, this is madness."

"Only a madman would ignore the evidence of his own eyes," Klaus replied. "I know what I've seen and I know what I believe. We have made allies with creatures of the devil himself. What does that make us?"

Heinrich rested a hand on Klaus's shoulder. "Let's say I agree with you–"

"Finally!"

"Let's say I agree with you. What do you suggest we do about it?"

"Tell Satzinger our suspicions, for a start."

"What proof do we have? Some ashes in a plane? Hardly enough evidence to convince me, let alone someone who wasn't here to see what happened. The major, he didn't want to hear what you had to say last time. Hell, neither did I, and I'm your gunner. Why should he believe us now?"

"Two voices are louder than one," Klaus insisted.

"Perhaps, but we need more support before we go to Satzinger with this," Heinrich insisted. "We have to talk with the rest of the Staffel, one on one. Find out if anybody else shares our suspicions about the Rumanians."

"They're not suspicions."

"Until we get some proof, that's all they are," the gunner replied. "I'll talk to the ground crew, see if they've noticed anything unusual about our guests. You approach some of the other pilots, see if they're on our side."

Klaus nodded, smiling at last. "Good. Let's get back to the landing field. The sooner we make a start, the better."

Heinrich nodded. "It's good to see you smiling again. You've been weighed down with all the troubles of the world lately."

"I was beginning to doubt my own eyes," Klaus admitted. "It feels good to have you on my side again."

"I was always on your side," Heinrich said. "I always will be."

CHAPTER EIGHT

JULY 21ST, 1941

REACHING THE EASTERN banks of the Dnestr was more than another simple river crossing for the men in Hans's unit. For most units along the Ostfront, the invasion of enemy territory had begun within hours of Operation Barbarossa's launch on June 22. But the Landser of Army Group South would only set foot on true Russian soil once they had crossed the Dnestr. Hans's unit had reached the river valley four days earlier. Several men from the Mosel region said that it reminded them of home, thanks to the valley's steep slopes and thick woods. Stukas ruled the skies as close air support, bombarding Soviet bunkers across the river, while 88mm German artillery guns destroyed the Russian defensive positions. The constant barrage went on for so long Hans wondered if he would ever know silence again. When the guns finally stopped, it was almost unnerving. No retaliation came from the Soviet side, all resistance apparently crushed by the onslaught from the sky.

The infantry were streaming across the Dnestr. While some crossed in rubber rafts, most used bridges – either those left intact by the retreating Red Army, or new spans hastily put in place by German engineers. Hans was among the first company to reach the eastern side, the soldiers swiftly and deftly taking possession of key defensive positions nearby to secure the bridgehead. Witte warned them to watch for booby traps or Soviet snipers left behind to attack the German flanks, but the lessons learned in Reni had become second nature for these Landser.

Once the crossing was judged secure, Hans and the rest of the unit were tasked with searching all the Russian bunkers to flush out any survivors. Hans was working in a twoman team with Franz Kral who insisted on wielding the hefty flamethrower, despite being considerably slighter of build. As they reached each bunker, Hans would shout a warning for anyone inside to surrender. If no movement was heard within a few seconds, Franz shot a sustained burst of flame into the confined concrete space. Hans would then burst into enclosure with his recently acquired MP 40 machine pistol, ready to finish off anyone still alive. It quickly became apparent someone had already carried out this grim task for them.

Each bunker the privates inspected offered the same spectacle. Where Russian soldiers had remained behind, they were cold and dead, their bodies pale and lifeless. A pair of puncture marks was visible on the neck of each corpse, a patch of dried blood mute evidence as to what happened to the Soviet troops. Some had managed to scratch warnings into the crumbling concrete walls of their emplacements, using the tips of bayonets or even their broken fingernails. "Djavo" and "Djavoli" were the most frequently seen words, but religious symbols also appeared on some of the bunkers' walls. It was the eyes of the dead men that perturbed Hans – glassy and staring, faces around them clenched with horror and fear.

"God in heaven," Franz whispered. "Who is doing this?"

"Fiends," Hans replied. He was becoming all too familiar with such sights, recognising them as symptoms of a battlefield appearance by Constanta or one of his kind. Hans had not seen the Hauptmann for weeks, but other Rumanians bearing the bat and swastika emblem were an all too common presence. "Desecrated bodies, drained of blood. We've seen this too often lately."

Franz pointed at the word "Djavo" written in blood beside a Russian corpse. "What is that? A warning? Or an accusation?"

"Both," Hans said bleakly. "Come on, we've one more of these to check." He marched out of the concrete tomb and straight into the next bunker, not bothering to shout a warning or let Franz incinerate the interior first.

Hans strode inside and felt something round and organic squash beneath his jackboot – he lifted the sole to see a cluster of garlic cloves crushed beneath it. At the same moment a circle of cold metal pressed against the back of his neck. "Scheisse!" he cursed, angry at himself for not following procedure. His haste could well cost him his life.

A quaking voice said something in Russian.

"I don't speak your language," Hans replied slowly, carefully.

The voice spoke again, this time using words he could understand. "Teeth... See... Teeth."

"You want to see my teeth?" Hans asked, pointing at his mouth.

"Da!"

Hans opened his mouth and turned sideways so whoever was behind him could look inside. He was startled to see a young woman in a Soviet soldier's uniform peering intently at his teeth. Hans had heard the Russians let females fight in their army, but was shocked to see one in person; the idea of German women joining the Wehrmacht was unthinkable.

Hans's captor relaxed a little when she saw his teeth were normal, removing the end of her pistol from the back of his neck. But when Hans smiled, her expression darkened. She snarled at him in her own tongue, rattling off as to what sounded like a string of insults and accusations.

Desperate to make himself understood, Hans dropped his weapon and held up his hands in surrender. "I don't want to hurt you." He tried to remember one of the few Russian phrases he had learned in a month of fighting the enemy. He vaguely remembered captured Soviets talking with each other, while awaiting transportation to a prisoner of war camp. What did they call friends? "Tovarisch."

The woman glared at him uncertainly. "Tovarisch?"

Hans nodded, his thoughts racing. Somehow this woman had survived, whereas Constanta's men had slaughtered all the other Russian soldiers in bunkers nearby. The question was how. "Djavoli?"

"Djavoli!" The woman's eyes flashed angrily. She pointed the pistol directly between his eyes, her finger moving to the trigger.

"No, no, not me," Hans protested, waving his hands, hoping his body language would speak for him. He made a series of awkward gestures to ask the Russian a question. "How... did you... stop the... djavoli?"

She looked at him, obviously confused. "Shtop?"

"Stop," Hans said. He pressed a hand out sideways, as if trying to halt traffic. "Stop! Err, halt. Prevent. Stop them. How did you stop the djavoli?"

The woman stared at Hans, then her face lit up, as if finally grasping what his strange words and gestures might mean. She pointed at a string of garlic bulbs hanging over the narrow doorway of the cold concrete bunker. "Chyesnok!"

"Chairs-nook?"

She nodded. "Chyesnok."

"You mean garlic," Hans said, pointing at the bulbs. "Garlic."

"Chyesnok!"

"Garlic keeps them out? Interesting…"

The Russian soldier cracked open her pistol and removed one of the bullets inside, showing it proudly to Hans. "Syeryebro."

He peered at the round. It appeared normal but for the tip, which had been crudely coated with a different metal. "Is this silver?"

"Syeryebro," the woman said, nodding vigorously. She replaced the bullet in her pistol and then aimed the weapon at Hans's head once more. "Bang! Myortvi."

"Myortvi?" he asked. The word sounded a little like "Mord", the German for murder. His mind raced, trying to interpret what she was saying. "You can kill them with a silver-coated bullet?"

The Russian began talking excitedly to Hans, her words racing away, pistol still pointed at his face. Over the woman's shoulder Hans could see Franz creeping into the bunker, the flamethrower ready to fire. Franz jerked his head sideways, his eyes urging Hans to jump out of harm's way.

"No, no, don't do it," Hans urged. "She's not–"

But his words and actions had alerted the female soldier to danger behind her. As she spun round to face Franz, Hans jumped aside. Franz let loose with the flamethrower, burning the woman alive, shouting in triumph as she turned into a human torch. She screamed and howled – flames melting her skin and flesh – before collapsing on to the cold floor, black smoke and the stench of scorched flesh choking the air inside the claustrophobic chamber.

Hans could not bring himself to look at the charred corpse as he staggered out of the bunker, his eyes streaming from the fumes. He had known the woman for a few minutes, yet had formed a bond with her, however fleeting – just as he had with the Russian about to kill him at Reni, before the intervention of those mist creatures. She had been plain-faced and rather dumpy in her ill-fitting Red Army uniform, but she was no different from him. They were both scared, both looking for a way of stopping the Rumanian fiends. Now she was dead, another statistic in a war where thousands were dying every hour, every day. I don't know who will weep for her passing, Hans thought, but I may owe my life to her.

IT WAS SEVERAL hours before he encountered Franz again. The little private was still bragging about how he had saved Vollmer from the Russian femme fatale. "Give it a rest, Kral, okay?"

"Why? It's the bravest thing I've ever done," Franz protested.

"She wasn't going to kill me," Hans said. "We were talking."

"Talking? She was waving a gun in your face."

"Yes, but not to…" Hans gave up, realising it would be too difficult to explain without sounding unbalanced. "Forget it, it doesn't matter."

"It matters to me," Franz insisted. "For once I'm a hero, not the unit mascot. Let somebody else have the glory for once, will you? We can't all be Witte's favourite."

Hans watched him go, bemused by Kral's final statement. I'm the sergeant's favourite? When did that happen? But the call of a familiar voice pulled his attention away from further wonderings. A column of cavalry was crossing the nearby bridge, followed by an armoured reconnaissance vehicle. Standing on top the Panzerspähwagen was Brunetti, waving and calling to Hans, beckoning the soldier to come nearer.

Once the vehicle had crossed the bridge the war correspondent jumped down to the ground, his camera in
one hand, a small kitbag slung over the opposite
shoulder. Brunetti shouted his thanks to the Panzerspähwagen's driver and then smiled at Hans broadly.
"We meet again! I've been hoping to find you somewhere along this road. How goes the war with you?"

Hans pointed at the steady stream of vehicles that
rolled past. "I can hardly hear you. Let's go some place
else, where we can talk without shouting ourselves
hoarse."

The Italian nodded, his warm eyes twinkling with
intelligence. "Good idea." The two men retreated from
the road, strolling through the devastated Russian
defences while Hans related his encounter with the
Soviet soldier. Brunetti was intrigued by what he heard.
"That matches other reports I've had from sources along
the Ostfront. Seems none of the Rumanians under Constanta's command are fond of silver, sunlight or symbols
of faith. Garlic, you say? Remarkable. I wish I'd known
that before I wrote my report."

"What report?" Hans asked anxiously.

"I filed copy three days ago about rumours of a malevolent new force committing atrocities in this war. I
couldn't be too specific, for obvious reasons, but anyone
who reads between the lines will guess what I'm talking
about."

"Was that wise?"

Brunetti shrugged and smiled. "Perhaps not, but
people deserve to know the truth. Even in war, a writer's
duty is always to tell the truth as he sees it."

"But if word of what you've written reaches Constanta
or one of his men–"

"The Rumanians are a tiny part of the Axis forces,
and Constanta's troops from Transylvanian are the
smallest fraction of the Rumanian contingent fighting
alongside Army Group South. According to some of the

documentation I've seen, the Hauptmann had little over a hundred men at his command when Operation Barbarossa was launched. How much influence can one man have?"

"Constanta is not like other men," Hans replied tensely. "His eyes, his voice... It's as if he can reach inside your soul, twist your thoughts to do his bidding. I'm still not sure how I managed to resist him in Reni."

"Vollmer! Why aren't you on patrol with Kral and the others?" The shouting voice belonged to Sergeant Witte, anger all too evident in his tone. He was striding toward Hans and the war correspondent, his face a scowl of anger.

"I was talking to–"

"I can see who you're talking to," Witte spat. "It's Brunetti I was looking for, not you. Get about your business, Vollmer, before I put you on report."

Hans nodded a hasty farewell to the Italian before marching away. Why would the sergeant be looking for Brunetti? The two men did nothing but argue on the few occasions Hans had seen them together.

IT WAS ALMOST dusk when the staff car transporting Giovanni Brunetti stopped outside an abandoned farmhouse, some twenty miles behind the frontline. Soldiers standing guard outside the battered building motioned for the Italian to get out. Witte had said the staff car was personally despatched by Generalfeldmarschall von Rundstedt to collect the war correspondent. No reason was given for the summons, but the sergeant made it clear that refusing the invitation to meet Army Group South's leader was not an option. So Brunetti had let himself be driven back across the Dnestr to von Rundstedt's field HQ.

Once inside the farmhouse, the Italian was escorted to a sparsely furnished room and told to wait. When he tried the door, Brunetti was surprised to discover it was locked. The sole window in the room had been boarded up, remnants of shattered glass on the floor evidence of the battles fought around the structure. The only illumination came from a smoky oil lamp on a wooden table, its fumes creating a greyish pall in the air. Brunetti sat on a lone chair and waited. Whatever happened next would happen, so he might as well be comfortable.

A cold chill of dread had been sinking into Brunetti's heart since talking with that German private, Vollmer. The Italian liked to think of the young soldier as an ally in his quest for the truth about Constanta and the Transylvanian troops, but Vollmer had looked aghast when told about the war correspondent's most recent story. The colour drained from the private's sun-bronzed face, making his blonde hair and blue eyes even more prominent. It had never occurred to Brunetti his article could have gone too far, that someone other than military censors might be reading everything he had filed.

I've been a fool, he realised belatedly. I did not believe the powers that be would concern themselves with my writings. What's the worst they can do? Deport me back to Italy, put me under house arrest? I haven't written anything that could be considered remotely treasonous, he decided. Besides, von Rundstedt is a legend in the Wehrmacht. I doubt he fears anyone but the Führer himself. Everything will be fine, it will all blow over, given time, Brunetti reassured himself.

But the creeping terror rising within his chest would not listen, instead is grew colder with each passing minute, as if someone was scooping him hollow.

It was almost a relief when the sound of approaching jackboots broke the silence. A key twisted inside the lock and the door swung inwards, admitting two armed guards. They glared at the Italian, who hastily vacated the sole chair. The third and final man to enter was Generalfeldmarschall Gerd von Rundstedt, a figure Brunetti had seen once before during a military parade. Viewed up close, the Italian was surprised how tired the German officer looked. True, von Rundstedt was already sixty-five and had served during the Great War, but the burden of commanding Army Group South was plainly weighing heavily on his shoulders.

The Generalfeldmarschall removed his peaked cap and smoothed down his silver hair, the same hand then adjusting the Knight's Cross hanging below his throat. He looked at Brunetti, his eyes displaying a piercing intelligence, while one hand pointed at the chair. "May I?"

"Err, of course," the Italian replied, stepping aside.

The German officer sank into the seat, resting his cap on a nearby table. "You have caused me considerable difficulty," von Rundstedt began. "I should be concentrating all my energies on sealing off the Kessel at Uman. Instead I find myself here, talking to you. Others have long argued that allowing a non-German war correspondent to mingle with our troops was a mistake, but I supported your presence on the Ostfront. How else are we to prove the worth of our mission if independent observers are not allowed to report on the good we are doing, yes?"

"Yes," Brunetti agreed.

"However, others have not seen it this way. As a result, your reports have been filtered through the offices of our propaganda minister. Goebbels has not been pleased by your writings, but was willing to permit their publication – until the most recent article." The Generalfeldmarschall clicked his fingers and one of the guards produced several sheets of yellow paper, folded twice. "I will not dignify the fanciful claims you make on these pages by reading them aloud. Suffice to say they will not see print and any attempt on your part to repeat such nonsense or have them published elsewhere shall be dealt with severely. Step beyond the guidelines of our propaganda ministry again and I shall have no choice but to expel you from the war zone. Charges may yet be brought against you. I understand the Führer himself has expressed interest in your case," von Rundstedt added, holding up a hand to still Brunetti's voice before the war correspondent could ask a question. "Trust me when I say this interest is neither favourable, nor best sought by one in your position. Do I make myself clear?"

Brunetti thought of protesting but was all too aware of the soldiers on either side of the Generalfeldmarschall, their fingers poised over the triggers of their machine pistols. "Yes, sir."

The German commander smiled thinly as he stood once more. "Very well. Now, before I have you returned to the field, one of our allies wishes to have a word with you. Perhaps they can reassure you about the nature of this conflict." He strode from the room, followed by the two guards. The door remained open, but Brunetti made no attempt to leave. He was too busy digesting what he had been told, desperately trying to burn it into his memory. When this war was over, he would write about this day and he wanted to have perfect recall of its events.

So preoccupied was the Italian with his thoughts, he did not notice the lone figure appear in the doorway. It was only when he heard the voice, with its familiar thick, throaty Rumanian accent, did Brunetti look up. A gasp fell from his lips, along with a cry for help from the heavens.

Hauptmann Constanta chuckled as he walked into the room, closing and locking the door behind him. "Praying for mercy will do you little good," the Transylvanian officer sneered. "And the Germans are pulling out of this location as I speak, so screaming is also of no use. But if either activity gives you comfort, I suggest now is a good time to start."

Chapter Nine

JUNE 25ᵀᴴ, 1941

RALF HAD HEARD rumours about two new Russian tanks creating havoc for Panzer divisions along the northern frontier of the Ostfront, but had yet to see either of them for himself. According to rumour, one of the Russian monsters was a heavy tank called the KV. Its armour was said to be the equal of anything in the war, while its main gun was superior to anything the Panzerwaffe possessed. Tales abounded of a single KV squatting on a causeway, holding back an entire Panzer division for a day. Even when artillery guns were brought up to bombard the vehicle, the KV simply shrugged off their rounds.

Having spent so long inside medium tanks, Ralf was more interested in the other Soviet innovation, a design known as the T-34. According to frontline reports it also had a 76mm main gun, but had been seen travelling at speeds far in excess of any German battle tank. Most impressive of all was the T-34's angled plates of armour, giving it a resilience the equal of any heavy tank. The Wehrmacht's anti-tank crews reported their projectiles

merely bounced off the T-34. Only chance hits on the
turret ring or rear drive-sprockets disabled the vehicle.
However, a single shot from the T-34 was capable of
blowing off the commander's cupola from a Panzer III
and there were multiple cases of German tanks being
split apart by frontal hits from the formidable main gun.
The mere appearance of these Red Army behemoths was
said to induce Panzerschreck in German ground troops,
but so far Army Group South had not encountered them,
so "tank terror" remained an unseen phenomenon
below the Pripyat Marshes.

Ralf could not understand why these Soviet vehicles,
supposedly so superior in their firepower, armour protection and mobility, were not stemming the German
advance. He and his crew had discussed this question
frequently in recent days, after finding themselves
without a battle to fight. The attack on Kiev had been
postponed on orders from Berlin, despite the 13th
Panzer Division being within sight of the city. Instead
the armoured forces had been sent south, giving Ralf's
crew plenty of time to speculate about the superior
Soviet armour. So far, Russian battle tactics had been
inexplicable and frequently inept, with few indications
of communication or co-ordination between individual
tanks. Bizarrely, they often did not have any radio
aerials. Some had even been seen communicating with
flag signals, to the amazement of German crews.

Ralf finally caught sight of a T-34 during manoeuvres
to encircle the Russian 6th and 12th Armies at Uman,
south of Kiev. He immediately recognised the tank's
sloping armour and brutish appearance, but was surprised to see the T-34 travelling as part of a Panzer
column. As it rumbled nearer, Ralf could see the Soviet-
built vehicle had been repainted in German colours. He
used his binoculars to study the insignia on the new
arrival. The T-34 bore the black and white cross seen
on all Panzers, but it also had another emblem clearly

visible on its turret: a bat with wings unfurled, clasping a swastika in its talons. Ralf had seen that emblem before, on Gorgo's uniform. The commander called his Panzer to a halt, urging the crew to get a clear look at the passing T-34.

"Is that what I think it is?" Gunther asked.

"Look at the size of that gun," Willy said admiringly. "The damage I could do with that."

Helmut was the last to emerge, having been busy on the radio. "Apparently half a dozen T-34s were captured at Dubno-Brody. The Reds abandoned them after running out of fuel. The Rumanians claimed the tanks for their own, had them refitted and repainted. Erfurth's radio-operator says Gorgo has been put in charge, forming his own little Panzerverbande."

"Just what we need," Martin muttered darkly. "Battle tanks full of blood–"

"Quiet!" Ralf snarled. "Remember our agreement. Nobody mentions what we saw in that village or what we suspect. It's for our own safety."

"But–" the youngest crewman protested.

"But nothing," Gunther interjected. "You heard what the commander said. If you can't follow orders, you don't belong in this crew. Got it?"

Martin nodded, still scowling as a Kette of Stukas flew over. The planes dropped into a dive-bombing attack beyond the next ridge.

"Seems the Russians are not that far away," Ralf said. "Let's roll."

The Panzer surged forward, falling into formation behind the converted T-34 as it raced after the Ju 87s. The Rumanians might have stolen the Soviet's own tanks to use against them, but Ralf still believed his crew was the equal of any within one hundred kilometres.

THE BATTLE WAS fast and furious. Two more Rumanian T-34s joined their compatriots to act as a crude spearhead while Ralf led a wedge of Panzers round to attack the enemy position from one side and Erfurth drove in from the opposite direction. The Stukas had disabled half a dozen Russian tanks and armoured vehicles, but several more remained mobile. Ralf studied the Soviet positions and strength from the vision ports in his cupola.

"Seems our Rumanian allies have an advantage over the Reds," he noted. "The captured Soviet tanks are better than anything the Russians have at their disposal." An enemy artillery shell landed a few metres behind the Panzer, showering the German vehicle with soil and shrapnel. "That was close."

"Too close," Willy agreed. "Time we gave them a taste of our German steel." He traversed the turret sideways and took aim at the cluster of Russian anti-tank guns. "Ready to fire."

"Fire!" Ralf roared and was rewarded by the sight of enemy casualties screaming and dying. "And again!" Another blast from the main gun and another direct hit on the Russian positions. "Good shooting. Gunther, take us closer."

"Already rolling in," the driver responded, his hands deftly manipulating the Panzer's controls to swivel the tank to its right.

Ralf kept his gaze fixed on the enemy positions, watching as all three T-34s barrelled towards the Russians. "Looks like the Rumanians are taking the direct approach." The first T-34 drove directly over the top of the first Soviet artillery crew, crushing the anti-tank gun beneath its tracks. "God in heaven," Ralf gasped. "That would be suicidal in any other vehicle." Another T-34 thundered into the Soviet positions, smashing through the remains of a burning tank. The third tank reared up as it drove over another artillery gun, squashing the crew beneath as the tank slammed down atop them.

Ralf's gaze slid sideways to the inferior Russian tanks under attack. The main gun of one was dropping to zero elevation, so its long barrel was parallel to the ground. The first T-34 was almost upon them, but still the crew did not fire. "Scheisse, why are they waiting?" Ralf wondered.

"They're either brave or stupid," Gunther replied. He was also watching the drama unfold in front of them. "The Russians must know what it takes to stop one of their own T-34s."

"It'll be on top of them any second," Ralf said.

Finally, when the barrel of the T-34 was almost touching that of the anti-tank gun, the Russian tank fired. At point blank range, they could hardly miss such a large target, but the effects were no less spectacular as a result. The shell slammed into the narrow gap between the T-34's turret and hull. The turret exploded into the air, somersaulting across the sky, accompanied by a blizzard of metal and black smoke. The Rumanian tank died screaming, but as it did another cry shrieked throughout the air, an inhuman wailing that chilled the Panzer crew to the bone. When the clouds of smoke cleared, the unearthly cry was suddenly cut short with a final, fatal shriek of protest.

In a bitter irony, the victorious Russians had mere moments to enjoy their triumph. While the turret of the T-34 was flying into the sky, the mighty hull of the tank was still rolling forwards. It crushed the weaker vehicle, armour crumpling like brittle paper beneath the T-34's weight and momentum.

Ralf realised his own tank had stopped to watch the mismatch, turning itself into a sitting target. He slapped his hand on Willy's shoulders, jolting the gunner back to the present. "Fire!" Within moments the Panzer's main gun was joining the battle ahead of them, firing shell after shell at the rapidly diminishing Russian force. "Gunther, get us moving, before the Reds see we've stopped."

The Panzer lurched forward, accelerating into the melee. Blood stained the once peaceful valley's grass red and the stench of spent cordite tainted every mouthful of air. Ralf pressed his eyes against the nearest vision port and called the position of their next target. The skirmish was merely beginning.

THE BATTLE WAS both bloody and brutal, with fewer than a dozen Russians being taken prisoner once the last shots were fired. The Rumanians had driven their converted T-34s with suicidal fervour, plunging through the Soviet ranks before turning round for another attack, using the fearsome tanks as naval tacticians once used the cannon of tall ships against each other. What the Rumanian drivers lacked in skill they more than made up for with death-defying enthusiasm.

By dusk it was all over, and Ralf was discussing the battle's conduct with Erfurth. The Feldwebel was preparing a report for division HQ and felt obliged to seek Ralf's input, despite rarely mentioning the name Vollmer in despatches. Ralf did not care, since he did not share Erfurth's lust for glory. The sooner this war was over, the sooner he could go home and forget it. God knows he would not miss the killing or the quiet, gnawing terror that grew with each successive battle. Having made his contribution, Ralf gratefully strolled back to where his tank was parked for the night. Martin and Helmut were loading fresh supplies of fuel and ammunition aboard, while Willy was arguing with Panzerwarte engineers about firing problems he had been having lately, blaming the ubiquitous red dust for insinuating itself into the main gun's mechanism.

Ralf took care not to be dragged into this perpetual disagreement and approached the crew's radio operator instead. "Helmut, where's Gunther?"

"Eyeballing the T-34's wreckage. He went for a closer look with Hoepner. They went about ten minutes ago, leaving us to do everything, as usual. If you find Gunther, tell him to get his lazy arse back here, and fast!"

Sure enough, Ralf located the ruddy-faced driver and his counterpart from Erfurth's crew standing beside the broken remains of the shattered T-34. The two drivers were debating the merits of the tank over their own vehicles. Gunther had clambered on top of the hull and was rapping his knuckles against its shell. "The armour is not much thicker than anything in the Panzer, but the extreme angle must double its effective thickness. Our standard anti-tank gun would be as useful as a pea-shooter against these plates."

Hoepner was pointing inside the gaping hole where the turret should have been. "How many crew does it take?"

Gunther counted the shredded seats in the wrecked interior. "Four, by the looks of what's left. Driver, radio operator, loader and gunner. The gunner must also be the tank's commander." He searched the surrounding battlefield but the missing turret was nowhere in sight. "I didn't notice any cupola or vision ports. I wonder how they see out?"

"We use a periscopic sight," a thickly accented voice replied. Sergeant Gorgo appeared from the twilight, his uniform now similar to those worn by Ralf and his Panzer crew, but with the bat and swastika emblem prominently displayed. "It is too dangerous to ride with our heads exposed as you prefer, because the turret hatch pivots forward, not backward. We would have to sit on the turret roof to see where we are going."

Besides, your kind doesn't like being caught in sunlight, Ralf thought.

Gorgo glared at Gunther standing on the T-34's hull. "I must ask you to climb down. My countrymen died inside that tank and I wish to recover their personal belongings. I know you are interested to see inside the T-34, but please show my fallen brothers some respect, yes?"

Gunther took another glance inside the burnt and blistered hull and then jumped down to stand beside Ralf on the grass. The two men walked away, leaving Hoepner behind, still studying the T-34's exterior.

Once they were out of earshot, Ralf nudged his crewman in the ribs. "What did you see inside? What did the Rumanian bodies look like?"

Gunther frowned. "That was the strangest thing – there weren't any bodies. I guess they could have been sucked out when the turret blew off, but..."

"But what?"

Gunther stopped, looking back at the tank's carcass silhouetted in the moonlight. "There was a pile of ashes in each crew member's position, almost as if someone had individually cremated them where they sat."

"Spontaneous human combustion?" Ralf asked disbelievingly.

"Combustion? Yes. Spontaneous? Maybe. Human – I don't think so." The driver grabbed his commander by the arm and pulled him further away. "Do you remember the moments after the turret was blown off?"

"Of course."

"After the clouds of smoke from the T-34 had cleared away I heard a strange noise, a noise unlike anything I've ever heard before."

Ralf nodded. "Like the death shriek of an animal."

Gunther grimaced. "I haven't been able to get that sound out of my mind. I keep replaying those moments, over and over, in my head. The smoke clears and sunlight floods the exposed interior of the T-34. That's when the screaming started. It wasn't the explosion or the turret being blown off that made the Rumanians cry out. It was being exposed to direct sunlight."

"You think they burned alive where they sat?"

Gunther nodded. "And so do you, Ralf. I can see it in your eyes. We both know what these creatures are, what they can do. Gorgo couldn't care less about recovering the personal effects of his fallen comrades. He wants to remove any evidence that proves his Transylvanian countrymen are vamp–"

Ralf clamped a hand over his driver's mouth. "Don't say that word," he said. "Not here, not at night and certainly not out loud. We had an agreement. As long as the Rumanians are fighting on our side, we're safe from them."

Gunther wrenched Ralf's hand from his face. "Maybe, but how long do you think that's going to last? Gorgo and his kind are arming themselves, learning from us, from our methods. Why? What happens when the war is over? Why would his kind even want to fight alongside us? What do they have to gain?"

"You think somebody somewhere has made a deal with the Rumanians," Ralf said quietly. "They help us defeat the Bolsheviks now, and in return..."

"Who knows? But I don't want to be among the poor bastards who find out. We need to think about defending ourselves against them, if the worst should come to the worst. If the time comes, we need to be ready."

Chapter Ten

JULY 29ᵀᴴ, 1941

HANS WASN'T SURE how long it had been since Sergeant Witte had taken half the unit away down a narrow gully that curved out of sight to the north. Red Army activity was supposed to be light in the area, but intelligence reports on enemy numbers was frequently wrong. Hans and the others maintained their position in a small copse of trees close to the end of the gully.

Hans was starting to believe that much he had been told about the Soviets was less than accurate. All through basic training it was drilled into them, over and over again: the Bolsheviks were inferior fighters, godless sub-humans without the will for a long or tenacious war. The mighty Blitzkrieg of Panzers and Stukas would sweep all before it and conquer the Red Army, crushing the bulk of the Russian forces within a month of crossing the border. Then the Landser would move in, mopping up any lingering pockets of resistance that might remain.

Reality had proven a different matter. The infantry of both sides was bearing the brunt of the fighting. The Red Army was tenacious in defence, always ready to counter-attack and willing to continue fighting long past the point where soldiers of other armies would have surrendered. Communism might have rejected religious beliefs, but its soldiers fought with a passion equal to any zealot's.

They were not inferior and weak-willed, Hans thought ruefully, watching grey clouds drift across the moon overhead. Its light filtered through the trees, dappling the Germans in tones of blue and slate, casting a death-like pallor on their nervous faces.

A scream disturbed the men. Distant shots rang out, answered by the characteristic *rat-tat-tat* of a German machine gun. More shots and more screams followed. Then, only silence, cold and foreboding. The cluster of men beneath the trees shifted nervously, uncertain how to respond.

"God, I need a cigarette," Ulrich muttered, hands scrabbling for his tin of tobacco.

"No naked flames, no lit cigarettes," Hans said. "We don't announce our presence here."

"Who died and put you in charge?" Ulrich replied.

"No one, hopefully." Hans fell silent, listening to the night. In the distance a familiar sound was becoming audible, drawing closer. "Footsteps. That must be Witte and the others coming back."

"I'll signal them that we're here," Siegfried volunteered, about to move out from the copse. Hans pulled him back into the shadows.

"Wait," Hans whispered. "That doesn't sound like the sergeant. He makes much less noise when he moves."

Siegfried tilted his head to one side and listened. "If that's not the sergeant, then who?"

"Scheisse, it's the Reds," Hans realised. "Down! Get down!"

The infantrymen dropped to one knee, fingers nervously gripping the triggers of their weapons, eyes searching their surroundings for movement. A few seconds later, a single figure emerged from the end of the gully, creeping forwards into the open. The pale moonlight made it difficult to identify the colour of his uniform, but the style was obviously Russian.

Ulrich raised his rifle and took aim, but Hans intervened again. "He won't be alone. Let him think he's safe and the rest will follow. Then we attack."

Ulrich nodded. Sure enough, the lone Soviet soon made a discrete gesture and a dozen of his comrades emerged from the gully. Several Russians began moving toward the copse.

"If they'd seen us, they would already be shooting," Hans whispered. "Hold your ground, let them come to us." He could feel Ulrich trembling alongside him, the private's hands rattling the rifle in his grasp. Hans reached across and stilled the movement, keeping his own gaze fixed on the nearest Russian. Soon the Soviets were within spitting distance, the moon casting harsh shadows on their pallid faces. Hans was about to open fire when the enemy troops changed direction, moving slowly and deliberately towards the German camp in the west. Hans waited until all of them were facing away from the copse, then bellowed a single word to his comrades: "Fire!"

The Landser killed half the Soviets with the first volley, wounding many of the others. The Russians spun in the air, their bodies jerking and twitching. Those who were not killed instantly threw themselves to the ground and returned fire, spraying the copse with ammunition. Hans took a round in his right thigh, the leg folding beneath him. Others were not so fortunate, with Ulrich's brother Siegfried losing half his jaw and the back of his skull.

Seeing his twin slaughtered, Ulrich screamed in fury and charged the Russians. He shot two soldiers dead, then bludgeoned a third with the butt of his rifle, reducing the Soviet's face to a viscous red pulp. The

remaining Russians fled into the darkness, put to flight
by his raging onslaught. Other members of Ulrich's unit
had to drag him away from the corpse to stop him
beating the lifeless body any further. Even then, his
thirst for vengeance was not sated.

"I'm going after the rest," he announced, reloading his
rifle as blood dripped from his crimson-spattered features. "Who's coming with me?"

"The sergeant told us to hold this position," Hans said
weakly from where he had fallen.

"Witte is probably dead," Ulrich snarled. "You saw
where those murdering bastards came from. They
slaughtered the sergeant and the others, and then they
tried to do the same to us. But we'll show them, won't
we?"

Most of the others nodded their approval. Only Kral
stood aside from the mob mentality. "Hans is right. We
should stay here and tend to our wounded. We don't
know Witte or the others are dead."

Ulrich pushed past Franz, striding off in the same
direction the enemy had fled. "Stay here if you want.
I've got Russians to kill." The others went after him,
leaving Franz and Hans behind.

A few minutes later gunfire sounded in the distance,
staccato rhythms of death peppering the air. Then
nothing. An eerie silence covered the copse like a
shroud, not even a gust of wind to shuffle the leaves on
the trees.

Hans bandaged his leg wound, the Russian bullet
having only creased the side of his thigh. Franz kept
guard beside Hans in the shadows, having gathered all
the abandoned weapons and ammunition around them.
"Better safe than sorry," he explained.

Hans stayed on the ground, resting his back against
the nearest tree trunk. He found it hard to believe Witte
was dead, but the sergeant had never been missing in
action this long before. Hans had come to depend on

Witte for guidance, using him as a mentor. When faced with a problem he couldn't resolve, Hans had taken to pondering what the sergeant would do in the same situation. Using that same logic, his choice had been clear when Ulrich wanted to pursue the Russians. Hans could almost hear Witte's voice inside his head, gravelly tones passing judgement on the dilemma.

"Never pursue a hostile force over unknown territory, especially at night. Fight the enemy with your head, not your heart."

Before Hans could ponder what the sergeant would suggest, he felt Franz's hand closing round his arm. "Someone's coming," the little soldier said.

"From where?"

Franz made two gestures: one in the direction Ulrich and the others had gone, the second down the gully from where the Russians had come. Hans pulled his MP 40 closer, gently sliding the thirty-two round magazine out of the machine pistol to check it was fully loaded. He then slotted the metal clip back into position and flicked the safety catch off.

"Aim low. Put your man down," Hans whispered to himself, repeating the words in his mind again and again.

Franz breathed in deeply as the first group of Russian riflemen appeared, cockily sauntering back from where Ulrich's group had ventured. There were half a dozen of them; several more than had fled the field before. It must have been a trap, Hans realised, a feint to lure us into chasing them. Then a second group of Soviet soldiers emerged from the gully, ten in all. The Russians were talking loudly and warmly, laughing and making extravagant hand gestures to describe their night's work.

How long before they remember to check the copse for survivors, Hans wondered. How long before Franz and I die here?

A noise got the enemy troops' attention, a sound Hans had not heard since visiting a zoo as a child. It was the growling of wild animals, low and savage, the feral noise of a hunter closing on its prey. Hans and Franz watched in amazement as five wolves emerged from the shadows, creeping out from among the scrub and long grass to surround the Soviet riflemen. Another wolf paused as it passed Hans, glaring into his eyes hungrily, lips curling back to reveal bloodstained teeth. There was something chillingly familiar about the animal's expression, as if it recognised him.

It then joined the others, all six of them, stalking the Russians in a broad circle, keeping the men clustered tightly together. One of the soldiers fired at the lead wolf, but it danced around his aim, moving with a speed that cheated the eye. Nothing can move that fast, Hans thought, certainly not any animal I know. The only thing I've ever seen move so quick was those creatures at Reni.

"What do we do?" Franz whispered, terror quaking his voice.

"Nothing," Hans replied, licking his dry lips. "We do nothing." He glanced up at the sky, where a thick bank of dark clouds was about to cover the moon. Then darkness fell on the copse and the Russians started screaming.

WHEN THE MOONLIGHT returned, the wolves were gone. Where the Russians had once stood was a pile of dead bodies, arms thrown across faces, eyes glinting lifelessly wetness soaking the front of their uniforms. Only one man was standing and he wore a long, dark cloak with a high collar and a peaked cap. He smiled with satisfaction at the sixteen dead Soviets and then turned to face Hans and Franz. It was Constanta.

Kral had fainted; the sound of men screaming and animals feasting was too much for the private to bear. But Hans watched it all, peering into the darkness to catch glimpses of the wolves at work. The animals' shapes blurred in the blackness, seeming to mutate into shadowy figures that flung themselves upon the Russians. So fast was the attack that the Bolsheviks did not have time to fire another shot, their protests of "Nyet! Nyet!" dying with them in the dark.

Constanta strolled towards Hans, the Rumanian officer wiping smears of moisture from the ends of his moustache with a gloved finger. "Private... Vollmer, isn't it? I thought I recognised you."

Hans felt a shudder of terror soar through his spine. The monster recognises me, it knows my name, he thought. What else does it know about me?

"You needn't be afraid of me or my men," Constanta said, almost as if in reply to Hans's thoughts. "We received word of a Russian counter-attack planned for this evening and made our way to this area. You can count yourself lucky we intervened before the enemy realised you were so close at hand. I would not like to think what would have happened otherwise." The Rumanian smiled, letting Hans see the points of his fangs glisten in the moonlight. "I wouldn't be surprised if your commanders give you a medal for single-handedly wiping out a Russian patrol like that, particularly when you've already been wounded."

"But I didn't–" Hans protested.

Constanta silenced him with a gesture. Hans wanted to cry out, to shake Franz back to his senses, but something was crushing his will, preventing him from moveing. "Hush, my boy, hush. Enjoy your moment of glory when it comes, for they are few and far between in the lives of mere mortals. How is your wound, by the way?" The Hauptmann crouched beside Hans and pressed a gloved finger into the bloody bandage, pushing into the moist fabric.

The German private wanted to scream in agony but his voice and lips were frozen, unable to respond. Constanta removed his finger from the wound and lovingly licked the tip, savouring every last drop of blood. "Hmm, delicious. A shame my men and I are not allowed to feast on such sweet succour. These Russians are a foul-tasting foe, their blood tastes of vodka and potatoes." The Rumanian stood up again, wrapping his cloak around himself. "Remember what I have said, Vollmer. You will take credit for killing the Russians, whether you like it or not. Circumstances require my men and I to keep a low profile in such matters. Besides, it is good for German morale to make heroes of its men."

With that Constanta was gone, fading away into the darkness, the slightest wisp of mist remaining where he had stood.

Franz shuddered on the ground beside Hans, slowly lifting his head to see what had happened. "Where are the Russians?"

"All dead," Hans replied numbly.

"And the wolves?" Franz glanced about them anxiously, fear in his eyes.

"What wolves?"

"Those wolves before... You saw them, didn't you? I can't remember what happened after that. I must have passed out. Come to think of it, I'm not sure about anything anymore."

"That's probably just as well," Hans decided. He could hear several people running towards them from the gully. "Over here. We're over here."

"Are you insane? How do you know they're on our side?" Franz demanded.

"I doubt there's a Russian alive within ten kilometres." Besides, Hans thought, having someone on your side doesn't make them any less deadly.

Witte was the first to emerge from the gully, followed by seven more members of the infantry unit. The pile of Russian corpses surprised the sergeant, but he was even more astonished to find that Hans and Franz were still alive. "We've been pinned down by the Russians for hours," he explained. "It's taken us this long to work our way back to your position." Witte noted Siegfried's body beneath one of the trees. "Where are the others?"

Hans explained most of what had happened, but glossed over the final confrontation with the Russians. "Hauptmann Constanta and his Rumanian Mountain Troops intervened, though he seems to think we should get the credit."

"Does he?" the sergeant said thoughtfully. "He shuns the limelight as much as he shuns the daylight." Witte noticed the puzzled look on Franz's face. "Don't worry, Private Kral, I was merely thinking out loud. It's time we got you and Vollmer back behind our lines, yes? You've both served with distinction tonight."

IT WAS ALMOST midnight when Hans returned to his tent. He was looking forward to falling asleep but Brunetti was waiting for him inside.

The war correspondent shook Hans's hand as if the two had never been introduced. "My name is Brunetti, Giovanni Brunetti. I'm an Italian reporter covering the Ostfront."

"I know," Hans said, baffled at this opening gambit. "We've met before."

"Have we? Well, I meet so many troops, all the faces begin to blend together after a while," Brunetti said, his sad eyes twinkling. "I hope you won't be offended if I don't recall you straight away."

"No, of course not."

"Good. Well, I'm told you've had a busy night. According to my source you and another private wiped out an entire Russian patrol by yourselves."

"How did you hear that?" Hans asked.

The war correspondent tapped the side of his prominent nose. "A good journalist never reveals their sources, you know. So please, tell me what happened."

Hans did his best to answer the question, but Brunetti had to prompt him through the details – how the devious Bolsheviks had lured the rest of Hans's unit into a trap, how Hans had been wounded in the fighting, how Hans and Kral had managed against all odds to overcome the Russian patrol.

When the questions were concluded, the private complemented Brunetti on his grasp of events. "It's almost as if you were there in person."

The Italian smiled. "I pride myself on trying to see these battles through the eyes of those who took part. It gives the necessary verisimilitude." Brunetti pocketed his notebook and pencil. "Well, I'll be filing my copy tomorrow. I wouldn't be surprised if you get a medal for this incident." He shook hands with Hans, but the German refused to let go of Brunetti.

"Giovanni, I have to tell you something, about what happened tonight."

"Yes?"

"I didn't kill all those Russians. It was Constanta, him and his men. They slaughtered the Reds, tore them apart like wild animals. Everything you said about the Rumanians, everything you told me – it was true, all of it!"

Brunetti looked at Hans as if the German had lost his mind. "You're not making much sense, private. I'm certain we've never met before this evening. As for this nonsense about Hauptmann Constanta, you must be mistaken. It was him who supplied me with the information about your heroics."

"No, don't you understand?" Hans protested. "It was–"

"I think that's enough excitement for one evening," another voice cut in. Constanta stepped inside Hans's tent. "Brunetti, perhaps you'd like to wait for me outside?"

"Of course, Hauptmann," the Italian replied. He nodded to Hans and stepped out of the tent, leaving the two men together. Constanta advanced on Hans, backing him against one of the tent poles.

"I'm growing rather fond of my war correspondent," the Rumanian said, smiling wolfishly. "He was a troublesome creature, but since I had a little talk with him he has been a model of propriety. I wouldn't wish to see him come to any harm, would you?"

"No," Hans agreed, shakily.

"Very well then," Constanta continued. "You will accept whatever praise or commendation offered to you for tonight's events. You will do so cheerfully and without hesitation or reservation, and you will forget anything unusual you witnessed this evening. Do I make myself clear?"

Hans could feel the Rumanian's eyes boring into his own, Constanta's will pressing itself down upon his. "Yes, Hauptmann."

"That's better. I would hate to have to send Brunetti out into no-man's-land, alone and unarmed, to face the guns of our Bolshevik enemies. I doubt he would last a few seconds against the Red Army. But that is what will happen, unless you obey my will. Now, let's say no more about this incident, shall we? You had better get some rest, so that wounded leg of yours can heal. I fear we both still have a long war ahead of us. Goodnight, Private Vollmer. I trust we shall not have cause to meet again any time soon." Constanta turned on his heel and departed, like a shadow passing across the moon.

Hans sank to his knees, shivering uncontrollably.

Chapter Eleven

AUGUST 2ND, 1941

KLAUS WOKE UP and screamed twice. The first was one of terror. A single image was fixed in his mind's eye: a grinning, evil face looming towards him, its thin, cruel lips pulling back to reveal a mouthful of fangs. A wet, lascivious tongue slid out like a black serpent to lick them and then returned to its home in the darkness. The massive jaws got closer and closer, larger and larger, as if it was about to swallow Klaus whole, making him disappear forever into oblivion.

The second scream was born of pain; every muscle and sinew in the pilot's body cried out in agony as he jerked awake. Klaus sank back into the makeshift bed, aware of its coarse blankets and creaking metal framework. The stench of rotting flesh and misery filled his nostrils. Battling against the blackness that wanted to consume him, Klaus let his eyes slide from side to side, taking in his bleak surroundings. What he saw did little to comfort him.

Judging by the canvas walls and ceiling, it was a field hospital of sorts, with portable cots standing in lines. Each bed held a wounded man, most swathed in bloody bandages, their limbs or eyes missing, skin burnt or charred. A few moaned constantly in pain, others were mercifully unconscious, some stared sightlessly at nothing. Medics moved from cot to cot, checking pulses and temperatures, administering what care they could. An artillery shell exploded nearby, showering the outside of the field hospital with earth, but not one medic flinched. A few of the wounded cowered, while those asleep stirred, mumbling curses or prayers under their breath.

In the cot opposite Klaus, three orderlies were holding down a patient, while a surgeon was taking a hacksaw to the wounded man's leg. The soldier was howling in agony, hurling as many swearwords as he could at the physician.

"God in heaven, somebody shut him up!" the surgeon snarled, redoubling his efforts to saw through the bone as blood poured on to the floor.

One of the orderlies retrieved the wooden shaft of a stick grenade from the ground and shoved it between the patient's teeth. Biting into the wood, his eyes bulging in pain, the soldier could only convey his agonised sobbing and guttural moans to torment the other wounded.

Klaus decided he was in hell, but he had no idea how he had got there.

The medics were too busy dealing with a dying patient to notice him. When he had expired, the medics snapped off the identity disc and pulled a sheet over the corpse's face.

Once these brief formalities were concluded, the medic wearily approached Klaus. "Yes?"

"Where am I?"

"A field hospital, between Bratslav and Uman."

The names meant little to Klaus. "How did I get here? What happened?"

The orderly sighed and reached for Klaus's chart. "You were brought in yesterday, unconscious and unresponsive. Few visible injuries, except your leg and chest."

"My leg?" A creeping horror engulfed the pilot, daring him to look down and see if his body was still intact. "Oh god, you didn't–"

"Amputate? No. You dislocated your left knee. The bones remained out of place for several hours, causing damage to the muscles and tendons. We'll have to wait for the swelling to go down before the doctors can assess how much damage has been done. You also took a piece of shrapnel in the chest, close to the heart. The surgeons believe they got most of it out, but you'll need a second operation to make sure. Now, if you'll excuse me."

The orderly was already turning to leave, but Klaus grabbed his wrist, forcing the sad-faced medic to stay put. "My gunner, Heinrich. What happened to Heinrich?"

The orderly shrugged. "Have a look around. Maybe you'll see him." He prised his arm free from Klaus and walked away.

The pilot quickly scanned the faces of all the nearby patients he could, but Heinrich was not among them. Klaus let his head drop back to the bed, straining to recall how he came to be there. The last thing he could recall was receiving orders to give aerial support for the ground troops encircling the Russian forces near Uman. Beyond that was nothing, only darkness and the image of the fanged jaws closing around him. Already he could feel exhaustion, claiming him for its own. Then the darkness enveloped him again.

KLAUS OPENED HIS eyes and found himself outside Major Satzinger's tent at the airbase, in the cool air of dusk. Căpitan aviator Stefan Toma was striding towards him, the Rumanian pilot's face livid with anger. "Why have you been spreading these lies about me and my men, Vollmer?"

"What lies? I don't know what you're talking about," Klaus protested.

"Other members of your Staffel are not so devious as you. They told me how you and your gunner had come to them, asking questions about us, creating rumours, suggesting we have some ulterior motive for helping you fight the Bolsheviks."

"Heinrich?" Klaus glanced about, trying to catch sight of the gunner, his mind filled with unanswered questions. Was this memory or a hallucination? "Please, I need to find Heinrich."

"Forget about him, Vollmer," Toma snarled. "You and I have our own matters to discuss. You will stop these lies."

"What lies?"

"Whispered conversations with other Stuka pilots, suggestions that my countrymen and I are somehow tainted by evil."

Klaus gave up trying to rationalise the situation. "Prove me wrong. At dawn tomorrow I dare you to stand in the sunlight. Show yourself in the daytime like any normal person."

"We are not children. We do not play games of truth or dare," Toma spat, his eyes glinting maliciously. "Tomorrow the Führer himself will publicly thank myself and my brethren for our contribution to the Ostfront, saying we are a vital part of the war against the communists. After that, few will give credence to your tales of supernatural happenings in the sky. Cross us again and I will not hesitate to act against you, Vollmer. Consider this your first and final warning."

The Rumanian fighter pilot strode away, acknowledging Heinrich with a curt nod as the gunner approached.

"What was all that about?" Heinrich asked when Toma was out of earshot.

"Seems one of our fellow flyers has been telling tales to the Rumanians." Klaus did not share the rest of the conversation with his friend, not wishing to worry him.

"Well, Căpitan aviator Stefan Toma and his associates won't be our problem much longer. Word among the ground crew is that the Hurricanes leave tomorrow at dawn, heading off to form a new Rumanian Staffel."

"Good," Klaus sighed, realising he had been holding his breath during the confrontation with Toma. "The sooner they're gone from here, the better." His legs sagged beneath him, so Klaus grabbed hold of Heinrich's arm for support.

"What's wrong?" the gunner asked anxiously.

"Tired..." Klaus murmured. "So tired..." Then the blackness had him again.

"VOLLMER? VOLLMER, CAN you hear me?" Klaus felt himself floating upwards through darkness towards a light, the nearby voice guiding him to the surface. He opened his eyes to find Satzinger standing nearby, the major gingerly stroking the black leather patch over his left eye. "Ah, you're awake. Must be on the mend."

Klaus shuddered, not sure what was real and what was a hallucination. He was still in the field hospital, but he had no way of knowing how long he had been unconscious. "Heinrich. Where's Heinrich?"

The major frowned, his hands nervously twisting a cap. "Your gunner didn't make it, unfortunately. Seems there was a problem with the canopy of your Ju 87, so when you tried to bail out, he went down with the plane."

Klaus wanted to grieve for his friend, but instead felt so detached from reality the news of Heinrich's death was hard to grasp. "I don't remember what happened. I don't even remember the mission."

Satzinger nodded. "The doctors told me you suffered a concussion, along with the damage to your leg and chest. You should recover, given time. When your mind is ready, I'm sure it will recall what happened."

"I need to know," Klaus said quietly. "Please."

The major sighed. "Very well. You and the rest of the Staffel were doing night bombing runs above the Uman Kessel – what the tacticians like to call vertical envelopment. But there was a mid-air collision, between your Stuka and the Hurricane of–"

"Cãpitan aviator Stefan Toma."

"That's right," Satzinger replied. "How did you know that?"

"I guessed," Klaus said. "What happened next?"

"We don't know, to be honest. Other pilots in the Staffel witnessed the collision; said Toma flew into you headfirst, then his Hurricane flipped over on top of yours. We think that's when the canopy jammed. As your plane went down, you were wrenched free. That's probably when you sustained these injuries. Luckily, your parachute still opened. Heinrich wasn't so fortunate." The major rested a hand gently on Klaus's arm. "He would have died the moment the plane hit the ground."

"What about Toma?"

"Parachuted to safety, somehow. I swear he has the luck of the Devil."

More than you can know, Klaus thought. He wanted to share his fears about the Rumanians with someone, but could not bring himself to trust Satzinger. Something the major once said had stuck in Klaus's mind: "I would make a pact with the Devil himself if I thought it could end this war without another person dying. Since the Devil does not grace us with his presence, we must do our best."

At the time it seemed merely a passing remark, but now Klaus was wondering if the Devil himself was fighting alongside the Wehrmacht.

"Is there anything I can get you?" Satzinger asked.

"My brothers. I need you to get word to my brothers that I'm all right. I don't want them hearing about my plane going down and thinking I've died."

"Of course." The major extracted a notebook and pencil from his pocket. "Where can I find them?"

"My elder brother Ralf is a tank commander with the 13th Panzer Division. Last I heard he had the rank of Obergefreiter. My younger brother is called Hans. He was still doing basic training when I had a letter from him, but he could be stationed with the Landser by now." Klaus could feel his strength fading once more. "Get them news about me, please. I'd like to see them, but…"

"I'll do what I can," Satzinger said. "You should rest now. We need all the pilots we can get, believe me. I'll find you a new gunner too."

Klaus nodded, not wanting to think about Heinrich now – the wound was too fresh, too raw. When he felt stronger, then he might face the loss of his friend.

Chapter Twelve

AUGUST 3ᴿᴰ, 1941

HANS WAS SHOCKED when he saw his older brothers. It was months since his last meeting with Klaus, when they had parted on good terms. But it was more than a year since Hans and Ralf had spoken and longer since they had sat down together. Then the eldest of the Vollmer brothers had come home on leave from the war, his hair shaved close to the scalp and his skin bronzed by the sun. Hans had spent all his time pestering Ralf to talk about the glories of war, but the Panzer commander had refused. When Hans proudly announced he was getting a promotion within the Hitlerjungen, Ralf had sneered and cursed the Führer's name. Hans had agonised long and hard before deciding against reporting his brother to the authorities, putting the incident down to battle fatigue.

As Hans walked into the field hospital, he had difficulty recognising either brother. Ralf looked like an old man, his skin lined and leathery, his close-cropped hair now rapidly receding. There was a bitterness about his face, a taciturn set in his features that defied anyone to engage him in conversation. Klaus looked even worse, but at least he had the excuse of being a patient. The flyer appeared feeble in his hospital cot, one leg swathed in bandages, while more bandages circled his chest and dark rings underlined each eye.

"What a place for a family reunion," Hans said as he approached them, trying to inject some lightness into his voice.

The previous evening he had been pulled from the frontline and told to report to the field hospital west of Uman, where one of his brothers was a patient. No other details were passed on. It was only after arriving that Hans learned his journey had a double purpose. There was to be a medal-giving ceremony later today and he was among the soldiers getting their citations from the Führer himself. The Uman Kessel battle was all but over, and Hitler was attending a briefing at Army Group South HQ, using the chance to thank some of the Wehrmacht's brave fighters.

Klaus smiled when he saw Hans coming. "Both of you! This is some sort of miracle, both of you coming to see me on the same day."

"It's no miracle," Ralf replied sourly. "Hans here is a war hero, so the Propaganda Kompanie thought it was a good idea to reunite us all."

"A war hero, eh? What did you do?" Klaus asked.

"Very little," Hans admitted. "I certainly don't deserve a medal. They say I wiped out a Russian patrol almost single-handed, despite having been shot in the leg."

"So what really happened?" Ralf sneered. "Don't tell me the golden boy is getting disillusioned of his glorious war."

Hans shook his head. "I can't believe you, Ralf. How can you deride everything we're trying to achieve? Millions of men fighting for the Fatherland and all you do is act like we're committing war crimes."

"Despite what our glorious leader might tell us, there's nothing holy or righteous about this war – about any war," Ralf snarled back.

A medic shouted at the three brothers to keep the noise down. "You're disturbing the other patients. If you can't be quiet in here, I suggest you take your problems outside. There's a wheelchair over there."

"That's a good idea," Klaus said, easing his legs over the side of the cot. "I've been dying to get out of this place. You two can take turns pushing me. It might stop you arguing. For once."

Hans fetched the rickety wheelchair while Ralf helped Klaus off the cot carefully. Once the siblings were outside, Klaus pointed at a nearby tree offering shelter from the sun.

When all three were beneath the shade, it was Klaus who broke the bitter impasse between his brothers. "Will you stop arguing long enough for me to say what I need to say? Look, there's something I need to talk about and you two are the only ones left I can trust." Ralf and Hans glared at each other, but both nodded their agreement. Klaus sighed with exasperation, then began telling them about his encounters with Căpitan aviator Toma and the other Rumanians.

Hans listened with amazement as Klaus talked. "I thought I was the only one of us who had met these monsters," he said.

"You've seen them, too?" Klaus asked.

Hans did his best to summarise his brushes with Constanta – the mist creatures at Reni, the tales Brunetti had told him about the Rumanians having a village slaughtered, what the Russian woman soldier had said about garlic and silver hurting them and the pack of wolves that slaughtered the Soviet patrol.

"That's why I'm getting a medal, for something I didn't do," Hans admitted. "Constanta wants me to have the credit for the killings, but I still don't know why." He glanced at Ralf. "Go ahead, gloat, I know you're dying to. Tell me how you always said there were no heroes in war."

But the Panzer commander simply shook his head. "You're finding that out for yourself, little brother. You don't need a lecture from me."

"What about you, Ralf? Do you believe what we're saying about these creatures, these Rumanians?" Klaus asked.

Ralf grimaced. "Unfortunately, yes. My crew had one of the Transylvanians in our tank for twelve days, so he could learn about armoured warfare." He told of his experiences in the village courtyard, his suspicions about Gorgo attacking the Russian snipers. "What came out of our Panzer, it sounds like the same mist you saw in Reni."

Hans nodded. "I know it seems insane, but the mist seemed to have a will of its own, an... intelligence. I don't know how else to describe it."

Klaus had been biting his fingernails while the others talked. He looked up at the sunlight filtering through the leaves and branches over their heads. "These creatures – they only come out at night. We know sunlight is deadly to them, that silver and garlic and religious symbols repel or even harm them and it seems they can transform themselves into mist, or bats, or even wolves. There's a name for things like this."

"Don't say it," Hans whispered.

"How can we ever hope to fight such monsters?" Ralf asked. "How can we ever hope to defeat them?"

"Why should we?" Hans asked. "Aren't they on our side in this war?"

"Only when it suits them," Klaus said, his voice thick with emotion. "One of them killed Heinrich, my gunner, and they were trying to kill me, too – because we were asking too many questions. Because we knew them for what they were: nightwalkers, the undead... Vampyrs."

The three brothers looked at each other, letting the name and all its implications sink in. Hans found it hard to believe they were discussing such creatures, monsters he had thought existed only in legends. But he knew all too well everything he had said was true, and he did not doubt his brothers' word. Constanta and his kind were vampyrs.

"So what do we do now?" Hans asked.

Klaus bit his bottom lip. "The way Toma spoke before the plane crash, he was suggesting the Führer already knew what the Rumanians were and that Hitler had made some unholy pact with these devils."

"I can't believe that," Hans maintained. "Why would he?"

"To win the war," Ralf replied. "But I suspect the vampyrs have greater ambitions, plans for what happens after the fighting stops."

"We can't know for certain whether the alliance with these creatures was forged in Berlin or with the Führer's knowledge," Klaus said.

"I could ask him," Hans offered. "I'm receiving my medal from him tomorrow. I could ask him then."

"Don't be a fool," Ralf snapped. "Do you honestly believe that madman would tell you the truth?"

"The Führer is not a madman," Hans replied. "He is founding a Reich that will last a thousand years. He is the father of our nation. You'd do well to remember that."

"The bloody Reich will be lucky to last another thousand days," Ralf spat back.

"Stop it, both of you. This bickering is getting us nowhere," Klaus protested. He waited until his brothers had calmed down before continuing. "Ralf is right. To even consider talking with the Führer about this is madness. If he is in league with these monsters, you will be taken away and shot, at best. If he isn't in league with them, Hitler will merely think you insane and the consequences will likely be much the same. You must promise not to mention what we've talked about with the Führer."

Hans frowned. As the youngest, he had endured eighteen years of being told what to do. It went against the grain to keep doing so, now that he was a man. But even his stubborn streak could not stop him seeing the sense in what Klaus was saying. "I doubt the opportunity will arise," he said. "Even if I wanted it to."

Ralf rasped a hand across the stubble on his chin. "We don't know who to trust when it comes to Constanta and his men, so we can't trust anyone. Hans, you told us how that Italian war correspondent became a lapdog for the vampyrs. And that driver, Cringu, he's another servant of the nightwalkers, doing their will while the sun is in the sky. How many more thralls do the Rumanians have at their beck and call? We have to assume we're on our own. For now, the Rumanians may be fighting on Germany's side, but I believe we must prepare for the day when that's no longer the case."

"Why?" Klaus stared at his elder brother intently. "What do you think is going to happen?"

"It was something my driver said, after we saw the vampyrs driving some captured T-34 tanks. Gunther wondered why the Rumanians were even fighting in this war, let alone using armoured vehicles as their weapons. The more I thought about that, the more it worried me. What have Constanta and his men got to gain from helping us?"

"Constanta said the Russians were as much their enemy as ours," Hans recalled. "That made us allies in this war."

"That explains how the Rumanians got drawn into the fighting," Ralf agreed. "But what happens after the war? Let's say we defeat the Bolsheviks, push them into the Volga and claim the steppes as our Lebensraum, our living space – what will the vampyrs do then? Go quietly back to their homes in the Transylvanian mountains? I don't think so. There will be a price for their help, and we'll be paying it in blood. These monsters are learning our ways of war, studying the tactics of Blitzkrieg that we developed. What happens if they apply these tactics to their own ambitions? The vampyrs are learning how to fly fighter planes and bombers, learning how to drive and fight battle tanks, learning how to turn their thirst for blood into a weapon of absolute terror. What chance would we have against an army of creatures like Constanta, especially if they were armed with planes and tanks and God alone knows what other weapons?"

"I hadn't thought of that," Hans admitted. "But Witte thinks Constanta had only a hundred men when Operation Barbarossa began. They can't have created more vampyrs out of thin air." Then Hans remembered something he hadn't told the others. "My sergeant, he burnt the bodies of the Russians slaughtered by the mist creatures. He said they could resurrect their victims, turn them into more vampyrs."

Klaus shuddered. "There could be hundreds of them, maybe thousands."

For once, Ralf was more positive than his siblings. "I don't think so, not yet. Constanta and his kind have been staying deliberately behind the scenes, not wanting to advertise their presence in this war. The greater the number of vampyrs, the greater the chance of them being noticed by ordinary members of the Wehrmacht, like us. We can't be the only ones who suspect there is something strange about these Rumanians. It's a guess, but I think the vampyrs will not start recruiting men into their ranks until there is a need for them.

"I hope you're right," Klaus whispered fearfully. The three brothers fell quiet, contemplating all they had gleaned from each other. It was Hans who broke the silence.

"So what do we do? There are only three of us and at least a hundred of them that we know about. There could be more for all we know. We're guessing at numbers, grasping at shadows, trying to figure out their motivation. Even if we're right, what can we do about them?"

Ralf undid his tunic to reveal a silver crucifix hanging on a chain round his neck. "For a start, we can protect ourselves. My crew have been wearing these since our last encounter with Gorgo. Gunther figured any kind of protection was better than none. We're safe from the vampyrs during the hours of daylight, but this may not be enough. What we need are weapons that can hurt these monsters."

"How many crosses do you have?" Klaus asked.

Ralf shrugged. "Half a dozen, I suppose. Why?"

The pilot's face was a mask of concentration. "We're of the understanding that silver is actually fatal to these fiends. So, what's to stop us collecting all the silver we can, then turning it into bullets? You could even use silver to coat the shells for your Panzer's main gun."

"That would take a lot of silver," Ralf replied. "Better to coat the tips instead. But we'd still need a way of smelting the metal."

"Many villages we've marched through had a smithy for shoeing horses," Hans observed. "The bigger towns and cities probably have foundries."

Klaus nodded, his smile returning slowly. "We should start stockpiling silver, in case the worst comes to the worst. In the meantime, avoid contact with the Rumanians whenever possible. Get hold of some garlic as protection for when you're asleep. Ralf, your crew already believes in these monsters, that makes your task easier. Hans, you need to find someone you can trust as an ally. What about this sergeant?"

"Witte? Maybe," Hans agreed. "He suspected the Rumanians long before I did. But whether he'd be willing to act against them, that's another matter."

"Try sounding him out, but be careful. We cannot be sure of anyone besides each other. Anybody could be a thrall of the vampyrs," Ralf said. "Even unwittingly."

"What do you mean?" Klaus asked.

The tank commander frowned. "There's something that's bothered me since we rolled into Soviet territory – where have all the Russian prisoners of war gone?"

"They're being transported to detainment camps, behind our lines," Hans said.

"Yes, but where are those camps?"

"In Rumania," the infantryman replied, realisation slowly dawning in his face. "I heard the biggest camp was not far from Sighisoara, in Transylvania."

"Exactly," Ralf muttered.

"I don't understand the significance," Klaus interjected.

"That's where Constanta comes from," Hans replied.

Ralf nodded. "You've got to wonder what's happening to all those Soviet POWs."

AN HOUR LATER Klaus was back in his cot at the field hospital, failing to get any sleep. It had been a joy to see Ralf and Hans, but the pilot's body was making him suffer for spending so long in the wheelchair. The pain from his injuries was excruciating, but it was the disturbing conversation with his siblings that kept him from sleeping. Separately, the three brothers had encountered parts of a puzzle far larger than any of them realised. They had compared experiences and the picture was becoming far clearer and infinitely more frightening. If their suspicions about the Rumanians were true, each of them was in danger. Klaus felt certain that there was something far greater at stake than the lives of the three brothers.

The sour orderly who had sent them outside paused to check Klaus's condition. "Good news," he announced. "You're being transferred to another hospital for another operation, then on to a rehabilitation centre. Guess you can thank your brother the war hero for that."

"Where am I going?" Klaus asked weakly.

"I'm not sure which hospital is performing your surgery, but the rehabilitation centre is in Rumania, at a place called Sighisoara," the orderly replied. "You'd better get some rest. I'm told the journey can be hellish."

Klaus watched him go. If the journey is hellish, he thought, what would Sighisoara be like?

Chapter Thirteen

AUGUST 4ᵀᴴ, 1941

HANS WAS GRATIFIED to see Ralf among those at the medal ceremony. Despite their frequent clashes, he felt closer to Ralf now that they had a shared enemy. The ceremony was taking place in a cobbled courtyard on the western outskirts of Uman, not far from an airfield captured by the Germans several days before. The square was flanked by tall stone buildings, two large archways providing the only entrances to the enclosed space. Hans could see his brother among the guests stood along the north and south sides of the courtyard. The medal recipients waited for the Führer along the eastern wall.

As dusk approached, the sound of an approaching staff car announced the imminent arrival of the German Army's Supreme Commander. The black vehicle swept into the courtyard, small flags fluttering on the bonnet. It braked smoothly to a halt and a Leutnant emerged, saluting crisply as he opened the rear door. Everyone in the courtyard snapped to attention, a thousand boots stamped loudly on the cobbles. The Führer emerged, smiling and holding up a hand to acknowledge them.

Hans had seen Germany's leader in the flesh once
before. At the age of twelve he had been among 54,000
boys and girls from all over the Fatherland chosen to
take part in the Adolf Hitler March, a gathering at
Nuremberg stadium. He counted himself fortunate to
have been chosen and luckier still to be within sight of
the main podium. It was filled with adults, but, like all
the others, Hans only had eyes for one person – the
Überwavter. When he appeared, everyone began
shouting with one voice, crying out: "Heil Hitler!" The
roars of adulation continued for many minutes before
drum-rolls and fanfares brought the noise back under
control. To Hans's eyes, the Supreme Commander had
appeared like a god. He had loved Hitler more than his
own parents, then.

Six years had elapsed since that glorious day. Now he
was to be personally introduced to the Führer and
receive a medal he did not deserve. The experience felt
beyond reality, yet all Hans could think about was what
he and his brothers had discussed the previous day.
Hans knew he would never get another chance like this.
Surely it was his duty as a good soldier of the Fatherland
to alert his Supreme Commander to the vampyr threat
against the Reich?

Hans compared his memory of the Führer from that
glorious day in September 1935 with the man stepping
from the staff car. Back then Hitler had been a giant to
Hans's boyhood eyes, not in height but in stature. Now
the Supreme Commander of all Germany appeared little
different from the men in uniform clustered around him.

Hans waited patiently as the formalities were observed
and the other men of the Wehrmacht received their
medals. He glanced sideways to see how close the
Führer was and felt his blood run cold. Constanta was
among those waiting to receive their medals. The
Rumanian officer appeared composed and solemn as
Hitler approached. Hans could not understand why he

had not seen Constanta sooner, until he remembered how long they had all waited. No doubt the Rumanian had stayed indoors until there was no danger from the setting sun. Constanta twisted his glance sideways and locked eyes with Hans, raising a finger to his lips and smiling.

The message was clear: be careful what you say.

Hans tore his eyes away and looked across to Ralf, but his brother was busy talking with one of the other guests.

Fearfully, Hans turned toward Constanta. The Haupt-mann was bending forwards to allow the Führer to slip a medal over his neck. When Constanta straightened up, Hans could see that he had received the coveted Iron Cross. Did Hitler realise what sort of creature he was honouring? Soon it was Hans's turn to have his moment with the Supreme Commander. He could feel his heart beating hard, with a strange sense of pride and fear. Hans was clearly intimidated by the sheer presence of the Führer, the immaculate uniform, the way he addressed each soldier. As the Führer stepped up to him, Hans saluted crisply. The medal was pinned to his chest and then they shook hands.

"Congratulations," the Führer said, his voice full of formality. "I understand you wiped out an entire Russian patrol almost single-handedly. With men like you at the front, it shall not be long before these Bolsheviks crumble completely."

Hans smiled and did his best to accept the praise gratefully, trying to avoid his nerves coming through in his voice. "I did what any good soldier would do. There are others who deserve the credit far more than me."

Hitler raised an eyebrow at this, apparently amused by Hans's answer. "And so modest! Truly, a credit to your unit."

The Führer was about to move on, but Hans somehow found the courage to speak again. "Excuse me, sir, but there is something I wanted to ask you."

"Yes? What is it?"

Hans took a deep breath, not sure how to phrase his thoughts. "How far should we go for victory? What means must we be willing to use to defeat the Russians?"

Hitler smiled, but his eyes were cold. "We must win," he replied, "by any means necessary." The Führer's gaze flickered sideways to Constanta. "By any means."

Chapter Fourteen

JUNE 16TH, 1941

NEARLY A FORTNIGHT had passed since Hans's medal ceremony. Ralf had returned to his tank and told the others
all he had seen and heard. For Ralf, the most disturbing
moment was seeing the Führer laughing with a man
bearing the emblem of the vampyrs. His disquiet had
deepened further when he discovered the identity of that
austere figure: Hauptman Constanta, leader of the 1st
Rumanian Mountain Troop. Any lingering loyalty Ralf
felt for his Supreme Commander died then. If Hitler was
in league with the undead, nobody was safe until the
vampyrs were destroyed.

Gunther and the others vowed to follow Ralf into hell
itself, if necessary. They had no qualms about collecting
silver rings from the bodies of fallen comrades, nor
about looting any silver they discovered between battles.
With the Uman Kessel closed around the Soviets and the
13th Panzer Division waiting for fresh orders, the last
few days had been uneventful. Ralf's crew had busied
themselves searching for silver, slowly accumulating a
stockpile of the precious metal. When another Panzer

crew questioned this, Gunther explained Ralf wanted to be rich when he went home for Christmas. The driver even had the nerve to encourage other crews to follow their example. A single tank could only carry so much extra weight and they needed all the silver they couold get.

Ralf believed he would have to enlist the aid of other Panzer crews, but could see no easy method of convincing them about the Rumanians. Ironically, it was Sergeant Gorgo who provided the answer. The 13th Panzer Division was despatched towards Dnepropetrovsk, a town on the western bank of the Dnepr River. Gorgo's five T-34s had joined the German armour for the journey. Soviet forces were falling back to the eastern bank of the Dnepr, seeking to protect its key crossing points. As usual, the retreating Russians left pockets of men and armour to slow the German advance.

It was such a pocket that ambushed the Panzers and T-34s. The tanks had stopped for the night at the remnants of a hilltop village. Few walls stood more than a metre high and no signs of life remained when Ralf led his crew on a hunt for silver. Their search proved fruitless, but it did mean they were away from their tanks when the Russians attacked under cover of darkness. Soviet shells rained on the encampment. Each explosion flung out a devastating hail of shrapnel. Ralf and his crew had dived for shelter at the first distant boom of the enemy artillery, but many others were not so fortunate.

The shelling continued for thirty minutes, only ceasing after a Schwarm of Stuka was called in to bombard the Soviet artillery positions. But the sound of men dying or weeping with pain was audible long afterwards. It was Martin who stumbled over Hoepner in the darkness, the driver from Erfurth's Panzer clutching a tunic round his left thigh. Hoepner screamed in agony, bringing Ralf and the others to his side.

"What happened?" Gunther asked, gently lifting the tunic to look at the wound.

"Shrapnel sliced right down to the bone," the driver replied weakly. "It was… bizarre."

"What was?"

"I was arguing with Gorgo's driver, Iliescu. He was between me, and the shell that it exploded. Shrapnel hit Iliescu in the throat, decapitating him."

Ralf could see no sign of the dead Rumanian. Then he remembered what Gunther and Klaus had said. "What happened next?"

Hoepner shook his head. "You'd never believe me."

"Try us," Willy urged.

The wounded man shuddered. "Iliescu just… turned to dust before my eyes." Hoepner searched the faces of the five men watching him. "I said you wouldn't believe me."

"Did he turn to dust, or to ashes?" Helmut asked.

"I don't know," Hoepner said. "I wasn't paying that much attention, because the same piece of shrapnel embedded itself in my leg. It's still in there."

Ralf looked to the others. "We need to get that shrapnel out."

Gunther nodded. "The sooner the better."

"What are you talking about?" Hoepner demanded, all colour draining from his face.

Ralf knelt beside the driver. "We believe Gorgo and his men are carriers for… an infection. If any part of Iliescu is still on that shrapnel, you could also be infected."

"Infected? With what?"

"Vampyrism."

Hoepner stared at Ralf as if the tank commander had gone mad. When Ralf did not recant his suggestion, Hoepner turned to the others. They all nodded in agreement.

"You're insane, all of you," Hoepner said. "There are no such things as vampyrs."

Gunther gripped one of Hoepner's hands. "We're friends, have been for a long time. Have I ever lied to you?"

"No, but–"

"But nothing. This is the truth. How else do you explain Iliescu exploding into ash?"

"I can't, but what you're suggesting is…"

"Beyond belief? Maybe," Ralf agreed. "But it's also the truth."

Mercifully for Hoepner, he passed out when Gunther began removing the shrapnel. As it came free something squirmed on the bloody surface of Hoepner's leg, the crimson stain coalescing into a shape. No, not a shape, Ralf realised, a face. Eyes and a mouth appeared in the moist redness, grinning evilly. Ralf had already sent Martin back to Panzer for a flask hidden beneath the commander's seat. The loader almost dropped it when he saw what was on Hoepner's leg.

Ralf twisted the lid off the flask, then poured the contents over the wound. "Who's got a match?" he demanded.

Gunther pulled a packet from his tunic pocket and lit one.

"Throw it on the alcohol," Ralf said. "Do it!"

Gunther dropped the lit match on his friend's leg, turning away as the mixture of blood and alcohol caught fire. As it burned Hoepner jerked awake and cried out, but his voice was overwhelmed by the unearthly screams of Iliescu. The Rumanian's face appeared in the black, greasy smoke rising from the burning leg, a chilling keen issuing from the writhing mouth. Gunther used Hoepner's tunic to put out the fire, while the injured man stared in disbelief at the vision hovering over him. Then the face faded away, the smoke floating into the night sky, disappearing into the heavens.

"What in God's name was that?" Hoepner asked weakly.

"Our real enemy," Ralf replied quietly. "And it walks among us."

Gorgo appeared from the shadows, demanding to know where Iliescu was. "We don't know," Gunther replied. "Perhaps he took a direct hit from one of the Russian shells." The Rumanian sergeant glared at the Germans suspiciously before leaving. Once he had gone, Ralf examined Hoepner's leg.

"The fire seems to have cauterised your wound. It needs a medic, but you'll survive."

The driver was shaking his head, struggling to comprehend the situation. "I saw that thing with my own eyes and yet…"

"Now you know what we're up against," Helmut said.

Two HOURS LATER, Erfurth called an assembly of all the Panzer commanders and drivers. Once they had gathered in two lines, he stepped forward to address them.

"It's been a tough night, but for the most part we have been fortunate. My own driver is injured but the medics tell me he'll pull through, thanks to Vollmer and his crew. Sergeant Gorgo has not been so lucky. His driver is missing, presumed dead, and the Rumanian T-34s are needed to help another division nearby. One of you will be seconded into Sergeant Gorgo's tank until he can acquire the services of another driver. Are there any volunteers?"

Ralf suppressed the urge to laugh. The Rumanians had made themselves exceedingly unpopular with the Panzer crews, thanks to their malevolent attitude. Rumours were already spreading about what had happened to Hoepner and gossip travelled fast in armoured divisions. Besides, each crew was bound by a loyalty forged in the cauldron of battle. Nobody would willingly abandon their own crew to join that of Gorgo.

"Very well then," Erfurth said unhappily. He made an impatient gesture and the Rumanian sergeant emerged from the darkness. "You may choose a replacement from among the men, but I reserve the right of veto. I do out-rank you," the Feldwebel added.

Gorgo bristled at this comment before turning his attention to those assembled. He strode along the two lines, muttering something in his own language as he passed each man. Finally Gorgo stopped behind Gunther. "I want this one. He is impertinent, but has shown some skill as a driver."

"Charming," Gunther whispered to Ralf. But his smile vanished when Erfurth agreed to Gorgo's choice.

Ralf broke ranks to approach the Feldwebel. "Permission to speak with you in private?"

Erfurth nodded, beckoning Ralf away.

Once they were out of hearing by the others, Ralf pleaded the case for exempting his crewman. "Gunther's the best driver in our division and you know it. It's bad enough they have laid claim to the abandoned T-34s, we shouldn't let the Rumanians steal our best men as well."

The Feldwebel was not convinced. "Perhaps, but I'm under direct orders from Berlin to show them every consideration."

"Gunther saved your driver's life tonight," Ralf replied. "If you don't believe me, ask Hoepner yourself."

"I've already talked with my driver, thank you," Erfurth said prissily. "He was full of praise for the quick thinking of your men." He sighed. "Very well, I will spare your driver. But do not consider this any sort of precedent."

"Thank you."

The Feldwebel nodded regally, then returned to the men. "I have decided to exempt Gunther Stiefel from this duty. Sergeant Gorgo, you must choose again."

"I have already chosen," the Rumanian snarled angrily.

"Be that as it may, you must choose again."

Gorgo glared at the Feldwebel, but Erfurth would not give way. Eventually, the sergeant gestured at the nearest man, a driver called Muller. "Him, he will do."

"Very well. Gefreiter Muller, you will gather your personal items and report to Sergeant Gorgo within the next fifteen minutes. The rest of you are dismissed."

TWENTY MINUTES LATER, Gunther was still thanking Ralf for his timely intervention when a man's scream was heard in the distance.

"That came from the Rumanian tanks," Ralf said.

He and Gunther raced to where the T-34s were clustered. Men from several other Panzer crews joined them, arriving in time to see Muller emerge from Gorgo's tent. The ashen-faced driver was wearing a Rumanian uniform, one hand holding a dressing over a wound on his neck. When the others asked what was wrong, Muller waved away their questions.

"I'm fine," he insisted. "Something flew into me in the dark and I scratched my neck. It's nothing to worry about."

Gunther approached Muller, offering to shake his hand. "I'm sorry about what happened, that you got chosen instead of me–"

"I don't want your pity and I don't need your sorrow," Muller said with sudden vehemence. "Gorgo told me all about you, how you've been trying to poison the other crews against us. Your day will come, Gunther Stiefel. You can be certain of that."

"Poison the other crews against you? What are you talking about, Muller? You're one of us," Ralf interjected.

"Not anymore," the driver replied, grinning broadly so all the men could see his teeth. Twin fangs caught the moonlight as Muller licked his lips.

Gorgo appeared from his tent. "What's going on out here? Muller, I told you to ready the T-34. We leave in twenty minutes." The others drifted away, muttering darkly about Muller.

"Yes, sergeant," the driver responded, before striding away obediently into the night.

Gorgo glared at Ralf and Gunther. "I don't know how you changed that fool Erfurth's mind, but challenges to our authority do not go unpunished."

Ralf undid the top two buttons of his tunic, letting the silver cross slip out so it caught the moonlight. "We can and we will protect ourselves from your kind."

The Rumanian sneered at Ralf, shaking his head dismissively. "You have no faith in that symbol, so it has no power in your hands."

Gunther took out his own silver cross. "He may not believe anymore, but I do. What do you say to that, nightwalker?"

Gorgo retreated slowly from the glinting crucifix, a hand held in front of his face to keep its light from his eyes. "Your time will come, Christian. He can't save you forever."

Then Gorgo was gone, vanishing into the darkness, the sounding of flapping wings fading into the night.

Ralf breathed out again, shivering as the air left his lungs. "Thank you," he whispered.

The driver smiled and shrugged. "Now we're even." The two men walked back to their tank. "What happened to Muller – that could have been me."

"It could still be any us unless we do something," Ralf replied. "Gorgo knows we're on to him. We must be twice as watchful from now on."

Chapter Fifteen

AUGUST 25ᵀᴴ, 1941

THE REHABILITATION CENTRE in Rumania was based at an abandoned private school on the outskirts of Sighisoara, housed in an old baronial castle. Klaus was grateful to reach the towering stone structure during the hours of daylight. It stood on the brow of a hill that offered magnificent views of the black, brooding Transylvanian mountains. Klaus shuddered involuntarily as he was wheeled inside. There was something malevolent about those peaks, almost as if they were alive.

Inside it was cold and draughty, with high ceilings and plaster crumbling from the walls. The acrid stench of disinfectant filled the rooms, mingling with the stale scent of dust and mouse droppings. The building had seen better days, as had most of the staff. Wehrmacht medics were responsible for overseeing the patients. Only those with a realistic chance of full recovery came to the centre, while more serious injuries were invalided back to Germany. Klaus soon noticed menial jobs such as cooking and cleaning were done by a handful of elderly Rumanians. He tried asking them about the local area, but they refused to answer or did not understand his questions. He mentioned the name Constanta to a wrinkled washerwoman. The colour drained from her face and she kissed a crucifix, which was hanging round her neck.

Klaus's curiosity soon came to the attention of the centre's director, Doctor Sheybal. The thin-faced, pallid physician paid an early morning visit to the pilot's bedside, waking him from a dreamless sleep. "I understand you've been asking my staff a lot of questions. May I ask why?"

The pilot shrugged, wincing at the pain that he still felt in his chest. His wounds were healing well, but that didn't stop them hurting. "Those mountains outside intrigue me. Where I come from in, it Germany is mostly flatland, we don't have anything to rival such peaks."

Sheybal pondered his reply, one hand nervously smoothing a few greasy strands of hair across his balding pate. "Perhaps that is true, but I'm told you've also been asking about a local dignitary, Lord Constanta."

Klaus fought to keep the panic from his face. "One of my brothers met Hauptmann Constanta on the Ostfront and they talked about Sighisoara. When Hans heard I was coming here, he asked me to pass his regards to the Hauptmann's family."

"Did he?" The doctor pursed his lips thoughtfully. "Well then, you are in luck, Oberleutnant Vollmer. Lord Constanta is passing through Sighisoara today. In view of your interest, I shall make a request for him to visit us. I'm sure he will want to meet you in person."

"I'll look forward to that," Klaus replied, forcing a smile until Sheybal left the private room. His mind raced, trying to plot some way out of this situation before realising the encounter was unavoidable. Klaus closed a trembling hand around the silver cross on his bedside table.

I'll simply have to hope this does its job, he decided, gripping the crucifix tightly between his fingers.

IT WAS DARK when Klaus stirred from sleep, the last light of the day tinting clouds red. The pilot watched night claiming the sky for its own though the tall, lead-lined windows of his room. Something was nagging at the back of his mind, trying to force its way past the drowsiness clouding his thoughts. Then a voice in the darkness jolted him awake.

"I understand you've been asking for me."

A lone figure appeared from the shadows. A high-collared cloak of black surrounded the man like a shroud, casting darkness across his clothes. Black leather gloves encased his hands, creaking as the newcomer clenched and unclenched his fists. A peaked cap above the cold, patrician features bore the familiar emblem of the vampyrs. There could be little doubt that this was Hauptmann Constanta. Cold, numbing fear chilled Klaus as he stared into the stranger's face, unable to tear his gaze from those hooded eyes. The pilot felt himself drawn deeper into those black pupils, as if they were somehow sucking the spirit from his body.

Klaus forced himself to blink, breaking contact between them. He looked at his open hands, but the cross was gone. A hurried glance confirmed it had not fallen from his grasp while he slept, or slipped to the floor. It must have been taken while he dozed, his sole form of protection deliberately removed. He realised that he was alone, with no means of fighting off this monster. Constanta was glaring at him, so Klaus repeated what he had said to Doctor Sheybal about passing on Hans's regards.

"Is that so?" the Hauptmann replied. "Private Vollmer is your brother? How interesting. I wonder, do you have another sibling fighting in this war?"

Klaus tried to lie, but was unable to with Constanta's gaze boring into his own. The Rumanian's eyes seemed to scour his soul.

"Yes," Klaus said. "Ralf, my elder brother. He's a Panzer commander."

Constanta smiled. "I thought as much. One of my underlings reported an icident involving an Obergefreiter Vollmer. The same surname, recurring so many times... I knew it had to be more than mere coincidence." He stepped closer to Klaus, gently resting a gloved hand on the edge of the bed. "A trio of brothers, all stationed along the Ostfront, all causing trouble for or asking questions about me and my men. One might almost think the three of you were planning to pit yourselves against us."

"Why would we?" Klaus asked, struggling to keep the fear from his voice. "We're all on the same side in this war, we share a common enemy."

"Precisely." Constanta smiled wide enough for Klaus to see the tips of his fangs. "We are allies, we should act that way."

"Then my brothers and I have no reason to fear you or your men."

"Fear us? Why should you fear us?"

"One of your pilots tried to kill me," Klaus said, his anger over the death of Heinrich finding an outlet at last. "He crashed his plane into mine, murdering my gunner in the process."

"The official inquiry found the collision was an unfortunate accident."

"It was no accident," Klaus snapped.

Constanta's hands flashed forward and grabbed Klaus by the neck, gloved fingers closing over his windpipe. The Rumanian leaned closer, fixing the pilot's gaze. "You will listen to me, Oberleutnant Vollmer. I am a patient man. When you have lived as long as I in the service of my sire, you learn these passing conflicts are but a moment in the vast span of history. Millions will die in

this war, as millions have died in wars past and wars yet
to begin. Your life and the lives of your brothers are less
than nothing in a conflict of this scale. Whether or not
you see the end of this war is in your hands. Keep silent
about what you think you know and you might survive.
Continue spreading sedition about my men and you will
leave me with no alternative. Do I make myself clear?"

Klaus nodded hurriedly, anything to get Constanta's
rancid breath away, to escape the curving, crimson-
tipped fangs that hovered within biting distance.

The Hauptmann straightened up and smiled, apparently satisfied. "Very well, then. Let's us say nothing
more about it."

He clapped his hands and Doctor Sheybal scurried into
the room like an obedient dog.

"Ah, my dear Vladek. I want you to ensure young
Vollmer receives the finest possible care. The sooner he
is back in the air with a new Stuka, fighting the good
fight for Germany and Rumania, the better for all of us.
Don't you agree, Oberleutnant?"

"Yes," Klaus whispered.

The Hauptmann wrapped an arm round Sheybal's
shoulders and led the physician out of the room. "Now,
doctor, I need to talk with you about medical supplies
for the prisoner of war camp on the other side of
Sighisoara. I was visiting there earlier today and saw a
severe shortage of vital equipment. We don't wish the
Russian prisoners to die needlessly, do we?"

Once they were gone, Klaus let his head sink back into
the pillow. He became aware that his bedclothes were
soaked with sweat. He began shivering uncontrollably,
his hands shaking like those of an old man. Why hadn't
the vampyr leader killed him when given the chance? It
would look suspicious if he had died while recovering at
a rehabilitation centre, but these things happened. Eventually, he abandoned trying to understand the
Hauptmann's actions. Klaus decided he could not think

his way into the Hauptmann's head, nor did he want to. Besides, something else was bothering him. Why would Constanta care about the welfare of Russian POWs if the Rumanians hated the Soviets as much as they claimed? Again, he could find no obvious answer to that question. But the pilot did come to a decision: he would pay a visit to that camp and see those prisoners with his own eyes.

Chapter Sixteen

SEPTEMBER 1ST, 1941

FOUR WEEKS AFTER his brief encounter with the Führer, Hans realised he was one of only three survivors in his unit from all those who crossed the Prut in June. Nearly a dozen had died in that first day of fighting to claim Reni. More had fallen during intermittent skirmishes with the Soviets since, but the midnight ambush had cost the most lives. Both the Held twins fell that dark, bloody night, along with many others Hans thought of as friends. Since returning from the medal ceremony he had watched the casualties mount up, fresh-faced youths brought in from Germany to fill the gaps cut down as quickly as their predecessors. The losses had seen him promoted to Gefreiter, as much by default as on merit. Hans dreamt of such promotions when he first put on his private's uniform, but the reality had made little difference to him.

Only Witte, Kral and himself remained from the Originals, as Franz liked to call them. Seventy-three days of fighting and only three survivors. It was a chilling statistic, but one Hans could not help dwelling upon. The threat of the vampyrs was always at the back of his mind, a troubling shadow on his subconscious, but he had only ever seen Constanta's men killing the enemy.

In this bitter war of attrition, Hans thought, perhaps the presence of such ruthless warriors was as much a blessing as it was a curse. Then he remembered the sudden change in Brunetti, the attempt on Klaus's life, the things Ralf had told them about the vampyrs. How could you balance one enemy against another? He was a simple soldier. He would do his duty for the Fatherland and let history be the judge of his actions. It was the only decision he could make without driving himself mad.

Hans's unit had been progressing slowly since the launch of Operation Barbarossa. Isolated from much of Army Group South, they had been busy keeping their Axis allies out of trouble and providing flank cover for the 17th Army. Recent battles had captured a bridge-head across the Dnepr River at Berislav. It didn't take a genius to realise the Crimea would be their next objective. Happily for Hans, his encounters with the vampyrs had been few, reassuring him their numbers remained small among the millions of men fighting along the vast-ness of the Ostfront. The majority of the Rumanian soldiers were like him – ordinary men trying to get through the war alive. But Hans's belief was shaken when his unit was ordered to help expand the Berislav bridgehead.

The target was to secure a wide road through the set-tlement on the Russian side of the river. Constant aerial bombardment from Stukas and German guns had devas-tated buildings on either side of the road, but had also turned the scarred structures into perfect hiding places for snipers.

Witte was grim-faced when he briefed the men in the early afternoon sun. "We are bait for a trap, charged with advancing down the road, attracting hostile fire. A

strike force will use us as a way to pinpoint the enemy
locations and wipe them out, making the road safe."

"What about us?" Franz asked nervously. "Who keeps
us safe?"

"We have to keep each other safe," the sergeant
replied.

When the men began muttering in protest, Witte
snapped at them for silence. "Perhaps you have forgotten pledging your life to the Fatherland?" He ordered
them to look at the square alloy buckle on their waist
belts, embossed with a Wehrmacht eagle set inside a
wreath of oak leaves. Surmounting the wreath were
three words, "Gott mit uns".

"God is with us," the sergeant reminded them. "Now,
get yourselves ready. We move out within the hour. Dismissed!"

Hans went from man to man, checking that each had
two clips of ammunition in their pouches, along with a
full Feldflasche and several stick grenades. Franz started
at the other end of the unit, reminding the conscripts the
safest ways to advance and how to provide cover for
their comrades. The two men met when Hans reached
Private Ludwig Blomberg, a nervous youngster with
spectacles. His father had been a hero in the First World
War.

"I begged him for some way out of this," Ludwig told
Franz. "He said if I didn't do my duty, he would have me
shot for being a coward."

Hans and Franz exchanged a look of despair. It was
soldiers like Blomberg who got good men killed.

"You stay beside me," Hans said, trying to reassure the
raw recruit. "Together we'll prove your father wrong,
okay?"

Blomberg nodded weakly, mucus hanging from one
nostril. Hans got the boy to wipe his nose and collect his
equipments while Franz went on to the next man.

• • •

LESS THAN TWO hours later Blomberg was dead. His head
had exploded like a rotten grapefruit, bone and brain
spraying the air. He and Hans had been at the rear of the
infantry unit as it advanced along the road. An eerie
silence enveloped the men. The snipers only opened fire
when every German soldier was completely exposed.
Then the slaughter began, a volley of shots that seemed
to come from every direction. Hans sprinted to one side,
dragging Blomberg along as he sought the shelter of a
doorway. Both men had nearly reached sanctuary when
a sniper fired.

A wet aerosol hit Hans as Blomberg's terrified whimpering was stopped by a dull, moist thud. Hans kept on
running, dragging the body behind him, but he knew it
was too late for poor Ludwig. When he glanced at the
young soldier, little remained of Blomberg's face. The fool
must have taken off his helmet, Hans realised. He
searched the road where they had stood. The dead youth's
helmet was still there, but the chinstrap was broken.

"Guess I did you a disservice," he said. "Not that you
care much now."

Hans snapped off the bottom half of Blomberg's identity disc. He read the dead man's date of birth and
laughed. Blomberg had been five days older than him.
After three months on the Ostfront, Hans felt as if he'd
been fighting the war for three years. Being among so
much devastation aged a person in ways that nothing
else could.

Across the road, he could see Witte make his way back
along the opposite side, sniper bullets spitting up cement
chips from the broken pavement. The sergeant made a
hand gesture and asked if Hans was wounded. He shook
his head, then pointed to the windows above, indicating
there was a sniper overhead. The sergeant nodded, then
disappeared into an open doorway.

Hans was removing spare ammunition from
Blomberg's body, when he noticed movement in the

building opposite. Witte was creeping past a window on the first floor, but there was another person two levels further up. Hans realised he couldn't call out, as it would draw attention from the sniper. But he couldn't get a clear shot either because he needed more elevation. He leaned against the door behind him and felt it move. A twist of the handle and the door swung inwards. Plaster dust covered everything, while shattered glass cracked beneath Hans's jackboots.

Another sound was audible.

He stopped and listened. Somewhere above him was another sniper, waiting for a clear target. Hans crept to the nearby staircase and quickly removed his boots. They did a good job of protecting his feet, but made too much noise. Hans crept up the stairs, his MP 40 ready to fire.

The first floor was empty so Hans ascended another level, aware of every movement in the shattered building. A German shell must have exploded in the next home, as the adjoining walls had collapsed sideways into this house. Fragments of mortar were strewn across the wooden floor like pebbles. Hans tiptoed to a window and looked across the road. He could see Witte and the sniper grappling, both men clawing desperately at the other's face.

A shot rang out from directly above Hans, startling him.

Abandoning all attempts at stealth, he ran for the staircase and sprinted upwards, opening fire before he reached the top step. The sniper spun round, caught in the act of reloading. Hans emptied all thirty-two rounds from his machine pistol into the Russian soldier, who fell sideways against the window frame, then crumpled face-first to the floor, blood covering the floor and walls.

"That's for Blomberg, you bastard," Hans snarled as he approached the dead sniper.

He kicked the body so it rolled over, a heavy cap that had hidden the Russian's features falling aside. The sniper was a woman. Her pale face was remarkably beautiful, despite the blood oozing from her mouth and nostrils.

"Oh, God," Hans whispered, the dead woman's blood pooling round his feet.

"Vollmer," a voice said. "Vollmer. Are you all right?" Hans recognised the voice. Witte was waving from the far side of the road, one hand nursing a shoulder wound.

"What happened?" Hans called back.

"Your sniper's shot went through my arm and hit this one in the throat. What about you?"

"This one's dead," Hans replied emotionlessly.

The sergeant gave the thumbs up signal. "There's at least four more along the road. They've got Kral and several others pinned down."

Hans nodded his understanding and went back downstairs to retrieve his jackboots. He didn't look back at the dead sniper, didn't want to see her lifeless eyes staring at him accusingly. He told himself that he did not kill a woman; he killed one of his enemies. But he couldn't help wondering if the war was turning all of them into monsters of one kind or another.

FRANZ WAS PINNED down with half a dozen men in a doorway, caught in the crossfire of three snipers secreted across the road. Half the conscripts died in the first twenty minutes, picked off by precise Soviet fire. The rest learned the lesson and kept out of harm's way. Franz had seen so many men die he no longer bothered remembering the names of newcomers, unless they survived past the first week. Of the three who were crouched around him, Franz recognised only one – a tall, gangling youth called Raus. He had arrived nine days earlier and kept his head when others panicked. The other two were unknown to Franz. He nudged a pale-faced private with black hair and a broken nose on his right. "Hey, what's your name?"

"Jodl. Kurt Jodl."

Franz nodded towards the other soldier, a slightly overweight youth with strawberry blonde hair and crimson cheeks. "And him?"

"That's Zeitzler," Jodl replied. "I don't know his first name. Sorry."

"Hey, Zeitzler," Franz said. "What's your first name?"

But the newcomer was dead before he could answer. A single bullet neatly punctured his chest. He fell to the ground as a sucking sound escaped from the gaping hole. The others flinched. Jodl clutched at the front of his trousers. A dark, wet stain spread from the crotch, the smell of warm piss filling the air.

"Scheisse," the private muttered, his face flushing red with shame.

"Let's hope not," Franz replied, returning fire at the sniper. "Otherwise that smell is only going to get worse." He glanced up and down the road that had cost the lives of half the unit in a single afternoon. "Where the hell are our reinforcements?"

HANS HAD JOINED Witte on the opposite side of the road, then the sergeant led him towards where Franz and the others were pinned down. The two men had to stop twice along the way to deal with Soviet snipers. As soon as they had flushed one out, another appeared.

Like Kral, Witte wondered aloud about the support they had been promised. "We're getting slaughtered out here and there's no sign of them," he said angrily.

When the two men stopped to reload, a grim thought occurring to Hans. "Did anyone specify where our support was coming from, what company or battalion?"

Witte shook his head. "Some new unit, trained in stealth and covert tactics, that's all I was told." His eyes widened. "You don't think... We haven't seen Constanta or his men for weeks."

"That's what worries me," Hans agreed, slapping a fresh magazine into his MP 40.

A lone voice called out from the German-held end of the road. A figure was approaching Hans and Witte, waving to them cheerfully while walking down the centre of the street. "Hello, soldiers. How goes the war for you?"

Hans squinted to see the madman's face in the gloaming. "Is that Brunetti?"

The Italian waved again, ever closer to the firing range of the snipers. He seemed oblivious of the danger he was walking into. "Have either of you see Hauptmann Constanta? We've arranged to meet here, but I can't seem to find him anywhere."

"Brunetti, get out of the road," Witte said. "This area is swarming with Soviet snipers."

But the Italian kept coming, smiling and waving. It was as if he was in a trance, like somebody sleepwalking to their own death.

"Giovanni, stop," Hans said. "Don't come closer!"

Still Brunetti continued walking. He raised a hand to his mouth and shouted into the air. "Hauptmann Constanta, are you here? Hauptmann Constanta, can you hear me?"

One of the snipers blew a hole in Brunetti's chest. The Italian stumbled and fell, blood leaking from his wound. Despite the fact he was dying, the war correspondent began crawling on all fours. "Please, Hauptmann. You said you'd be here. You told me I had to come this way." Hans looked away as another shot rang out. Brunetti did not speak again, but his body twitched for several minutes afterwards.

RAUS DIED NEXT. The sound of Brunetti's bizarre demise tricked him into leaning forwards, to see who was approaching. A fusillade of rounds set Raus dancing like a rag doll. It was a relief for Franz when the conscript died. He collapsed into an untidy heap, but the casualty proved too much for Jodl.

The black-haired soldier was weeping uncontrollably, tears streaming down his face. "I don't want to die," he whispered weakly. "Please don't let me die here."

"Shut up a minute and let me think," Franz snarled, losing patience with the boy. He already knew the door behind him would not give way, having tried it several times already. Trying to run was suicidal. All they could do was wait. The sun was setting and night offered their best chance of escaping this death trap. A flapping sound overhead forced Franz to look up.

"What's that noise?" Jodl sobbed. "What is it?"

Franz pointed into the darkening sky. "Bats."

A pair of winged creatures was circling above the street, beating their wings in time with each other and observing the impasse.

"How can they help us?"

Franz didn't reply. He was content to watch the bats descending in slow circles towards the snipers' positions. A few seconds later and the Soviets started screaming.

HANS HAD ALSO seen the bats fly overhead. When a cry echoed along the road, Hans sprinted towards Franz.

"Vollmer! What are you doing?" Witte shouted after him, but Hans kept running. By the time he reached Franz, the last Russian voice had fallen silent.

"Franz, are you–"

"Your friend is fine," a familiar voice interjected. Hauptmann Constanta appeared behind Hans, emerging from the building where one of the snipers had lurked. "I am only sorry we did not arrive soon enough to save the rest of your unit."

"What about Brunetti?" Hans asked quietly. "Are you sorry about his death too?"

The officer shrugged. "Consider his loss a lesson, a pawn who was sacrificed to make a point."

Hans stepped closer to Constanta, dropping his voice so only the vampyr leader could hear his next question. "And what point is that, Hauptmann?"

"Nobody is indispensable. He served his purpose."

"Where the hell have you been?" Witte demanded of Constanta, having reached the doorway where Franz and the others had sought refuge. "My men have been getting butchered while you waited to make a bloody entrance!"

The Rumanian officer regarded him coldly, his eyes narrowing. "I do not answer to the lower ranks, nor do I appreciate being shouted at by them. I suggest you moderate your behaviour, otherwise it will go the worse for you."

Witte spat on the ground in front of Constanta. "You don't frighten me. I know what you are and I know how to deal with the likes of you."

"Really?" Constanta lashed out with the speed of lightning, the back of his gloved hand smashing into the sergeant's face, sending Witte sprawling to the ground. Hans stepped between Franz and the Hauptmann to stop his comrade getting involved. As Witte scrabbled at the buttons of his tunic, reaching the silver cross within, Constanta stepped on the sergeant's hands. His black leather boots pressed remorselessly on Witte's fingers, breaking the bones in them, one by one. The crack of each successive bone was accompanied by a fresh scream of agony from the prostrate soldier, his face contorting in pain. "You were saying?"

Another Rumanian emerged from the buildings opposite, wiping his mouth clean. "Hauptmann, we're needed elsewhere."

"Very well," Constanta replied. He gave one last stab downwards with his heel, breaking another two bones in Witte's hands, then removed the black boot. The officer glanced sideways at Hans, arching an eyebrow at him. "I am gladdened to see you are beginning to understand where the true power lies in this war, Gefreiter Vollmer. Congratulations on your promotion, by the way. I only hope your siblings share your good sense."

With that, Constanta strode into the gloom. His footsteps echoed on the road surface. The other Rumanian fell into step behind him. The darkness engulfed them both.

Franz stepped past the hysterical mess that was Jodl to confront Hans. "Why did you let that happen?" he demanded. "Between the two of us we could have done something to–"

"No, we couldn't," Hans replied. "You saw what Constanta did to the sergeant." His gaze shifted to Brunetti's body further along the road. Crows had already gathered beside the corpse, studying it with interest.

Hans thought that the message from Constanta had been loud and clear. Even the vampyr thralls were no more than equipment, to be used and then tossed aside once their worth had passed. When the war was over, all of humanity could become like Brunetti and the Russians – slaves or prey for the vampyrs. The Rumanians had to be stopped.

Hans crouched next to Witte. The sergeant had curled into a foetal position on the ground, his broken hands quivering by his white face. "God, what a mess."

Chapter Seventeen

SEPTEMBER 7ᵀᴴ, 1941

KLAUS WOULD NOT have believed what was happening at the prisoner of war camp if he had not witnessed it himself. Even then, the horror within the walls was the stuff of nightmares.

Rumours had long been circulating among the Wehrmacht about what happened to people in conquered territories. It was said that the Einsatzgruppen moved in and ruthlessly cleansed these areas for German occupation. Klaus found such tales hard to believe until he went to the POW camp near Sighisoara. After that he could believe anything was possible.

He had spent twelve days at the rehabilitation centre before Doctor Sheybal gave him permission to fly again. The director congratulated Klaus on making such a speedy recovery. "Most of our patients need weeks or even months to recover from such injuries, but you have shown remarkable resilience." They met in Sheybal's office, Transylvanian mountains filling the windows behind his sturdy oak desk. The doctor consulted his calendar. "Now, let's see. You've missed the last train east today and tomorrow is a Sunday. You can wait here until Monday if you wish."

Klaus had insisted he didn't want to needlessly occupy a bed any longer. Sheybal volunteered to drive the pilot into Sighisoara and even recommended a clean, hospitable tavern for the next two nights. Klaus risked a remark about Constanta's visitation, but Sheybal seemed to have little memory of the incident. Perhaps it was a side effect of being in thrall to the vampyr, Klaus speculated. He gambled on asking Sheybal about the prisoner of war camp. "There must be hundreds of Russians there, even thousands. Aren't you worried about them escaping?"

The doctor did not hesitate before replying. "I doubt they have the energy to think of escape, let alone to try." Sheybal pointed at a distant hillside. "It's on the other side of that. Only military personnel are allowed within a kilometre."

"Why's that?" Klaus asked lightly. He noticed Sheybal's tic spreading across his pallid face.

"It is..." the doctor began, but words seemed to fail him. "It is... forbidden." The effort of saying this was beginning to affect Sheybal's driving, making it more erratic. Klaus quickly changed the subject and Sheybal's twitching eased.

It was Sunday morning and Klaus was striding towards the camp's front gates in full dress uniform. His nostrils were filled with the stench of burning fat. He thought that there must have been a tannery or slaughterhouse upwind. If only military personnel were allowed inside the camp, perhaps his rank would find a way in. Whatever was happening within the barbed wire fences was of great importance to Constanta. Klaus needed to see for himself, to discover whether the camp held any secrets he and his brothers

could use against the vampyrs. Four Waffen-SS soldiers stood on the other side of the gate, armed with
machine guns.

Their leader, a sergeant with the top button of his
tunic undone, sneered at Klaus as he approached. "What
do you want? No unauthorised personnel are allowed
inside."

Klaus smiled. He had played plenty of cards
between sorties, enough to know a bluff only succeeded if you got a psychological edge over your
opponent. The pilot folded his arms and studied the
four guards. "Never in all my days have I seen such a
slovenly, disgraceful of insubordination. How dare
you address a superior officer in such a manner. What
is your name, soldier?"

The sergeant frowned, suddenly uncertain of his own
authority. "Erwin."

"What?" Klaus asked.

"Sergeant Erwin, sir." The soldier snapped to attention, saluting the new arrival. The other three hastily
followed his example.

"Why are the buttons of your uniforms undone? Do
you always turn out for duty in such a slovenly manner?
The four of you are a disgrace to this camp and to your
unit."

Erwin scrambled to fasten his buttons, gesturing for
the others to do the same. "Sorry, sir. It won't happen
again, sir."

"I should hope not. Well, are you going to open this
gate or not?"

The sergeant ran forward to unlock the gate, but
paused as he reached the heavy metal bolts. "Excuse my
asking, sir, but we weren't expecting your visit."

"Surprise inspections are being instituted at all POW
camps. There have been reports of slackness and failure
to follow procedure. It seems such reports are doubly
true of this place," Klaus snarled.

"It's just that, well, we need to see written authority before we allow any personnel to enter. Standard procedure, you see."

"I should hope so too," Klaus agreed. Now was the moment of truth, when his bluff would be pushed to its limit. "My staff car broke down between here and Sighisoara. I left my driver to make repairs and walked the rest of the way here but, alas, I left my paperwork in the vehicle. If you wish to confirm whether or not I have permission, I suggest you contact Hauptmann Constanta in person."

A single mention of the Rumanian officer's name was enough to have the gates open within seconds. The four guards saluted crisply as Klaus walked inside. He demanded a tour of the facility, choosing Erwin as his guide. "I understand you've been running low on medical supplies for the prisoners. Has this situation been resolved?"

"I'm not sure," the sergeant admitted, leading him up a slope past the guards' barracks. "But a doctor from the rehabilitation centre delivered fresh supplies a week ago."

Erwin reached the crest of the hill and gestured at the buildings spread across on a plateau below. "That's the POW camp. But we call it the Blood Bank."

"My God," Klaus gasped.

Row upon row of wooden huts stretched out below. There were close to fifty buildings in all. A metal box on legs, the size and shape of a small water reservoir, stood beside each, with pipes connecting it to the barrack.

Hundreds of naked men, and a few women, were shuffling outside the huts. He could see that their jaundiced skin was hanging from their malnourished bodies. They resembled the living dead as they slowly circled the barracks. Sentries tormented the prisoners with machine guns and leather whips. Some of the POWs rested arms on each other for support, while a few lay twitching on the dusty ground.

Klaus watched as another prisoner collapsed, her body surrendering to exhaustion and starvation. A sentry stepped forward and lashed the woman with his whip, its metal-tipped strands of leather slicing through her bruised, yellowing skin. When the prisoner did not respond, the sentry ordered two inmates to carry the body inside. "Drain her, then put the carcass in the ovens," he snarled.

"Impressive, isn't it?" Erwin asked.

"I've never seen anything like this before," Klaus admitted, battling to keep his revulsion from showing. "How many Bolsheviks do you have here?"

"Up to twenty thousand, with at least two thousand new prisoners arriving every day."

"Your barracks must already be beyond their capacity. Why are no new huts being built?"

Erwin shrugged. "Few prisoners last more than a week. We've been keeping the ovens burning round the clock lately, thanks to all the POWs captured at Uman."

Klaus nodded, not wanting to think about the implications of that. But he could not avoid asking another question. "And why do you call this place the Blood Bank?"

The sergeant frowned. "I'm surprised you don't know, since the Hauptmann sent you."

"He told me the trip would be... educational."

Erwin laughed. "That sounds like Constanta. Lord Constanta, I should say. He prefers to be addressed by his ancestral title when he visits the camp, you see."

"I can imagine," Klaus said. "I notice you have both sexes together here. Does that cause any problems?"

"Not that we've noticed. Once the prisoners have been inducted and drained for the first time, they put up little resistance." The sentry paused, then sniggered. "When we need a little entertainment, we borrow one of the females for a few hours. We show her a good time. We usually do it as a group. That way we're all involved and they're not going to complain when there're a few of you around them. We were amazed that the Reds actually allowed women in their army, but those Bolshevik bitches have their uses, if you know what I mean. It's strange that many of them don't scream. It's good if you don't look at the eyes. That can really put you off."

"Show me one of the barracks," the pilot replied, resisting the urge to attack the smug animal. And our leaders call the Russians sub-human, he thought. "I would like to see this 'draining' for myself."

"Of course. This way," the sergeant replied.

They marched down the hill towards the huts. He led Klaus to the nearest building and nodded curtly to a sentry, who was standing outside the main door. Once inside, Erwin stood aside to let the visitor get a good view.

What Klaus saw turned his stomach and the stench was almost too much.

Dozens of prisoners were bound to wooden cross-beams by their wrists. Their naked and emaciated bodies were hanging like wet laundry. He noted that their faces seemed unreal. They looked far older than they should, as if they had been just saved from a famine. None of them were moving, but he could tell that they weren't quite dead. One or two of the prisoners had their eyes open and they were staring off into a dark corner of the room. He could quite identify the musky smell, but he tried hard not to hold his nose.

Needles had been jabbed into each of the prisoners, and Klaus could see red rubber tubes extending from them to tall glass bottles. Orderlies in white coats marched up and down the rows, examining the inmates. After a few moments, Klaus realised the rubber tubes were translucent. The red colouring came from the blood that was being drained from the prisoners' bodies.

Erwin folded his arms proudly. "Initially the POWs were drained of blood until they died, but then one of our medics suggesting taking only two pints a day. By the third day the body has begun to replace the lost blood, creating fresh supplies in the same donor. Some of them can now last up to ten days using that method. I think the record is sixteen days."

"Fascinating," Klaus said through gritted teeth. "And where does all this blood go?"

"Watch," the sergeant replied, pointing at one of the orderlies. They removed a full bottle from beside a prisoner and poured its contents into a pipe. Erwin led Klaus outside to where the outflow pipe led into a metal reservoir tank.

"Those are emptied everyday and the blood shipped out in a tanker."

"A remarkably efficient system," Klaus agreed. "Where is the blood shipped to?"

"I'm not certain," the sergeant admitted. "The Hauptmann told us the blood had to be purified before it could be recycled for use as part of the war effort." Erwin pointed toward the nearby Transylvanian mountains. "The purification plant is in those hills. At least, that's where the tankers go. They must have enough blood up there to fill a lake."

A lake of blood, Klaus thought with a shudder. If Constanta does have a hundred of his kind along the Ostfront, how many more vampyr were still in those mountains? The pilot realised he was being watched closely by Erwin.

"Excuse my saying so, Oberleutnant, but you've been asking a lot of questions. What did you say was the purpose of your visit here?"

"A surprise inspection. I was a Luftwaffe pilot until a crash ended my days in a Stuka. Rather than spend the rest of the war flying a desk, I volunteered for the Einsatzgruppen." He shared a conspiratorial smile with the sergeant. "It's a dirty job, but someone's got to do it. I'm still waiting for my new uniform, as you can see. Well, I've seen quite enough for one day." And enough horrors to last a lifetime, he thought as the sergeant escorted him back to the main gate. "Thank you, Erwin. A most impressive facility. I will pass my congratulations on to the Hauptmann when I see him next. Good day."

Klaus strolled out of the gate, willing himself to keep walking at an even, steady pace.

"Oberleutnant!"

Klaus turned back to face the four armed sentries. Erwin was holding out a clipboard and pencil. "You forgot to sign out. Every visitor to the camp must sign out."

"Of course." Klaus scratched an illegible signature with the pencil provided, then returned the clipboard to Erwin. "Anything else?"

"No, that's it," the sergeant replied.

"Good. My driver should've fixed our staff car by now." Klaus walked slowly away from the death camp, his face a writhing mass of emotion. Never before had he seen such degradation and witnessed brutality on such a vast and appalling scale. The Russians were their enemy, but no prisoner of war deserved to be systematically drained of their blood.

It was unspeakable and inhuman.

Then Klaus remembered who was behind this sickness: Constanta and his vampyrs. They weren't human, so why did he expect them to act like humans? They were monsters and this place was the proof.

Another thought occurred to Hans as he strode away, eager to get as much distance between him and the camp as possible. The sentries had the same, almost dazed expression in their eyes as Doctor Sheybal. If the rehabilitation centre's director was in Constanta's thrall, there could be little doubt Erwin and the other German troops running the POW camp were also under vampyr influence. How else could they become party to such barbarism? No decent soldier of the Fatherland would take part in such atrocities otherwise, it was beyond imagining.

Klaus quickened his pace. The sooner he got away from Sighisoara, the better. He would send letters to Hans and Ralf, telling them what he had discovered. Trying to put all he had witnessed into words that would not be censored was not going to be an easy job, but his brothers needed to know what they were facing. Merely protecting themselves from the vampyrs was no longer an option. They needed to take direct action against Constanta and his kind. To do that, they would have to find more allies. The soul of the Wehrmacht was at stake.

Chapter Eighteen

SEPTEMBER 12TH, 1941

IT HAD BEEN eighteen days since the 13th Panzer Division captured a bridge at Dnepropetrovsk that stretched nearly a kilometre across the Dnepr River. The bridgehead had been solidified with assistance from the 60th Motorized, the 198th Infantry and SS Division "Wiking", but fierce Soviet attacks continued from three sides. Dogfighting aircraft swarmed in the skies overhead, while Russian cavalry and riflemen flung themselves against the Wehrmacht's positions. Panzer crew casualties increased by the day, with the division reduced to half the strength that had begun Operation Barbarossa.

For once, Erfurth saw sense and ordered those under his command to dig in until fresh orders were received. To Ralf's eyes, the Feldwebel had been a changed man since the confrontation with Gorgo, as if he sensed there were other forces operating below the surface of this war. Where once Erfurth would have demanded suicidal fervour from the division, now he was more willing to listen to reason. The Panzers' lack of progress at Dnepropetrovsk also worked in their favour, allowing time for supplies of ammunition, fuel and other essentials to reach the crews. This included a backlog of post: parcels of food and favourite items, letters from loved ones and from siblings serving elsewhere along the Ostfront.

Ralf was delighted to receive some good German pipe tobacco at last. He permitted himself the luxury of a full pipe and retreated to his Panzer's interior to read a pair of letters, one each from Hans and Klaus. His younger brother alluded to a recent encounter with "our Rumanian allies" at Berislav, hinting he had been lucky to survive. That gave the tank commander pause and he studied the letter carefully, trying to read between the lines. Something had clearly rattled Hans. By comparison, Klaus's letter was a banal record of his time at a rehabilitation centre. Ralf was bemused, the florid style unlike the usual terse pages Klaus sent.

"Gunther, see what you can make of this."

The driver poked his head in through one of the hatches. "Make of what?"

Ralf passed across the letter. "This. It reads like something my mother would write."

Gunther read the letter, as bewildered at his commander by the prose style, then gave a smile of recognition. "It's an acrostic."

"A what?"

"An acrostic, a way of hiding coded messages within more mundane words." Gunther handed the letter back to Ralf. "Read out the first few sentences."

"Ralf, Death and destruction seem miles from here. It's like being at that camp where you and I went once for a holiday. My nightmares have now stopped, thankfully. All the pows and bangs are gone..."

"Now try reading out only the first words on each line of text from the top to the bottom, then read out the last words on each line from top to bottom."

Ralf glanced at the words Gunther suggested, his eyes widening. "Ralf... Death... camp... for... POWs... blood–"

"As a sentence," the driver prompted. "Read them out as a sentence."

"Ralf, Death camp for POWs. Blood being drained by our Rumanian friends. Need to meet at once. All in danger. Time running out. Klaus." He finished reading the acrostic message, his mind racing. "God in heaven, I knew the vampyrs were monsters, but this..." Ralf re-read the letter, checking the message again before looking at Gunther. "You're sure about this acrostic?"

"My brothers and I used them when we got sent away to different military academies, it was our own secret code. Childish, really, but a lot of fun at the time."

"This isn't fun," Ralf said quietly. "Gather the rest of the crew, they need to see this."

Within minutes the other three had seen the hidden message.

"Nothing surprises me about these fiends," Willy said. "Not after what they did to Muller, or those Russian snipers."

"The radio is buzzing with messages from Army Group North about seeing the first snow fall," Helmut said. "Sounds like we can expect an early winter, and a bitter one."

"Christ, it's only September," Ralf protested. "What happened to the autumn?"

"Well, autumn rains are due to start any day," the radio operator replied. "Once they do we'll all grind to a halt in the bloody mud, no going forwards and no way of retreating. At least, not until the mud freezes and the rain turns to snow. Then we've really had it."

"The war is the least of our problems," Willy interjected. "The closer we get to Christmas, the shorter the days become."

"And the longer the nights get," Gunther added. "The vampyrs can hunt more freely then, but their pickings will get thinner as our progress gets slower. How long before they turn on us?"

All the crew fell quiet, pondering the implications.

It was Ralf who broke the silence, scratching at the venomous rash that had spread across his body. Water shortages, overcrowding and insects had left most of the men with skin diseases. Gunther glared at him and Ralf reluctantly stopped scratching. "We have to do something. In a few weeks we will be entrenched in our winter positions, unable to move because of the cold. That's when the Rumanians will become our greatest enemy. We can't wait until that happens, we have to find a way to stop them before they turn on us."

"How?" Martin asked.

"I don't know," Ralf admitted. "How much silver have we collected?"

Helmut was in charge of storing the precious metal in the Panzer's nooks and crevices. "Enough to defend ourselves, but not enough to start a war – or even win a small battle."

"What about the others?" Ralf's crew had been actively building support, slowly convincing the rest of the division about the true nature of the Rumanians. Hoepner's tales of what he had witnessed helped convince the more sceptical crews. Almost every Panzer was collecting its own small hoard of looted silver.

Helmut shrugged. "Most started long after we did, so they don't have as much. In total, I'd say the whole division is carrying four times what we've got in this tank."

Gunther frowned. "It would help if we knew how many vampyrs there are on the Ostfront."

"I doubt Constanta is likely to volunteer that information," Ralf said wryly.

"Then we must persuade one of his kind to tell us," Willy decided.

"You're suggesting we capture one of the vampyrs and force them to talk?" Ralf said.

Willy and Helmut simply nodded.

"If we do this then there's every chance that Constanta will discover what has happened and what we've done. There'll be no turning back," Ralf pointed out.

"Do you have a better suggestion?" Gunther asked.

Ralf shook his head. He noticed that Martin had not spoken much. The commander rested a hand on the young loader's shoulder. "If you want out of this, now is the time to say so. None of us will think any the less of you."

Martin smiled. "I've come this far, commander. Do you honestly think I'd stop now?"

"Good answer," Ralf replied. "Helmut, use your contacts with the other radio operators to track down Hans and Klaus. Once we know where they are, it'll be easier to arrange a time and a place to meet. The rest of you are not to say a word to the rest of the division. I don't want to drag them in unless we have no alternative. This is one battle we can't afford to lose. For all of our sakes."

Chapter Nineteen

SEPTEMBER 13TH, 1941

HANS'S UNIT WAS in disarray, as were others nearby. The 11th Army had succeeded in expanding the bridgehead at Berislav, pushing Russian forces back from the eastern banks of the Dnepr. But confusion had engulfed everyone when the Army's leader, Generaloberst von Schobert, was killed when his aircraft landed in a Soviet minefield. One day on from that tragedy there was no clear indication from 11th Army HQ in Nikolaev who would take charge.

Hans was all too aware of the confusion gripping his unit. Sergeant Witte was still out of action, waiting for his hands to heal. In the meantime, Hans was promoted to Obergefreiter to fill the gap, raising him to the same rank as his eldest brother. He did not feel worthy of the promotion and it was sullied further by hearing it had been recommended by Constanta. The Rumanian officer appeared to take perverse delight in advancing Hans's military career.

"If he thinks such gifts will make me his servant, he's got another think coming," Hans muttered.

The new Obergefreiter took advantage of the lull in activity to make a late afternoon visit to Witte at the field hospital tent in Berislav. It was constructed from several tents joined together to create a long ward with makeshift cots lining each side. Hans walked slowly among the wounded. He talked with those from his own unit and nodded to any he recognised from other squads. He finally located the sergeant in the last bed but one on the left. Both of Witte's hands were encased in plaster, only the fingertips were visible.

The sergeant smiled as Hans approached. "I was wondering when you'd find time for me. Too busy enjoying the privileges of rank to visit your men?"

"What privileges?" Hans replied. "Do I get a better class of lice now?"

"Chance would be a fine thing."

Hans sat on the edge of the bed, studying his sergeant's face. "You look tired."

Witte nodded towards the cot opposite. "That one screams for hours every night. He thinks rats are coming to eat his eyes in the dark. You try sleeping through that."

"I've always thought field hospitals would be much better places to stay if they weren't full of the sick and wounded," Hans said.

"Amen to that," the sergeant agreed. He beckoned his visitor closer, then whispered in Hans's ear. "I saw one of them here last night."

"Them?"

"Not the Hauptmann, but one of his men – a leutnant. I think his name was Gulan."

"What was he doing at a field hospital? He can't have been visiting one of his own."

Witte shook his head. "He went from man to man with one of the medics, asking about each patient's condition, finding out which ones were the weakest." The sergeant gestured towards the last two cots. "This morning the men in those beds were transferred to another tent nearby. None of the orderlies will tell us why, nor whether the men are coming back." Witte let his head fall back on to the pillow, exhausted by the effort of talking. "Find them, Vollmer. Find out what's happened to them. Save them, if you still can."

"Of course," Hans agreed. He studied the face of his mentor, realising how small and weak Witte looked in this environment. On the battlefield, the sergeant's presence had belied his slight, wiry stature. But there, lying on a field hospital cot, he looked like an old man, feeble and infirm. "How are your hands? The doctors say you don't need those plaster casts anymore."

Witte could not meet Hans's gaze. "The doctors are wrong," he replied, looking away.

"Well, I'll let you get some rest," Hans said, standing up. "We need you back on the frontline with us, we need your experience."

He approached the nearest orderly. "Excuse me, I was hoping to visit the soldiers that were in those two cots, but they have been moved. Do you know where I could find them? I have letters from home for both men."

The orderly led Hans out of the main tent and pointed to another, smaller tent nearby. "That's where we keep patients who are unlikely to recover. The condition of both men has deteriorated rapidly in the last twenty-four hours. Our doctors are baffled, to tell you the truth. Neither patient is expected to survive much longer. Perhaps these letters you've brought will offer them some peace of mind."

Hans regretted his deception, but it was a necessary evil. He thanked the orderly, then walked across the grass to the tent. Inside were half a dozen cots, all with white-faced patients lying on them. Several of the men were strapped down, their bodies thrashing and fighting against the restraints.

A brown-haired soldier saw Hans and called him closer. Bandages swathed his chest and neck, but blood was soaking through the wrappings in several places. "Obergefreiter, you've got to get me out of here. The doctor is killing me!"

"What's your name, soldier?"

"Ostermann, Private Ostermann. I was wounded eight days ago, but that was getting better until this new doctor started treating me. Now the medics look at me like I'm ready to be shipped home in a pine box."

"I'm sure that isn't so, private."

"Ask them, go on. Ask them," Ostermann insisted. "No patient ever leaves this tent alive. Being brought in here is a bloody death sentence."

"Where is this doctor?" Hans asked.

The soldier's eyes slid fearfully to the tent entrance. "He's on the night shift, he should be here any minute."

"I'll have a word with him. What's his name?"

"Gulan," the private whispered. "Doctor Gulan."

Hans felt fear crawling up his spine.

Ostermann stiffened on the cot. "Oh God, here he comes."

The other patients in the tent began to whimper with fear, several sobbing into their pillows as a shadow fell across the tent's entrance.

Gulan entered like a hungry man in a butcher's shop, his gleeful eyes surveying the six patients. He wore the white coat of a doctor, but the emblem of the 1st Rumanian Mountain Troop was visible on his uniform's collar. Gulan had the same arrogant posture as Constanta, the same ageless quality to his swarthy features. He grinned broadly and his elongated canine teeth gleamed in the tent's dim lighting. "Well, how are we all feeling this fine evening? Ready for another night of intensive treatment, I hope."

"Doctor Gulan?" Hans asked, surprising the physician. "I wonder if I might speak with you."

The new arrival glared at him, one eyebrow arched enquiringly. "Who might you be, and what are you doing with my patients?"

Hans approached Gulan carefully. "I'm an Obergefreiter with the 11th Army. I was visiting the wounded. One of them has been making some wild claims about you."

The doctor sneered at the six patients. "You don't want to listen to the rants of a delirious man. Tell me which soldier made these claims and I will soon set him straight."

"In a minute. First, could we talk outside?"

"Very well," Gulan agreed. Hans glanced at the wounded men, noticing that all of them looked pale and wan, and that they all had bandages on their necks. There could be little doubt what was happening to them, not with one of Constanta's men in charge. Hans followed Gulan outside, where darkness was falling on the field hospital.

"Well, what is it?" the doctor demanded. "I'm a busy man, I have no time for idle chatter."

"This won't take long," Hans said with a smile, reaching into a pocket on his tunic. "I simply wanted to thank you for taking such good care of the men. It means a lot to us on the frontline, knowing our brothers in arms are being treated so well."

"You're welcome," Gulan replied brusquely.

Hans removed his hand from the pocket and offered it to the Rumanian. "Let me shake your hand, doctor."

Gulan smiled, graciously reaching forward to accept the proffered handshake. But his kindly expression melted as the two man clasped each other's palms. Hans forced a silver cross into the vampyr's flesh.

Gulan open his mouth to scream, revealing a pair of fearsome fangs. "Gahhhhh–"

"Call for help and I'll shove this crucifix down your throat, you bloodsucking bastard," Hans said. "I don't care if it burns a hole right through your hand. You're going to listen to every word I want to say. Do you understand me?"

The vampyr hissed venomously at Hans, his eyes blazing.

Hans tightened his grip on Gulan's hand, pressing the cross further into the Rumanian's flesh. Wisps of smoke were escaping from between their hands, carrying with them the stench of charring flesh.

"I said do you understand me?" Hans repeated.

"Yes," Gulan spat. "I understand you!"

"That's better. Now, why have you turned on these German soldiers? Why are you draining them of blood? Constanta told me your kind were on our side."

"We fight this war to win."

Hans tightened his grip further, eliciting another cry of pain from the nightwalker. "Answer my questions, parasite!"

"We will stop at nothing to win this war. You Germans waste resources keeping alive men who can no longer fight. We choose to take sustenance from them, to strengthen ourselves for the battles ahead. This way your wounded can still give their lives for everyone's ultimate objective – defeating the Russians."

"That may be the Fatherland's ultimate objective, but I believe your kind has another motive for joining this war. What does it matter to you who wins?"

"The victor does not matter," Gulan conceded. "The balance of power afterwards – that is what counts most. The longer this war continues, the better for our cause."

"Why?"

The vampyr shook his head. "I have told you enough. Everything will become clear in time. Now, release me or suffer the consequences, mortal."

"Not yet," Hans said. He jerked his head towards the small tent. "You will leave our wounded in peace from now on. They are not here to sustain the likes of you, monster. I will ensure each man is given a silver cross and has garlic hung over his bed. If I hear that one man dies in suspicious or mysterious circumstances, I will hunt down and destroy you."

Gulan laughed bitterly. "You are signing your own death warrant, human."

"Maybe," Hans agreed. "But I'd rather die fighting for the good of the Fatherland than as a light snack for the likes of you and Constanta." He released the Rumanian's hand, smiling with grim satisfaction at the cross that had been burnt into Gulan's bones. "Now, get away from this place and never return. Before I change my mind."

The vampyr's eyes narrowed as he nursed his burnt palm. "You can't stop us, human. We are legion. By the time this war is over, our kind will have been to every battlefield, planted our kind in the ranks of every army that fights. You will never overcome us."

With that, Gulan stalked off, his white coat swirling around him.

Hans told himself that he had won, but for how long? Even if Gulan never came back, there would be others. The vampyrs were becoming bolder all the time, less and less unconcerned that news of their presence would spread along the Ostfront.

He was still contemplating what he had done when his unit's radio operator appeared in the twilight. Private Weidner had joined in the last week, one of numerous replacements to cover for recent losses. "Obergefreiter, I've been looking for you everywhere. There's an urgent message." The portly private handed over a hastily scribbled note. Ralf had sent it. It summoned Hans to a meeting with Klaus in two days at a place called Ordzhonikidze.

"Private, have you heard of this location?"

The radio operator nodded. "It's a village between here and Dnepropetrovsk, on the western side of the river. You'll need transportation, but the road there is not dangerous."

"Send this reply," Hans said, chewing his bottom lip thoughtfully. "Will meet at noon on 15th, stop. Southern edge of village, stop. Much news to share, Hans, stop." He got Weidner to read back the message. The private was nervous about transmitting personal communications on military channels. "I take full responsibility for this," Hans assured him. Weidner turned to go. "Private, what religion are you?"

"Catholic, Obergefreiter."

"Good. Do you carry a Rosary?"

"Yes, always," Weidner replied, patting one of his pockets.

"May I borrow it?"

Doubt crossed the private's features. "Can I ask why?"

Hans nodded his head toward the small tent nearby. "The men inside are wounded badly, some are close to death. A Rosary would be of great comfort to them. I promise to get you another before we leave this area."

Weidner took the chain of one hundred and sixty-five beads from his pocket. He was careful to rest its silver crucifix on top when he pressed the Rosary into Hans's hand. "I'll go and send that message."

"Thank you, private." Hans held up the beads. "I know how difficult it is for you to part with this. If it's any comfort, this Rosary means more to those wounded than you can ever know. It could save their lives, as well as saving their souls."

Chapter Twenty

SEPTEMBER 15ᵀᴴ, 1941

KLAUS WAS FIRST to arrive at Ordzhonikidze, landing his new Stuka on a long, flat field to the west of the devastated village shortly before noon. If anyone questioned his presence, he would claim to have heard worrying sounds coming from the Ju 87's engine and had stopped to find the cause. He was flying solo, still waiting for someone to replace Heinrich in the cockpit. They had flown more than a hundred sorties together, developing an empathic ability to anticipate how the other would react to danger. Finding a gunner to match Heinrich would be close to impossible, Klaus was certain of that, but finding a gunner who would understand the threat posed by the Rumanians – that might be even tougher.

Having concealed his plane beneath a canopy of tree, Klaus walked into the deserted village. Ordzhonikidze had been the scene of fierce fighting earlier in the campaign, when the Russians were still falling back to the Dnepr. The village was shelled with incendiaries by the Soviets as they departed, razing most of the buildings to the ground, denying food and shelter to the advancing

Germans. The remains of Ordzhonikidze were like a husk. Those civilians who could flee had done so, while the rest died in the Bolshevik firestorm. Seeing such devastation at close range was a dispiriting experience for Klaus. As a pilot, he got a bird's eye view of his targets and little more. Once the bombs were dropping, impact zones became plumes of smoke and fire. Seeing a typical village after it had been bombarded was a stark reminder of the war's human cost.

The spluttering sound of an approaching motorcycle caught his ear. Klaus retreated to the shadows of a burnt out building, drawing his Luger while keeping watch over the nearby road. A cloud of red dust rose in the distance. Klaus wished he had brought a pair of binoculars to observe who was coming. Eventually the motorcycle was close enough for him to see it had a sidecar attached, a passenger sat low beside the rider. It was a Zundapp KS750. The motorcycle paused close to Klaus's hiding place, the engine's characteristic sputter slowing as the rider let it idle. The two travellers removed their helmets and goggles, revealing clean patches on their dust-covered faces.

"Hans!" Klaus called out, emerging to welcome his younger brother. The siblings embraced joyfully, happy to see each other again. Klaus offered to shake hands with Han's passenger, then realised the man in the sidecar had both arms in plaster. "Sorry, I didn't–"

"Don't worry," the passenger shrugged. "I'm Witte, Sergeant Josef Witte. You must be the flying Vollmer brother. Help me free from this death trap and I'll be in your debt, Oberleutnant." Once the sergeant was out, Hans hid the motorcycle from the view of passing vehicles or planes.

"What happened to your hands?" Klaus asked.

"Hauptmann Constanta," Witte replied grimly.

Hans returned, his eyes searching the surrounding area. "Any sign of Ralf yet?"

No sooner had he spoken than the sound of a Panzer rumbled into earshot, making its way through the ruins of Ordzhonikidze. Within a minute, the tank rolled into view, Ralf's head and shoulders protruding from the commander's hatch. He called something into his radio headset and the Panzer rolled to a halt. Several more hatches opened to reveal other members of his crew.

Once everybody was acquainted, Klaus pointed at the building where he had taken shelter. "I think that was the village Univermag, before the Reds torched this place. The interior looks sound and it still has a roof. Why don't we talk in there?"

Ralf and the others agreed. Gunther clambered back into the Panzer and drove it into the shell of another building nearby, where the remains of a mezzanine floor hid the tank from anyone flying overhead. By the time he returned, the other seven had assembled makeshift seats from broken crates and abandoned furniture. Cigarettes and pipe tobacco were exchanged, drinks from Feldflasche were shared and tunic buttons undone.

Once they were all settled, Ralf cleared his throat to talk. "Firstly, thanks for coming. I know it can't have been easy getting away. I persuaded our beloved Feldwebel we're busy searching for a Soviet fuel dump."

Hans said he was supposedly taking Witte to see a specialist about his hands, while Klaus explained his engine noise excuse. For the next hour they all talked about recent encounters with the Rumanians: seeing Constanta awarded the Iron Cross by the Führer; the POW camp where blood was being drained from thousands of Russian prisoners; the death by decapitation of Gorgo's driver and how Muller was turned into one of the vampyrs and the increasing boldness of Constanta's kind, as shown by Gulan taking blood from German wounded.

By the end of these recollections all eight men were grim-faced, any humour gone from their moods. Ralf stated his belief it was a matter of time before the vampyrs turned on the Germans. "The incident Hans witnessed at the field hospital is simply the beginning. These monsters need little justification for taking anyone's blood. Up to now they have chosen to attack the Bolsheviks because it suited their purposes, made them appear worthy allies to our leaders in Berlin. Mark my words – when winter comes and we can't advance any further, Constanta and his brethren will not hesitate to get sustenance wherever they can."

Klaus agreed with his elder brother. "But what can we do to stop them? There are eight of us, eight people we know we can trust. I don't know how many vampyrs there are along the Ostfront, but I'm willing to bet they outnumber us at least ten to one."

Hans nodded. "We can't plan to move against them without more facts."

Ralf smiled. "That's why my crew has brought a surprise guest to the party. Gunther, Willy, could you fetch our friend from the Panzer? Throw a blanket over him so he doesn't burn to a crisp in the sunlight, but you needn't be too careful."

Klaus waited until the driver and gunner had left before questioning his sibling. "Are you insane? You captured one of the vampyrs and brought them here – why?"

"Like Hans said, we need facts," Ralf replied. "Our friends with the fangs are the only ones who know the truth. This way we get our knowledge straight from the monster's mouth."

Gunner and Willy returned, pushing a screeching, cowering figure hunched beneath a blanket. Foul-smelling smoke rose from several holes in the fabric where the sun had burnt exposed skin. Once the two crewmen were inside the Univermag, they ripped the blanket away and shoved their captive to the floor. He was clad in a Leutnant's uniform, the bat and swastika emblem of Constanta's troops clearly visible. Hook-nosed and sallow-faced, the Rumanian had greasy black hair and cruel eyes. The vampyr was a repulsive thing, whimpering and pathetic. Both arms had been securely tied behind his back and a string of garlic bulbs hung round his neck, crudely sewn to the collar. Klaus hated the creature on sight.

"This one is called Dumitrescu," Ralf announced. "We captured him near Dnepropetrovsk. Claimed he was on a mission from Constanta to assess tank strengths in the area. We think he had been spying on our division, but we're not sure why." Ralf lashed out with a boot, kicking the Rumanian in the face. "You've been reluctant to talk so far, haven't you?"

Dumitrescu glared at Ralf. "You'll pay for what you've done to me," he sneered, then swept his gaze round the others. "All of you will pay."

Klaus ignored the threat. "How do we know this is a vampyr, not one of their thralls?"

Helmut produced a silver cross from round his neck. "We tested it." He grabbed Dumitrescu by the neck and pressed the crucifix against the captive's face. Dumitrescu howled as the cross burned its way through his skin and into his flesh, smoke rising from the wound. Helmut wrenched his cross away, wiping traces of scorched meat from its surface. "Our friend here is also rather squeamish about sunlight, garlic and holy water. For a creature of the undead, he has quite a few vulner-abilities."

"Good," Hans said. "We need all the help we can get to defeat them."

Dumitrescu laughed at loud. "Defeat us? You will never defeat us. We're immortal."

"Should we throw you out into the sunshine and see how immortal you are then?" Ralf asked. "Martin, I think our guest wants to leave." The loader pulled open a wooden door, allowing light to spill inside. Dumitrescu scuttled away, desperate to avoid another burning. Ralf laughed bitterly. "Not so cocky when somebody stands up to you, hmm?"

Witte cleared his throat. "I've heard about all the things these monsters can do – turning into wolves and bats, even into mist. How have you kept this one captive?"

"We discovered garlic disables his ability to transform," Gunther replied. "That's why he's wearing a garland of it, to stop him escaping."

"I will enjoy watching you die," Dumitrescu promised from the corner. "I will laugh as the Sire keeps you alive for centuries, to suffer in his service. Then, when he is bored of you as playthings, I will ask for the chance to kill you, one by one. You will beg me for death."

"Don't count on it," Ralf snarled. He reached inside one of his boots and pulled out a serrated knife. The blade was wickedly sharp, one edge brighter than the other. "I had this dipped in molten silver. Who wants to use it first?"

Dumitrescu peered at the knife uncertainly. "What are you going to do with that?"

Ralf grinned. "We're going to torture you until you agree to tell us everything we want to know about Constanta and the other vampyrs – their numbers, their locations, their plans, how they contact each other, everything. Then, once you agree to talk, we'll torture you some more, to make sure you're telling the truth. How does that sound, you bloodsucking piece of Scheisse?"

THEY BEGAN WITH Dumitrescu's extremities. Using the silver-dipped knife, they sliced off his toes one at a time. As each was severed a stream of black, foul-smelling

liquid spat from the wound. At first, the vampyr's body
tensed as he attempted to control the agony. Once all the
toes were gone, they moved on to his fingers.

Each of the men – bar Witte – took it in turns to attack
Dumitrescu's cadaverous body, the plaster casts on the
sergeant's forearms preventing him from wielding the
knife. Instead he made sure Dumitrescu did not black
out by spitting mouthfuls of holy water from Ralf's Feldflasche into the vampyr's, pleading face. Each drop of
consecrated liquid scorched a fresh hole, until there were
enough gaps that Dumitrescu's darting, blackened
tongue was permanently visible – even when his mouth
was closed.

The vampyr screamed and hissed at them, hurling
abuse in different languages. The noises he made sent
shudders through the soldiers' bodies like nothing they
had ever known. Ralf supervised the torture, making
sure nobody got too carried away. He explained a
theory he had about the vampyrs, that they only could
be killed by silver if the wound would have been fatal
if it had been inflicted upon a human. "That means we
can keep hurting this repulsive creature almost indefinitely, using my silver-edged knife to increase his
suffering."

Once all of Dumitrescu's fingers and toes were gone,
Ralf turned his attention to the Rumanian's wizened,
repulsive genitalia. He held them in front of the captive's
face. "Now, are you ready to talk or do I feed these to
you?"

The vampyr shook his head, long since past the point
of surrender. "I told you an hour ago I would talk," he
bleated pathetically. "Ask your questions."

Ralf grimaced. "I think he's ready. Hans, you start."

The youngest Vollmer stepped closer to the Rumanian.
"How many of you are there on the Ostfront? How many
vampyr?"

Dumitrescu shrugged. "I don't know–"

"Not good enough," Ralf said, wiping the knife clean on the captive's sleeve before holding the point close to the vampyr's left eyeball. "We want specifics."

"I don't know the specifics," Dumitrescu protested. "Only Constanta knows that."

Ralf sighed. "Seems we picked the wrong Rumanian. Everybody, say goodbye to our guest." He pulled back the knife, ready to stab it through the eye socket deep into Dumitrescu's brain.

"Please, let me finish!"

Ralf held back the killing blow. "Well, we're waiting."

Dumitrescu swallowed hard, his gaze fixed on the knife poised before him. "Constanta is our commander, the most powerful of the vampyrs on the Ostfront. He has ten lieutenants, almost as powerful as him, doing his bidding in different theatres of the war. They each have ten vampyrs at their command. Our numbers are divided among your army groups, with Constanta moving between them at will."

"What's your position in this hierarchy?" Hans demanded.

"I am one of the hundred. A foot soldier, you might say."

"A foot soldier without any toes," Gunther observed. A glare from Ralf silenced him.

The tank commander turned back to their prisoner. "What about the humans who work for your kind, who do your bidding? How many thralls do you have?"

Dumitrescu smiled. "Each of us has up to ten mortal slaves."

"That's a hundred and eleven vampyrs, plus a thousand thralls," Helmut calculated.

Witte shook his head. "These fiends can create whole armies by resurrecting their victims, raising the dead to feast on the living."

"Only Constanta and his lieutenants have that power," Dumitrescu said.

"I don't believe you," the sergeant replied. He tipped the rest of the holy water over the vampyr's head, smiling as it made the scalp sizzle and boil. Dumitrescu screamed and screamed again, his voice an eerie, high-pitched wail that nearly deafened his captors. Klaus slapped the Feldflasche out of Witte's hand, sparing the Rumanian more suffering for now.

"Why did you do that?" the sergeant snarled. "These bastards deserve every second of suffering we can inflict upon them."

"Maybe," the pilot agreed. "But we need to keep this one alive to find out what he knows."

Witte glared at Klaus for several seconds, then walked away shaking his head. Helmut took his place beside the prisoner. The radio operator slapped Dumitrescu's face until the Rumanian came round again.

"How do you communicate with each other? How do you co-ordinate your movements?"

"By radio."

"Impossible," Helmut snapped. "We would have heard you."

The captive smiled thinly. "Vampyrs can hear sounds that humans cannot."

"Like bats," Martin suggested from a corner. He had taken little part in the torture, watching quietly as the others attacked the Rumanian. "Or dogs."

Helmut nodded. "That makes sense. You transmit signals at high frequency, beyond the range of normal human hearing. How else do you communicate?"

"In rare cases we use the thralls as our couriers, to ensure delivery."

The threat of the blade prompted Dumitrescu to name his personal slaves, Gunther scribbling the names down on a cigarette paper for future reference. After that, silence fell on the room as the captors contemplated all the vampyr had said.

It was Ralf who spoke first, looking to each of the others in turn. "I've heard all I wanted. Does anybody else have any more questions before we end this?"

"What about the locations of all the vampyr units?" Willy asked.

Ralf shook his head. "You heard what he said – more than a hundred of their kind, plus a thousand thralls, spread along the thousands of miles of the Ostfront. If we attack each of those clusters one at a time, word will spread among the others and they will disappear."

"Or launch a counter-attack," Hans added.

"Exactly," Ralf agreed. "We can't find them all, we have to bring them to us."

"Why?" Dumitrescu asked. "What do you plan to do, human?"

"Wipe you bloodsucking bastards off the face of the earth," Klaus replied. When the others nodded, their prisoner started laughing. It was a chuckle of mirth at first, then a full-throated roar of hilarity, until tears ran down his face. Ralf soon silenced Dumitrescu by slicing off one of the vampyr's ears.

"You will never succeed," the Rumanian said to them. "Even as you strike us down, more will rise to take our place. Lord Constanta is all but invulnerable; his lieutenants are nearly as strong. We are your allies in this war, but betray us and we shall destroy you all."

"We'll see," Ralf replied calmly. "Gunther, Willy – let him go."

"What?" the two men said simultaneously.

"Let him go," the tank commander repeated. "We've learned all we can from this piece of undead filth. Get him out of my sight."

Hans and Klaus approached their brother. "Ralf, you can't be serious," the pilot protested. "The moment Dumitrescu leaves here he'll find Constanta and tell him what happened."

"We'll be dead men," Hans added. "Hunted by the vampyrs for the rest of our lives."

"Everybody dies of something," Ralf said. "Gunther, Willy, you heard me – get this little Scheisse out of here. Now."

The Panzer driver and gunner lifted Dumitrescu up to his feet. "Don't think letting me leave here alive will save you," the vampyr vowed. "Your suffering will be ten times what you put me through here today."

Ralf strode to the door and ripped it open, letting the late afternoon sun flood the room. "I said get him out of here. I never said anything about letting him leave here alive."

Gunther and Willy exchanged a smile, then propelled Dumitrescu out the doorway into the warm sunshine.

The vampyr screamed in agony, then collapsed to the ground. His body burnt in the light, his skin peeled away. Fat bubbled and boiled on the bones before the skeleton turned to smoke. Finally, Dumitrescu exploded, a cloud of ash and the echoes of his screaming all that remained in the air. A light westerly blew past and the ash was gone, along with the echoes.

The eight conspirators had killed their first vampyr.

"So WHAT DO you suggest we do?" Klaus asked his elder brother. Having got rid of Dumitrescu, the eight men sat down again to contemplate their next step.

Ralf sucked on his pipe and blew smoke rings into the air. "If what that thing told us is true – and we've got no guarantee of that – how can the eight of us take on a hundred vampyrs and a thousand thralls?"

"We don't have to fight the servants, just their masters," Witte said. "The vampyr are an army, little different from us. Kill the leaders, stop the flow of orders and the foot soldiers don't know what to do next. They lose focus, they lose heart and they give up. The thralls are being controlled by force of will. Eliminate the Rumanians and their slaves will no longer be a threat."

"I believe the sergeant is probably right," Helmut conceded. "But Klaus's question still stands. There are eight of us, and more than a hundred vampyr. Hardly even odds in a battle."

"Then we need better odds," Willy said. "Many crews in the 13th Panzer Division are already with us in spirit. If we can recruit a few of those to our crusade, that would make a significant difference."

"Don't forget all the silver we've collected," Gunther added. "We turn that into bullets, bomb casings and shell coatings, then we've got weapons we can use against the enemy."

Hans stood up. "Between us, Witte and I can probably convince our unit to join the fight. There may be more, once word spreads about what happened at the field hospital."

The sergeant nodded. "We eight are not alone in this fight. We are its generals, that's all."

"Before the Rumanians took me out of the sky and killed my gunner, I was building an alliance among the pilots," Klaus said. "I can convince at least half the Staffel to help us, but this level of activity will not go unnoticed. Someone will notice if planes, Panzers and infantry disappear off the map overnight."

Ralf nodded. "So we will form a Kampfgruppen, a special battle group to meet a specific military need. The Wehrmacht does it all the time. Our leaders pride themselves upon the unified structure of the armed forces, how easy it is to transfer whole units from one service to another. We will use that flexibility to create our own private army."

"How?" Martin asked, his face pale and nervous.

"Hiding behind the truth is usually the best defence," Witte replied. "We say there is a partisan insurgency operating behind our lines. The Kampfgruppen's stated mission will be to lure the insurgents out into the open, using our superior numbers to trap them in a Kessel and them destroy them. We volunteer for that mission, then use it for our own ends." The sergeant smiled wryly. "I once heard of an entire unit that went missing for twenty-seven days, supposedly going behind enemy lines to destabilise the other side's economy with counterfeit bank notes."

"What were they really doing?" the young loader asked.

"Oh, they went behind enemy lines, that much was true. But they were trying to break into a bank vault thought to be full of gold ingots. It would have worked too, if they had figured out a way of getting that weight of gold back home again."

Klaus waited until the others had finished laughing before speaking. "How long will it take to turn your silver hoard into bullets, shells and bomb casings?"

Gunther shrugged. "A week, at most. I've spotted an abandoned jewellery maker's factory near our current position. There's a small foundry at the back that seemed to have escaped bombing by either side so far."

The pilot nodded. "It would probably take as long to get the Kampfgruppen approved. Once that happens, we will have to strike against Constanta and his troops as soon as possible. We've no way of knowing whether any of the men in our units are collaborators with the vampyrs. The faster we act, the better our chances of success."

"Agreed. We can't expect to lure all the vampyrs from the length of the Ostfront, but we can cleanse Army Group South of these bastards," Ralf said. "This part of the war is their stronghold – wipe them out here and the rest will be cut off from their homeland. We know our enemy only comes out at night, so that gives us about twelve hours to achieve our mission objective: a single battle to secure the future. Is everybody ready for this?" He thrust one hand forward.

Hans was first to respond. He slapped his hand on top of Ralf's. Klaus joined them, the three brothers united.

Gunther, Helmut and Willy added their support. Martin was the last of the Panzer crew to step forward, biting his bottom lip but still pledging himself to the fight. That left only Witte, the sergeant. He was leaning against a wall, staring at the hands Constanta had crushed beneath his boot heel.

"Well?" Hans asked. "What do you say? Have you got one last battle left in you?"

Witte held up his plaster-encased forearms, hatred etched into his features. He smashed one arm against the wall, then the other, cracking both casts. The sergeant used his teeth to rip the plaster away from his hands, then used his fingers to remove the rest. When his arms were free, Witte smiled. "Let's wipe these parasite pieces of Scheisse off the face of the earth!"

Chapter Twenty-One

SEPTEMBER 27TH, 1941

IT WAS WITTE who chose Ordzhonikidze as the battlefield. He had observed that the surrounding forests would provide cover for the Kampfgruppen's tanks, guns and troops. The town itself was already devastated, with no civilians alive within twenty miles and no military activity any nearer. The only people in danger would be those fighting and no other force was close enough to intercede. Smelting all the silver had taken longer than expected, delaying the conspirators' plans. In the end Gunther sought help from other Panzer crews whose members had experience from working in foundries before the war. Bomb casings and shells had their tips painted with liquid silver, while rounds for rifles and machine guns were dipped in the molten metal.

Meanwhile Klaus, Ralf and Hans were masterminding the Kampfgruppen's creation, using contacts in other units to establish a plausible basis for its establishment. Feldwebel Erfurth insisted he should lead the Panzer contingent for this important mission, but his intervention ultimately helped confirm the need for the

Kampfgruppen. Erfurth never volunteered for a mission unless he felt it was important for the Fatherland and likely to advance his career. Martin and Willy took numerous Panzer crews into their confidence, recruiting twenty tanks for the Kampfgruppen.

Klaus discovered the vampyr pilots had been less than subtle in his absence, leaving a trail of bloodless corpses at every airbase they visited. He had little trouble recruiting several Staffel to the Kampfgruppen, creating an aerial squad of three-dozen Ju 87s and twelve Bf 109 fighters. Even Major Satzinger admitted he had been wrong about the Rumanians, and volunteered to fill the vacant gunner's seat in Klaus's Stuka. Between them, Hans and Witte enlisted an artillery unit and close to five hundred infantry. In total the Kampfgruppen had a fighting force of close to a thousand men and machines, giving them a ten to one ratio against the vampyrs. They could only pray it would be enough.

Once preparations were all but complete, Helmut had the job of baiting the trap. Reports from other radio operators along the Ostfront indicated Constanta was visiting the outskirts of Leningrad. Helmut used several unwitting thralls to send a message, supposedly from Dumitrescu, summoning his comrades within Army Group South to a mass gathering at Ordzhonikidze after sunset on Saturday, September 27.

After twelve days of frantic preparations, the waiting was over. The battle for the soul of the Wehrmacht was about to begin.

"Where are they?" Hans whispered, binoculars pressed against his face, his eyes searching the main road to Ordzhonikidze from the south. "The sun set half an hour ago, the bastards should be here by now." He was stationed on a hilltop to the southwest, a field radio at his side.

"Maintain radio silence," Ralf reminded his brother. The tank commander sat inside his Panzer in a small forest outside Ordzhonikidze, patiently waiting with the rest of his crew. A dozen more Panzers were clustered around them, while still more were positioned at other hidden locations around the ruined town. "Klaus will tell us when they're coming."

High above Ordzhonikidze a Ju 87 was trying to keep out of sight. Klaus watched the sky, looking for signs of approaching aircraft, while Satzinger studied the roads below for evidence of a vampyr convoy. The rest of the Kampfgruppen's planes were still on the ground some twenty miles away, waiting for a signal to get in the air. There was no point burning through precious fuel before the battle had even begun. "Nothing," Klaus muttered to himself. "I don't see anyone else up here. Maybe the message didn't get through? Or maybe the vampyrs realised it was a trap."

"If you have patience, you will be rewarded," Satzinger remarked. "I see two columns of dust rising from the ground, one approaching Ordzhonikidze from the north, the other from the south. Looks like our friends took the bait."

Klaus tipped his left wing slightly to see for himself. "You're right." He righted the Stuka. "And there's two Schwarm of Hurricanes approaching, a thousand metres below us. I'll take us up into the cloud cover." The Stuka rose steeply before levelling out. Klaus activated his radio. "We've got guests coming."

Ralf confirmed the signal from the sky, then reminded everyone to sit tight. "Let them wait. We attack only when they have stopped and their planes are on the ground."

CĀPITAN AVIATOR STEFAN Toma could not understand why Dumitrescu had called this gathering. Constanta was not due back for several days and only the Hauptmann had the authority to summon all the vampyrs together, except in extreme circumstances. Dumitrescu's message had offered no reason for the meeting. It stated a time and a place. Toma had tried and failed to contact Dumitrescu for clarification. Finally, unable to resolve this conundrum, he had gathered his Schwarm of four Hurricanes and flown over the rendezvous location. When he landed, the Rumanian pilot was startled to find four other planes, each bearing the vampyr emblem, already parked outside the devastated village.

Toma and his fellow pilots landed in the last glimmers of twilight as a column of T-34 tanks also bearing the bat and swastika symbol were arriving, followed by a company of cavalry and at least a hundred infantry. All the men on foot were thralls of different vampyrs. Their masters rode alongside on motorcycles or horses. None of it made any sense to Toma. He hadn't seen so many of his kind gathered in one place since they left Sighisoara a hundred days earlier. The pilot recognised a familiar face and hailed one of the tank commanders as they climbed down from their armoured vehicle.

"Toma, you old devil," the vampyr responded, his broad smile punctuated by a pair of deadly fangs. "What are you doing here? I thought you were busy tormenting the Russians at Melitopol."

"We were until Dumitrescu's message came through. Have you any idea why he summoned us here? Explaining our absence will not be easy, especially with the Red's Southern Front launching a new offensive."

The T-34 commander shrugged. "It seems I know as little as you. Where is Dumitrescu?"

"Nobody has seen him," Toma replied. "If I didn't know better–"

But the vampyr pilot never got the chance to finish his sentence. The tanks and guns of the Kampfgruppen opened fire from a dozen positions, raining shells upon the cluster of vampyrs and their thralls.

. . .

"FIRE!" RALF SHOUTED, slapping Willy on the back. The Panzer's main gun spat silver-tipped death at the vampyr horde, Martin already poised with the next precious projectile before the first had its spent shell ejected from the breech. "Gunther, take us in – full speed ahead. Helmut, once we're within range I want that machine gun firing non-stop." The crew shouted back their compliance, concentrating their focus on exploiting the element of surprise.

"FIRE!" HANS COMMANDED, pointing at the cluster of Rumanians gathered at Ordzhonikidze. On either side of him German guns pumped silver-coated shells into the air, paying special attention to the rear ends of the T-34s. That was one of the Russian-built tank's few weak spots. If they didn't hit it in precisely the right place, the Rumanians would have the chance to turn and charge the anti-tank crews' positions. The gunners had heard enough about the ruthlessness of this enemy and the effectiveness of the T-34 to know how painful that would be. "Keep firing!" Hans bellowed, struggling to be heard above the boom of the guns.

"DIVE, DIVE, DIVE!" Klaus ordered his Staffel, a dozen Ju 87s following his lead as he tipped the Stuka at the scrambling mass of men and machines below. His target was the collection of Hurricanes on the ground, his aim to blow them apart before the vampyrs could get back into the air. As his Stuka approached 300mph, Klaus remembered his distaste for bombing planes on the ground, during the first day of Operation Barbarossa. That was merely three months, but it felt like a lifetime. He grimaced at his former naivety. The cruel realities of this brutal war had beaten that out of him. He applied the plane's air brakes, for once enjoying the nerve-racking screech they created. "I hope it scares you bloodsucking bastards back to hell," he snarled, pressing the release button for his bombs.

THREE OF THE T-34s were destroyed in the first fusillade, well-aimed shots blowing apart the formidable tanks. Shrapnel flew sideways from the explosions, killing dozens of human thralls and sundering the flesh and bones of any vampyr it hit. The initial wave of dive-bombers accounted for all but two of the Hurricanes, blowing the Rumanians' aircraft apart on the ground. Toma had got back to his plane in time to avoid the Stuka, as did Locotenent aviator Zaharia. They taxied along the flat field past the burning, broken remains of the other Hurricanes, trying to find enough space for take off amid the carnage.

Toma could see a second wave of Stukas tipping over in the sky above them, beginning another bombing run. "Zaharia, get your plane in the air – that's an order."

Toma urged his Hurricane forwards, away from the plummeting Luftwaffe planes. But Zaharia's aircraft had become entangled with debris from another Rumanian aircraft. Toma glanced back in time to see his colleague killed by a direct hit from the Stuka. The vampyr managed to get his plane into the air, but he failed to spot one of the bombers that was still pulling out of its dive. The two aircraft collided a few metres off the ground, burning wreckage raining down upon a company of vampyr cavalry. The horses screamed, flinging their riders to the ground and trampling them underfoot before collapsing from shock.

Then came the Panzers, accelerating out of their hiding places beneath trees and burnt out buildings, catching the remaining Rumanians still on the ground by surprise. Twenty German tanks converged on the vampyrs, blasting shell after shell into the midst of the chaos. When the projectiles exploded, silver-flecked shrapnel was flung through the air. Every Rumanian hit by the metal fell shrieking, dozens dying or losing limbs within moments of the assault beginning.

Next to attack was a host of German soldiers on Zundapp motorcycles. Each had a sidecar passenger armed with a MG 34 light machine gun. Once the motorcycles were within eight hundred metres, the passengers opened fire, one hand pulling the trigger while the other fed a linked metal belt of ammunition into the weapon. Each round was silver-tipped, delivering a fatal wound when shot into the head or heart of a vampyr. The Rumanians had a moment to scream their rage before exploding into dust and ash. The motorcyclists circled around and around the vampyrs and their thralls, each machine gun accounting for a dozen or more of the enemy.

Last came the infantry, running into battle on foot, each man armed with a rifle or machine pistol, a silver-tipped bayonet protruding from the end of their weapon. They waited until the motorcyclists had withdrawn, then charged the bewildered vampyrs amidst the carnage. The battle ebbed and flowed, first one side gaining the ascendancy in this ground war, then the other. Eventually, the German's superior numbers began to make their mark, slowly reducing the Rumanians' strength. By the time the remaining Rumanians on the ground outnumbered their human thralls, there were less than fifty of each left alive. But vampyr crews had fought their way successfully back to the three intact T-34s and brought them to bear on the battle.

The tanks opened fire first with two machine guns, shooting anyone that moved. Germans, thralls, even other vampyrs were shot indiscriminately – but only the Rumanians were able to get up again. Then the T-34s began firing their main guns with devastating effect. Two Panzers were blown apart by the first salvo, while another was shredded by the second.

Inside his Panzer, Ralf was shouting orders at the men on motorcycles, exhorting them to get in closer to the T-34s. "Approach them from the rear. Use stick grenades on the track plates. If you don't put them out of commission now, they can still turn the tide."

Witte was among those riding a Zundapp around the edges of the battle. His sidecar passenger had been killed early on, forcing the sergeant to withdraw. Ahead of Witte, one of the T-34s and a Panzer were rolling towards each other, the Russian tank swivelling its turret round to take aim. The sergeant gunned his motorcycle's engine and surged forward, one hand reaching back to pull a stick grenade from his waist belt. A vampyr cavalry officer appeared in front of Witte, brandishing a curved sword and snarling something in Rumanian. The sergeant swerved slightly, using the empty sidecar as a battering ram against the vampyr's legs.

Witte was almost alongside the T-34. He shoved the head of the stick grenade under his arm and used his free hand to unscrew its base cap. When the looped cap came free, he yanked it hard, counted to three and wedged the grenade inside the tank's track plates. Witte was still turning his Zundapp away when the device detonated, the blast throwing him and his motorcycle into the air.

"No!" screamed Hans, who had been watching the sergeant through a pair of binoculars.

The moon was shedding pale blue light on the chaotic scene, but most of the illumination came from muzzle flashes and burning wreckage. Hans kept watching but saw no movement from Witte's crumpled figure; the sergeant's body was one amongst many. The T-34 targeted by Witte had been immobilised beyond it, its track blown apart on one side. But the turret, main gun and machine guns were still active. Hans watched as a Panzer rolled remorselessly towards it, perhaps ten metres away and getting closer by the second.

Moments before the two armoured vehicles would have collided, the German tank skewed sideways and opened fired at point blank range. Its shell punctured the gap between hull and turret on the T-34, exploding the turret into the air. Meanwhile, the German infantry were fighting their way through the wounded vampyrs on the ground, shooting some and bayoneting the rest when close enough for hand-to-hand combat. The battlefield was fast becoming a sea of maroon mud, blood saturating the once dusty soil.

Not all the Rumanians died alone, a cluster of them forming into a small circle, trying to fight and bite their way out of the Kessel. Any German foolish enough to venture within arm's length was grabbed and their throats torn open by the fiends. As the Rumanians moved they picked up any discarded weapon that came to hand, using these to blaze a path through the Germans. It was Erfurth's Panzer that put a stop to them, opening fire with both machine guns, shredding the last vampyrs on foot with a hail of silver-coated rounds.

That left the final two T-34s. Hans commandeered one of the Zundapps and launched himself towards the battlefield, determined to do his bit. He used a Luger to despatch several mindless thralls that lurched towards him, then abandoned the motorcycle when confronted by an oncoming T-34. Diving off the bike, he fell beside another German soldier. Hans was about to apologise when he recognised the face next to him. It was Kral and he was dead, clutching a Stielhandgranate as if his life depended upon it. Another of the originals gone, Hans thought sadly as he prised the weapon from Kral's fingers, but his loss would not be for nothing.

Each stick grenade had been augmented with a silver plug, designed to fragment when it detonated. Hans climbed the rear of the T-34 and tried to wrench open the turret hatch. It was secured from the inside, while the other hatches had plainly been welded shut, no doubt for the Rumanians' own safety. Hans's boot stubbed against a small circle on the roof of the turret, close to the hatch. He thought back to the briefing Ralf had given about vulnerable spots on the T-34. Didn't the Russians sometimes resort to using signal flags for communication? And wasn't the port for that on the turret roof? Having commandeered the Soviet vehicles, the Rumanians might not have thought to weld this port shut.

He crouched beside the turret and tried to open the port. After a moment's resistance it gave way, the circular hole offering enough space to accommodate a stick grenade. Hans undid the base cap on his device, then tugged on the cord inside. He rapped his knuckles on the turret to get the attention of those within. A pair of yellow, venomous eyes glared up at him through the small porthole.

"This is for Franz Kral," Hans said, shoving the stick grenade inside.

He took one jump down to the hull and then dived off the tank, clearing it as the Stielhandgranate exploded inside. Black smoke leaked from the turret port and the tank ground to a halt. Another soldier followed his example with the final T-34, putting that one out of action.

Ralf gave a shout of joy over the radio, nearly deafening everyone listening. "We did it! We stopped the bastards. We got them all."

Overjoyed by the news but still uncertain, Klaus flew his Stuka low over the battlefield, tipping one wing down for a better look. Once battle had begun on the ground it hadn't been safe to continue with the bombing runs, so the Staffel remained on patrol in the sky. He and Satzinger cheered as they passed the corpse-strewn field below. More than a hundred dead thralls littered the landscape, but too many brave German soldiers also lay unmoving in the mud.

Little remained of the vampyrs, beyond the vehicles in which they arrived, piles of ash and those who had been wounded but not yet finished off.

One by one, the Panzer crews emerged from their tanks. Erfurth and his men clambered out to get a better look at what little was left of this formidable foe, while Ralf and his men were busy clapping each other on the back, rejoicing at their victory. Others followed their example, cheering and singing. The infantry moved among the wounded vampyrs, despatching the last of the Rumanians with a single, silver-tipped shot into the skull. Hans was more intent on finding Witte, desperate to see if the sergeant was still alive. He was delighted to find the grizzled veteran leaning against a wrecked motorcycle, one leg folded awkwardly beneath him.

"First my hands, now this," Witte said with a smile. "I'm beginning to think you're jinxed."

"You should consider me a good luck charm," Hans replied. "You'd probably be dead by now if it wasn't for me." Ralf appeared and embraced his brother warmly.

"We did it," the tank commander said proudly.

Hans nodded, too happy to speak.

"What time is it?" Witte asked.

Ralf checked his watch. "Close to midnight. Almost Sunday."

"A day of rest," Hans said, his voice thick with emotion.

"Hopefully," Ralf agreed, before turning back to Witte. "Why do you ask?"

The sergeant smiled, a cunning malevolence in the corner of his eyes. "Because the real battle is about to begin. But this is one fight you have no hope of winning."

Chapter Twenty-Two

SEPTEMBER 28ᵀᴴ, 1941

HANS STARED AT Witte. He did not understand. "What do you mean? We've beaten the vampyrs and destroyed them all, and their thralls. It's over."

The sergeant shook his head slowly, while gesturing at the carnage around them. "This was merely a prelude, the rumble of distant thunder before the rainstorm begins. When that storm comes, you'll be washed aside."

Hans crouched beside his mentor. "You must be concussed, Josef. You aren't making any sense. Let me see if you've got a head wound–"

Witte grabbed Hans by the wrist, hissing a reply in the young soldier's face. "Fools. You thought you were luring the vampyrs into a trap, but they knew all along about this pathetic plan of yours. I told them. They let you have your little victory, knowing you would exhaust yourselves in the process, exhaust your supply of weapons. The vampyrs you defeated were the weakest, while the strongest were held back from the fray. Now midnight has come and the battle begins afresh. Only

this time you are the ones encircled and they are the
ones crushing you within the Kessel. If you believe in a
god, whoever he may be, then this would be a good time
to get down on your knees and pray."

Hans ripped his arm free. "I don't believe you. I don't
believe you are a traitor."

"Why not?" Witte asked. "I've been a servant of my
Lord Constanta since our first night in Reni. He found
me that night, turned me. I burned those dead Russians on his orders, to conceal the vampyr's presence
among you. I delivered that fool Brunetti to my lord
after one of his reports from the front line came close
to exposing the truth. But this has been my greatest
achievement – insinuating myself into your confidence, goading you and your brothers into this futile
attack."

"But Constanta attacked you on the road out of
Berislav, he crushed your hands."

"A small price to pay for confirming your complete
and utter faith in me. Every step of the way I have
manipulated you, boy. I used you to expose the elements
within the Wehrmacht who might one day have been a
danger to the vampyrs. And in one stroke you'll be
destroyed."

Ralf drew his Luger and aimed it at the sergeant's face.
"I saw you attack one of the T-34s, you immobilised it.
Hell, you even used a sidecar to cripple one of the Ruma-
nians."

"But I didn't kill any of them, did I?" Witte replied.
"Besides, my lord sent them here as sacrificial lambs.
What did you once call it? Oh, yes. Bait for the trap."

Helmut ran across the battlefield towards them. "Ralf,
your brother Klaus is on the radio. He says there are more
vampyr coming this way. Hundreds, maybe a thousand!"

Witte smiled, a quiet satisfaction evident on his face.
"My job here is done," he announced smugly. "And your
doom is at hand."

"Speak for yourself," Ralf replied tersely, and shot the traitorous sergeant through the brain. Ralf spun round, firing his Luger three times in the air. The other Germans fell silent, their celebrations abruptly muted. "We've been duped. All of this was a trick, a ruse to lure us out into the open, so the vampyr could attack us in force. Get back to your tanks and your guns. We've got to escape from here before they encircle us. Helmut, get back to the radio and call high command for help. We'll never survive the night without outside intervention."

Nobody responded. All of them were shocked by the sudden reversal.

"Didn't you hear me? Move!" Ralf bellowed.

The Germans started running. Vampyr planes appeared in the sky, wave upon wave of bombers and fighters passing before the moon.

"God in heaven," Hans whispered. "Have mercy on us all."

KLAUS RESISTED THE urge to soil himself when he saw what the vampyrs had ranged against them. Hours ago, before the first battle began, he had thought the Kampfgruppen's collection of thirty-six Stuka and twelve Bf 109 fighters would be overkill. They were outnumbered two to one by enemy aircraft, a blizzard of Hurricanes threatening to blot out the moon. On the ground below he could see three columns of vampyr tanks racing towards the killing ground, at least ten T-34s in each column. Swarming beside these were what looked like cavalry; company after company of riders on black horses. After that came the infantry. There were hundreds of them, marching towards the small field where his brothers were trapped.

Satzinger was whispering a prayer in the gunner's seat.

"I didn't know you were a religious man," Klaus said quietly.

"I'm not," the major replied. "But it seemed like a good time to start."

"There's so many of them. What do we do?"

"The Stuka will be slaughtered in minutes if we try to win this battle plane to plane," Satzinger said. "Better to use them for their true purpose: dive-bombing the enemy on the ground. Leave the dogfighting to Messerschmitts. At least they have a chance against the Hurricanes."

"But there must be a hundred Hurricanes, and only a dozen–"

"It doesn't matter," Satzinger insisted. "I doubt many of us will see the sunrise. Better we give those on the ground a chance. While our fighters engage the Hurricanes we dive-bomb the vampyrs and use the Stuka as tank-busters. One well-delivered bomb from us can stop a T-34 or decimate a company of cavalry." The major twisted round. "You must do it, Oberleutnant. It's the only chance any of us have."

ON THE GROUND, Erfurth and Ralf led a Panzer charge to the west, but they were met by a blockade of T-34s. The booming Soviet guns ruptured two of the German tanks, driving them backwards. The Panzers tried creating another salient to the south, but that was met with more T-34s and swooping Hurricanes.

After losing three more tanks and being forced into another retreat, Ralf accepted the inevitable. He activated his radio link to Erfurth. "We're surrounded. Better we form the best defensive position we can, than getting picked off one at a time."

The Feldwebel refused to listen to reason. "I am the senior officer in this Kampfgruppen," he insisted. "I decide the best strategy, Vollmer."

"For the love of God, we're being torn apart. Don't let your pride get us all killed, man."

"This is nothing to do with pride," Erfurth snapped. "This is about experience and tactics. If we form a Kessel, we will be destroyed. We must break out. All Panzers, follow me to the east."

"Panzers, ignore that last order," Ralf shouted. "Fall back to the battlefield. We can use the wrecks of the Rumanians' own tanks as cover, create a defensive ring to protect each other."

"All Panzers, this is Feldwebel Erfurth. You will ignore the transmissions of Obergefreiter Vollmer. Not only does he not lead this division, but if this battle is won he'll face a court martial for gross insubordination. Now, you will all follow me to the east!"

Erfurth sent his Panzer into oblivion, unaware that none of the others were obeying him. A single shot from a T-34 tore the tank apart, killing its crew outright. Ralf watched the tank's sad demise through the rear vision ports of his cupola as the fourteen surviving Panzers returned to the battlefield.

HANS HAD GOT halfway to the nearest German artillery position when he realised its guns were a sitting target for the Rumanian tanks. He started sprinting, frantically waving to the loaders and gunners who were still busy celebrating. "Run!" he shouted. "Get away from the guns! It isn't–"

The first shell blew apart the middle gun, the explosion sending a wall of shrapnel in all directions. Those standing nearest the blast were slain in an instant, shredded where they stood. Others were less fortunate, their injuries not enough to kill them outright. Death came in a form of a T-34 driving over the top of the artillery position. It crushed both men and guns beneath its twenty-eight ton weight. Those who tried to run were machine gunned ruthlessly. Hans escaped this by throwing himself to the ground when he saw the silhouette of a T-34 approaching.

He heard a rumbling, clanking sound and looked up to see one of the vampyr tanks almost upon him, its tracks about to crush his body. Hans rolled sideways into a groove created by the Panzers that had dragged the German guns into position. As the T-34 passed over him, he had the presence of mind to pull a stick grenade from his waist belt. He armed it and shoved the wooden shaft between the tank's wheels. The mechanical monster continued toward the battle until its left track exploded a few seconds later. Hans clambered up the tank's back and opened the turret porthole. He glimpsed two vampyrs arguing inside, then shoved the barrel of his Luger into the gap. "Say hello to Sergeant Witte when you see him in hell!" Hans emptied his pistol into the tank's interior, listening as bullets ricocheted around until they found targets. He jumped clear of the T-34 and ran to the battlefield, intent on reaching it before the encirclement was complete. If he died that day, he wanted to be alongside his comrades, fighting for what he believed in.

IN THE SKY the Bf 109s were dog-fighting brilliantly, the finely honed skills of the twelve Luftwaffe pilots accounting for dozens of enemy Hurricanes. But sheer weight of numbers meant the vampyrs could not fail to hit one of the Messerschmitts eventually.

Horst Lang was first to die. He had flown as escort for Klaus on numerous sorties, his cheerful optimism a source of comfort in many grim situations. His plane was strafed by enemy fire, flames blazing in the night sky. Lang got a final message off before the end. "Lang to Vollmer, I'm going down. Hals und Beinbruch!"

Klaus watched as his friend flew the dying Bf 109 into one of the enemy planes. Away to the east another of the Messerschmitts fell from the sky, its impact creating a fireball on the ground. Their defeat was only a matter of time now. Klaus called his Staffel into formation

behind him. Fifteen Stuka lined up to bomb the hell out
of the vampyr ground forces. "Begin your bombing runs
now!"

ALL THE REMAINING Panzers had pulled back to the battlefield, but the wrecked hulls of the T-34s only provided
cover for half a dozen of the German tanks. The rest
formed a defensive wall round the edges of the battlefield. When they were lost, their shattered hulks would
form another barricade, another obstacle for the vampyr
to overcome.

Ralf watched from his vantage point in the centre of
the killing field as the first of the outer circle exploded
beneath the onslaught of the T-34s. Then the men inside
the ruptured Panzer started screaming, howling for God,
for mercy, for their mothers. Then there was only the
sound of battle to crowd the ears, the sight of carnage to
fill the eyes. Many more men would die before the end,
but all of them would die fighting.

HANS GATHERED FIFTY German infantrymen, most from his
own unit. He split them into pairs. Each duo was issued
with a machine gun and all the ammunition they could
carry. The Kessel was collapsing in upon itself, the
vampyr hordes circling around them, compressing the
survivors into an increasingly small circle. Hans spaced
the teams evenly round the perimeter, telling them to
use anything they could find as cover – wrecked vehicles, shards of shattered armour, even the corpses of
their fallen comrades. "Don't waste your fire on thin air.
We have limited supplies of silver-tipped rounds, so
make each bullet count."

The wolves came first, feral animals that bounded
across blood-soaked soil towards the German positions.
When none of the machine gunners fired, Hans realised
they hadn't seen the vampyr transmute themselves into
different forms, different shapes. "Open fire!" he

screamed above the cacophony of battle. "If they get close enough they'll tear you apart!"

The first wolf bounded across the no-man's-land that was forming round the German defensive circle, leaping over the impromptu barricades to savage a two-man team. Hans ran across and shot the animal dead. As he did, it exploded into ash and dust, like all the other vampyrs when they died.

"Now do you see what we're up against?" he shouted. "Do as I say. Open fire!" The other teams needed no more prompting. They began strafing the circling pack of wolves, each animal giving an unearthly shriek as it died. After considerable losses, the four-legged vampyrs slunk away into the darkness, giving those on the ground a moment to regroup. The T-34s opened fired again, targeting the Panzers that formed the Kessel's edge. They exploded like fireworks.

ANOTHER WAVE OF Stukas plunged from the sky, dive-bombing the vampyr forces. Each plane accounted for a T-34 or devastated one of the cavalry companies, but as they soared back into the sky, the Stuka pilots were dismayed to discover a wall of Hurricanes waiting for them. The last of the Messerschmitts had fallen, wiped out by the superior numbers of vampyr planes in the air. From now on, the Stukas would have to fight their own battles. Klaus made his orders short and simple. "Use whatever weapons you have. Use your bombs, your machine guns, your planes if you have to, but we must protect those on the ground."

AFTER THE WOLVES came bats, swarms of winged vampyrs flapped like a cloud across the moon before they dived upon the German infantry. Hans screamed at the machine gunners to fire into the sky. Each bat exploded when hit by a silver-tipped bullet. So many of them died that the air became a choking dust cloud of stifling ash.

Then the bats retreated and a mist began creeping across the battlefield towards the valiant German fighters.

Hans quickly recognised the threat represented by this translucent vapour. "Activate your stick grenades, then throw them into the centre of the mist!" he yelled, leading by example.

His Stielhandgranate flew over the ring of exploding Panzers to the centre of the mist. A death shriek filled the air when the device detonated. Further cries followed as the other infantry hurled more stick grenades into no-man's-land. The vampyrs responded with another pack of wolves, and a colony of bats attacked at the same time, confusing the German tactical response. Little by little, each wave of enemy insurgents was whittling away at the defenders, creating gaps in the circle, weakening their numbers.

The last Panzer in the outer ring perished. Its hull burst apart like wet fruit beneath the T-34s' onslaught. Shrapnel from the exploding tank showered the machine gunners close by, driving them backwards, collapsing the Kessel still further. The inner ring of Panzers kept blasting away, each silver-coated shell accounting for a small pocket of enemy troops. The vampyr cavalry made its first charge. Black steeds raced fearlessly toward the German machine guns. Flecks of white foam fell from the animals' mouths. A hundred horses died in the first attack wave and as many in the second. And still they came, charging to their deaths, driven on by the remorseless Rumanians. The battlefield was a scene of carnage and devastation, the air thick with the stench of blood and ash, cordite and chaos.

IN THE SKY, Klaus was among the last of the Stukas still flying. The German Staffel had accounted for all but a few of the Hurricanes, but the aerial victory had come at a terrible price. Only four Ju 87s remained in the air, and that number was halved less than a minute later. One of the Stuka, out of ammunition and trailing black smoke across the clouds, lured two of the Hurricanes to their doom by engineering a three-plane mid-air collision. Another Stuka dove directly into the last of the T-34s and destroyed the final remnants of the vampyrs' armoured columns.

Only Klaus and Bruck were left of the forty-eight German pilots that had started the aerial battle.

"Theodor, how many bombs do you have left?" Klaus asked.

"None, and I'm out of ammunition for the machine guns too. You?"

"The same, and I'm flying on fumes."

"The sun will be up soon," Bruck said. "I'd like to see the sun once more before I die."

"Me too," Klaus agreed. "It would be–" He stopped transmitting, a sudden realisation halting him in mid-sentence. "Of course! We don't need to win this battle, we only need to keep the vampyrs fighting until dawn. The rising sun will save us!" In the distance the first faint glimmers of light were beginning to soften the sky above the horizon, black slowly becoming blue again. "Bruck, we can do it, we can make it."

"I'm not so sure," the other pilot replied. "Something's coming up to meet us."

Klaus tipped his wing over to look down. A black cloud was rising from the battlefield, like a choking black fog, but pulsating and alive. "Oh, God," Klaus gasped.

The cloud was made of bats, dozens of them swarming towards the two surviving Stuka.

"Evasive action!" Klaus peeled his plane away from the rising throng. Bruck did not react as quickly. His Stuka flew directly into the vampyrs. His engine stuttered and died as a curtain of bats covered every inch of his aircraft. The propeller stopped and the plane fell into a death spiral.

"Our Father, who art in heaven," Bruck prayed, transmitting his final words into the ether. "Hallowed be thy name. Thy kingdom come, thy will be–"

THE STUKA EXPLODED as it hit the ground in no-man's-land. The fireball incinerated nearly a hundred vampyr cavalry and their horses. Ralf watched with grim satisfaction from the cupola of his Panzer, knowing the end would not be long for him and his crew. May we take as many of these bloodsucking bastards with us when we go, he vowed silently. The tank had all but exhausted its supply of shells and the machine gun ammunition would not last long either, once the vampyrs got close enough to shoot. "Helmut! Where's our reinforcements?" he shouted.

"I still can't get through," the radio operator admitted. He had used every frequency, every trick he knew to try and get a signal out, but without success. "Something is jamming us."

"Something? Or someone?" Gunther asked, his usual cheerfulness bled away in the bleak reality of the battle. "We never had a chance."

"Nobody admits defeat inside my Panzer," Ralf snarled. "We fight to the death."

"But how do you kill a foe who is undead?" Martin asked.

"With courage, with heart and with your head," Willy replied. "When all that isn't enough, you give up your life to take theirs. Better we die stopping them than survive to see them prosper."

"He's right," Ralf said. "This isn't over yet. We can still…" His voice trailed off, his head tilting to one side, his face a mask of concentration.

"We can still do what?" Martin asked.

"Quiet!" Helmut snapped. "Listen."

The rest of the crew stopped and listened. An eerie silence had fallen outside the Panzer.

"I don't hear anything," Martin whispered.

"Exactly," Ralf replied. He reached up to open the hatch above his head.

Willy grabbed his commander by the leg. "Is that wise?" the gunner asked.

Ralf shrugged. "At this point, what have we got to lose?" He opened the hatch and peered outside. "They've stopped," he said with surprise. "The vampyrs have stopped attacking." The others scrambled to the nearest escape hatches and opened them to look out.

KLAUS PEERED DOWN at the battlefield. A single horseman was riding across no-man's-land towards the circle of besieged Germans. All the other vampyrs had assembled in a ring around the circle, three-deep in places but much diminished from when the battle had begun hours earlier. Even the bats had left the sky and returned to the ground, while the only remaining Hurricanes circled harmlessly below the Stuka. The battle had paused, but why?

"What the hell is happening?" a bewildered Satzinger asked.

"I was wondering the same thing myself," Klaus replied.

HANS WATCHED AS the lone cavalry rider stopped in the middle of no-man's-land, perhaps ten metres away from the German positions. Hans could not see the rider's face, but the upright posture and gently billowing cape suggested a single name: Constanta.

The vampyr lord had not been able to resist the lure of the battle, the chance to see his enemies wiped out in a single, bloody engagement. So much for reports the Hauptmann had been occupied visiting the outskirts of Leningrad. That must have been another lie, another deception. One more among so many.

"Men of the Wehrmacht, I salute you," Constanta called. "You have fought well, upholding the honour of your Fatherland. You can be proud of what you have achieved here. Nevertheless, your defeat is close at hand. I offer you the chance to surrender, to survive this battle and continue your fight for the Führer and the Reich. Join us and you will become ageless and all but immortal. With your courage and our blessing of eternal life, you would be a fighting force to rival any seen in this war or any other."

A murmur of disbelief spread among the Germans. Could the vampyr be offering them a way out of this death trap?

"Some of you will doubt this offer, but I have never lied in my long, long life. I consider my word to be a sacred bond. My Sire rewards loyalty with eternal life and I offer you the same. Join us and live forever, or die here on this battlefield, alone, unheralded and unsung. The choice is yours. I give you one minute to make up your minds." Constanta remained where he was, drawing a fob watch from a pocket on his uniform to take note of the time. His horse nodded its head up and down, as if approving his offer.

Hans spotted Ralf and the rest of his crew nearby, glaring at Constanta from the hatches of their Panzer. He ran across to them, clambering up the hull of the mighty tank to talk with Ralf. "He's lying. Why would the vampyr offer us a chance to join them? They have sacrificed hundreds of their kind to kill us."

"That could be the reason," Ralf replied. "We have wiped out so many of them, they need us to fill the gaps. But I've no intention of becoming Constanta's cannon fodder."

"There could be another reason," Gunther suggested, pointing at the horizon. "The sun will be up in a few minutes. If the vampyr don't leave before then, they will all die. If we can survive until sunrise, we've won."

Helmut had been relaying Constanta's message to Klaus in the sky. "Your brother says he can see the sun already, that's why the bats have come back down to the ground."

Ralf folded his arms. "That settles it."

Hans gestured towards the waiting vampyr leader. "What about him?"

"That Scheisse?" The Panzer commander smiled. "We'll hit him with everything we've got."

THE GERMANS OPENED fire on Constanta's position, bombarding him with the final few shells from each Panzer, a fusillade of machine gun rounds and stick grenades. When all the noise and explosions had cleared, the vampyr lord was still standing. His horse had been blown apart, but the Rumanian remained apparently unhurt.

"I can't be killed," he sneered at the Germans. "I can resurrect myself from the smallest speck of dust. That is the power of my Sire, the gift that you have spurned. Remember that on your way to hell."

KLAUS FELT HIS Stuka engine cough and splutter, its strength failing as the last ounces of fuel were exhausted. Behind him Satzinger had resumed praying, all too aware their time in the air was at an end.

Klaus nodded, wishing he believed in anything any more. "I'm glad you got to fly once more, major. If we have to die, better it be in the sky, doing what we've always loved."

"Amen," Satzinger replied. "It's time for our last dive, Vollmer. Choose your target and make it count." The Stuka fell silent, the only sound to be heard was the wind whistling past.

Klaus smiled as he aimed the plane's nose at a single figure on the battlefield below. "I'm coming for you Constanta!"

. . .

HANS AND RALF watched their brother's plane fall from the sky, the Stuka giving one last scream as it plunged to the earth, falling short of the vampyr leader's position. Constanta was still laughing at this heroic failure when one of the Ju 87's propeller blades sliced off his head. He exploded into a cloud of ash, a faint gust of wind carrying it away into the sky.

At the death of their leader, the vampyr hordes gave a wail of dismay, but it was as nothing to the cacophony that greeted the sun as it broke the horizon. A shriek rose up, louder and more terrible than any noise the German survivors had ever heard. On and on the cry went, rending the air, deafening in its volume, horrifying in its ferocity. The encircling vampyrs exploded, one after another, bursting into flame and ash, crying out to their dark lord.

Then they were gone, their last echo dying away on the wind. The undead army was reduced to a ring of ash on the bloody soil. Hans and Ralf looked at each other, disbelief clouding their faces. They were still expecting another attack, another wave to rise up and engulf them.

But none came. It was finally over.

Chapter Twenty-Three

SEPTEMBER 29TH, 1941

WHEN A FINAL count was made, only four of the Panzer crews and fewer than twenty infantry soldiers had survived. All the Kampfgruppen's planes had been lost, along with hundreds of men on the ground. But when the survivors returned to their own units they all found themselves facing charges of desertion and gross insubordination. With next to no evidence to prove what had happened, the accused were defenceless. Before leading his vampyrs into battle, Constanta had filed charges of mutiny against the Vollmer brothers and their co-conspirators. The fact that nobody could produce written orders to justify the existence of the Kampfgruppen only made matters worse. The unexplained loss of so many men and machines should have doomed the survivors to execution by firing squad, but a last minute intervention came to their rescue.

Hans and Ralf stood side by side as the verdict against them was read out at the court martial. "You two have been identified as the ringleaders of this bizarre and, thus far, inexplicable incident," the presiding officer said. "You acted outside orders, apparently costing the lives of hundreds of the Wehrmacht, not to mention some fifty valuable aircraft and numerous guns. Despite your actions, you have inspired such loyalty among your fellow accused that none of them will speak against either of you. I don't know what prompted this private crusade. That is a matter for another day. I do know this: but for the testimony of one high-ranking officer, both of you would certainly be facing the death penalty.

"Instead I find myself counselled to let you live. This I will do, but I cannot allow such gross insubordination to pass unpunished. Obergefreiter Hans Vollmer, you are hereby demoted to the lowest rank possible. You and all the other infantry involved in this incident are being reassigned to join Army Group North in the frozen north. Perhaps some time near the Arctic Circle will allow you to reflect upon the error of your ways. Obergefreiter Ralf Vollmer, you, your crew and all the other tank personnel will be demoted to become Panzergrenadiers. Since you are incapable of using your machines properly, you shall run alongside them into battle. Your presence beside the Panzers will be a constant reminder of what you have lost. Dismissed."

The two brothers were led away, baffled by the decision. Both had been resigned to facing the firing squad, but their spirits were buoyed by the knowledge their mission to wipe out the vampyrs had been successful.

However, they had been given another chance. But why? The answer came a few minutes later. One of the guards said there was a visitor coming to see them. The two brothers used the wait to say goodbye.

"I don't know what's worse," Hans admitted. "Seeing Klaus die like that or imagining how hard the news must have hit them at home."

Ralf nodded. "At least Klaus died for a good cause, a righteous cause. It was his Stuka that killed Constanta."

"I wouldn't be so certain of that," a familiar voice replied. The Rumanian leader appeared outside their cell, smirking at their shock and amazement.

"You died," Hans protested. "We saw you die."

"You saw me reduced to ashes, yes, but you didn't see me die," Constanta replied. "I told you, I can't be killed. I can resurrect myself from the smallest speck of dust. I let the wind carry me away before the rising sun achieved what you could not. The battle had achieved its goal: all but a few of those who would oppose my kind in this war were wiped out."

"I'll kill you with my bare hands if I have to," Ralf vowed, making a grab for the Rumanian.

Constanta easily eluded this clumsy attempt. "You should be grateful to me. Without my intervention, you would already be dead."

"You were the one who got to the court martial judges? Why?" Hans demanded.

"So you might spread a message on my behalf. Tell others about us, if you dare, but remember this: we cannot be beaten and we cannot be destroyed. We are legion. When this war is over, we shall rise up and claim our rightful place as the true master race. There shall be a thousand-year Reich, as your Führer believes, but we shall be its rulers. What you saw was a rehearsal for the war of terror we shall wage against all of mankind." Constanta tipped his peaked cap to the two brothers, offering one last thought before departing. "The battle for the future begins today, gentlemen. Enjoy the rest of the war."

About the Author

David Bishop was born and raised in New Zealand, becoming a daily newspaper journalist at eighteen years old. He emigrated to Britain in 1990 and was editor of the *Judge Dredd Megazine* and then *2000 AD*, before becoming a freelance writer. His previous novels include three starring Judge Dredd (for Virgin Books) and four featuring Doctor Who (for Virgin and the BBC). He also writes non-fiction books and articles, audio dramas, comics and has been a creative consultant on three forthcoming video games. If you see Bishop in public, do not approach him – alert the nearest editor and stand well back. Bishop's previous contributions to Black Flame are *Judge Dredd: Bad Moon Rising*, *Nikolai Dante: The Strangelove Gambit* and *A Nightmare on Elm Street: Suffer the Children*.

THIS KITTEN HAS CLAWS
(AND FANGS, AND GUNS...)

DURHAM RED

She is the last hope for a galaxy on the brink of extinction...

She alone can end the eternal war between mutants and humans...

She's a saint! An abomination! *A vampire!*

THE UNQUIET GRAVE
1-84416-159-5

THE OMEGA SOLUTION
1-84416-175-7

THE ENCODED HEART
1-84416-272-9

Available from all good bookstores or online at...

WWW.BLACKFLAME.COM
TOUGH FICTION FOR A TOUGH PLANET